CHANGE OF ADDRESS

HARTSBRIDGE  ISLAND

JORDAN S. BROCK

RIPTIDE PUBLISHING

Riptide Publishing
PO Box 1537
Burnsville, NC 28714
www.riptidepublishing.com

Change of Address

Cover art: L.C. Chase, lcchase.com/design.htm
Editor: Kate De Groot
Layout: L.C. Chase, lcchase.com/design.htm

ISBN: 978-1-62649-464-0

First edition
October, 2016

Also available in ebook:
ISBN: 978-1-62649-463-3

CHANGE OF ADDRESS

HARTSBRIDGE ISLAND

JORDAN S. BROCK

RIPTIDE
PUBLISHING

For my service dog, Darian. My dear friend. My helper. My companion.
You changed my life.

CONTENTS

CHAPTER
ONE

"Go through."

The unfamiliar voice was almost drowned out by the bell jangling over the front door. What a strange thing to say. Frowning, Josh peered through the kitchen doorway to the front of the shop.

"Dee's on break. Let me go get that," he told his ex-girlfriend-turned-accountant. When she waved him away, he got up from the prep table where they were working on the books and went out front. He was just in time to see a white taxi pulling away from the curb, which was odd. There was only one taxi service on the island, and those taxis weren't white. Someone from the mainland?

Shaking his head, he looked over at the front door. His new customer was standing there, and Josh eyed the guy for a second—T-shirt, jeans, sunglasses, messenger bag slung across his chest—before a swish of movement caught his attention. A dog?

No dogs allowed. He actually drew breath to say it before the dog's red vest registered. Service dog, then—and a handsome one too. Josh was no expert, but he could recognize a German shepherd and suspected this one was a purebred.

It took far too long for Josh to remember his customer-oriented manners. He put on a friendly smile and rested a forearm on the tall glass counter, saying, "Hey, welcome to Bagel End. What can I get for you?"

The guy took off his sunglasses, revealing warm brown eyes and high cheekbones. He was focused on the menu boards hanging over the counter, so Josh took a surreptitious second look. The guy was well-built, but thin enough that Josh's first instinct was to suggest a stacked brisket sandwich and a bowl of filling broccoli cheddar soup. Get some meat on those bones.

Not about to get caught staring, Josh took a couple of plastic gloves out of the box. He heard the guy approach, along with the soft *click* of dog toenails on the laminate floor. Josh turned back and met him at the order counter, which put them barely two feet apart, and there was no way he couldn't stare now. If not for the momentary distraction of the dog, he would've been staring the whole time, because *wow*. This guy was hot, especially when he gave Josh a shy little smile.

"Uh . . . let's do the corned beef," the guy said softly, his accent too indistinct for Josh to place.

"Bagel, white, wheat, rye, sourdough, or focaccia?" Josh asked, guessing he'd go for rye. He seemed like a traditionalist.

But he turned his attention to the bagel display, biting his lip. "Plain bagel," he said, glancing at Josh before looking back down. "I haven't had a good bagel in years."

A fellow connoisseur. Josh's smile brightened. "The recipe's from the family's old place in Brooklyn. You'll love it," he promised as he pulled out the plain basket. Indulging his need to feed his customer— and hopefully entice the guy to come back—he found the biggest bagel and dropped it into the automatic slicer.

The guy followed as Josh made his way down the counter to the corned beef. "Also, a half pound of roast beef. You can just wrap it in something."

Probably for the dog, Josh guessed. Lucky mutt. "Sure thing. What else did you want on your sandwich?"

"Only deli mustard."

"A purist." Josh grinned in approval and swiped a thin layer of spicy brown mustard on each half of the bagel. "This your first time on the island?"

The guy met Josh's eyes, though only briefly. Was it endearing shyness or skittishness? "I, uh, grew up spending my summers here."

"Oh! Well, welcome back, then," Josh said, trying and failing to slot the guy into the "rich asshole tourist" niche. He seemed friendly, despite the lack of eye contact.

"Thanks," he said, looking straight down, probably at the dog. Josh could barely see the brown tips of its ears. "It's good to be back."

Josh wanted to keep up the friendly chatter, but not while the guy was focused on the dog. Instead, he finished assembling the sandwich, sliced up a generous half pound or so of roast beef, then asked, "Anything else? The soup's really good today."

"Um, maybe later." The guy glanced at the empty tables by the front window. "Mind if I eat here?"

Why would he even ask? Probably because of the dog, though Josh knew better than to ask a well-behaved service dog to leave. Hell, the dog was cleaner and more polite than some two-legged customers. "Be my guest," he said, giving his friendliest smile. "Something to drink? A bowl of water for your pup?"

The guy's answering smile brightened a notch. "I've got a bowl." He glanced at the soda machine. "Uh, just water for me. She's fine, thanks," he added with a nod toward the dog.

Usually they used the small paper cups for water, but Josh filled a big cup, then capped it. He put the wrapped roast beef into a to-go container only because he wasn't sure if health department regulations would let him put a service dog's food on a plate. Was she even eating here? He arranged everything neatly on a tray and slid it down to the register.

The guy already had his wallet in his hands. He took out cash; so much for Josh seeing his name on a credit card. Josh got rid of the plastic gloves, rang up the order, and handed back the change along with a paper copy of the menu.

"We're setting up online ordering, but the kid doing the website is kind of flaky," he said apologetically. "But if you call ahead, we can have your order ready for you—for both of you," he added, stretching to look over the counter at the dog, who was politely sitting on her human's feet, attention focused on the door.

"Thanks." The guy smiled. "Do you do deliveries?"

"Technically only for catering orders," Josh said, lowering his voice. "But if it's not raining and I've got a full staff, I can get pretty much anywhere on the island within half an hour, give or take."

The guy's laugh was even nicer than his smile. "I won't tell anyone." He picked up the tray and told the dog, "Let's go." Together, they headed for the two-seat table in the front of the shop, where the guy sat with his back to the wall. The dog followed him, then turned neatly and sat at his side, mouth hanging open in a canine grin.

Cleaning up gave Josh a thirty-second excuse to linger, long enough to watch the guy crush the overstuffed bagel down to a manageable size. After the first bite, he smiled—always a good sign. Hopefully Josh had just gotten himself a repeat customer. Maybe even a regular.

The brisket was surprisingly good, which helped Michael to relax and concentrate on something other than watching his environment. That was Kaylee's job, and though she was young for a fully trained service dog, she was focused on the doors—a comforting reminder that Michael wasn't alone.

Not that he'd really been alone anyway. He glanced toward the back of the restaurant. On the customer side, there was a closed door with a bathroom sign. He could see straight through the open kitchen door behind the counter, where the cashier seemed to be working on a laptop.

Dark-blond hair fell to his shoulders in a mess of neglected curls. His back was rounded from leaning in close to the screen. His bright-blue polo shirt had short enough sleeves to show New Hampshire–pale arms. No desert tan. No hard muscles. No tattoos.

Being around a guy like this was the exact opposite of how Michael's life had gone for the last ten years. He'd never had trouble finding company, even before Don't Ask, Don't Tell was repealed, but they'd all been hard-bodied soldiers. And in DC, during his recovery, Michael had gravitated toward dark, anonymous clubs to find his one-night stands. Picking up a civilian in daylight would be a nice change—especially one with a welcoming smile and a charming laugh.

Had Michael returned that smile? He couldn't remember. He'd ordered his lunch on autopilot, too wary to do more than assess the cashier's nonexistent threat level. He hadn't even bothered to note the name tag.

"Next time," he murmured to Kaylee, reaching down to ruffle her fur. She gave him a doggie grin, tail *whooshing* over the floor. There'd definitely be a next time. Last Michael checked, Hartsbridge Island didn't have a big assortment of restaurants, and he wasn't going to live on his own cooking just to soothe his hypervigilant nature.

After polishing off the sandwich, he picked up the menu and unfolded the glossy paper. He didn't bother to take his reading glasses out of his bag. One side of the menu listed bagels sold by the baker's dozen, meat and cheese platters, and party-size soups and subs. The other had breakfasts, hot and cold sandwiches, and soups of the day. The shop's phone and fax numbers, too blurry for him to make out, were at the bottom. And hadn't the cashier said something about delivery?

Tempting, but no. Part of Kaylee's training involved reminding him when he hadn't left home for a couple of days. Heading into town for a bagel was a good way to keep from becoming a shut-in.

Kaylee sat up abruptly, ears perked toward the window, just as a young woman walked into the shop. Her polo shirt matched the cashier's, with *Bagel End* embroidered over her heart in a vaguely Elvish font. Another employee starting her shift or coming off break meant they expected a surge in customers, maybe an early dinner rush, which was Michael's signal to bail. He'd give Kaylee her roast beef at the town green across the street.

"Let's go," he told Kaylee, who pushed up to all fours and stepped away from his chair. He threw out his trash, then brought the tray to the counter, hoping to coax his cashier out of the kitchen, but no such luck. The young woman was already back there, tying on a green apron with the shop's logo covering the front.

"I'll get that. Thanks!" she said brightly, rushing close enough for him to see her name tag. *Dee.* Not the name he wanted to know. As she picked up the tray, leaving him the to-go box of roast beef, she grinned down at Kaylee and asked, "How was your meal?"

"Great," Michael said truthfully.

Turning her smile on him, she said, "Hope you two come back soon."

With one last glance through the open kitchen door, Michael promised, "We will."

CHAPTER

TWO

After an hour and a half on the train from Boston and almost an hour in the taxi, Michael welcomed the chance to stretch his legs on the walk to his new home. The bed in last night's hotel had certainly done his back no favors.

He crossed the town green, taking in the changes since he'd been here ten years earlier. The old town meeting hall had been turned into a museum, but the life-size bronze stag that was the town mascot, Hercules, still towered over the grassy field. The Stars and Stripes and the New Hampshire state flag snapped in the wind in front of the new civic center, with the island's tiny police station tucked into one side of the building.

East of the green, the Rocky Shores Diner was still in its old place, though it looked bigger than he remembered. The board of selectmen still hadn't put in a traffic light instead of the four-way stop at the corner. And the townies' houses hadn't been knocked down to make room for tourist bungalows and condos, which was comforting.

Despite the late-spring chill, the walk warmed Michael enough that he'd taken off his jacket by the time they reached the Baldwin family vacation home. The white colonial farmhouse was still surrounded by squared hedges, beds of bright flowers, and a green lawn, neatly striped from a lawnmower, that stretched from the road all the way to the bank above the rocky beach.

At the edge of the property, Michael took off Kaylee's service vest and unsnapped her leash. "Go play," he told her, and she rushed off to explore, nose buried in the grass. He watched her, smiling, and felt a weight slip off his shoulders. He was safe here, safe enough to let her play.

But when grass gave way to the manicured gravel driveway, Michael called her over and put the vest back on, a signal that she was on the job once more. Ears alertly perked, she trotted up the driveway at his side, rocks crunching together under her paws. Michael made a mental note to pick up some heavy booties and a warm coat for her. He'd never wintered on Hartsbridge Island, but he couldn't imagine the weather was at all gentle. In fact, they'd both need to be better prepared.

His parents had given him a house key when they visited in DC. Or, well, Mom had; Dad had spent the entire visit on the phone, making plans to have dinner and drinks with important political connections. Michael suspected a presidential bid in the near future, which was both unpleasant and convenient. A summer of campaigning meant there'd be no time for a vacation, leaving the house all to Michael.

So there was no trepidation in him at all when he pushed open the door, braced for a rush of stale air that never came. Instead, the house smelled like sunshine and flowers—but why? Who was here?

Suspiciously, he leaned down and unclipped Kaylee's leash. "Recon," he said, and she trotted into the house.

Apprehension drove him to pace along the sloped walkway between the garage and front door, though he couldn't see into the windows. If there was anyone inside, Kaylee would find them and give a warning bark. He was back home on American soil. He was *safe*.

He kept telling himself that for the endless minutes it took for Kaylee to return to him. She streaked past in a blur of brown and bright blue, turned on a dime, and sat, giving him the happy-dog grin that said it was all clear.

With a sharp, relieved exhale, he crouched down to pet her. "Good girl," he said, which was her signal that it was okay to break her sit and nose at his face. He laughed into her fur, reminding himself that this was proof he was safe. He could relax his vigilance. There was a perfectly reasonable explanation for everything—no need to be suspicious all the time.

But logic had nothing to do with emotion, so he was still a little apprehensive when he went into the spacious, remodeled house. The sound of Kaylee's nails changed between the warm wood hallway and the slate-floored kitchen, which had doubled in size. The patio furniture had been set up out back, and there were fresh-cut flowers everywhere, no more than a few hours old, so *someone* had been here.

Maybe his mother had arranged for the caretakers to air out the house before Michael's arrival? That would have been unusually thoughtful of her. More likely, her personal assistant had taken care of it.

Perfectly normal explanation, Baldwin. Get a hold of yourself. And this was a good reminder that the caretakers would be around every week or so. Michael would have to find out their schedule so they couldn't catch him by surprise.

Upstairs, he opened the door to what had been his childhood bedroom and froze. His classic sci-fi movie posters and framed comic books were gone, replaced by a blandly tasteful painting of the island's crumbling lighthouse. Instead of his old bed, there was a queen-size bed lost under decorative quilts and throw pillows. One of them, instead of being square or round like the rest, had a familiar contour.

Was that *his* pillow? The one shaped to help ease his tense neck and shoulders? Suspicious all over again, he went into the room and picked it up. Definitely his, though it was in an unfamiliar ivory pillowcase that matched the rest of the linens.

He spun and opened the wardrobe tucked into one corner of the room. His clothes, few as they were, hung from the rod. The drawers revealed his socks and underwear, along with the plastic box that held his service ribbons. Looking back into the room, he spotted the wooden box with his Purple Heart on a shelf near the valet stand.

Why the hell was his stuff unpacked?

Sure, he'd shipped most of his belongings to the house a couple of weeks ago, along with the SUV he'd picked up last winter in DC. But the caretaker was supposed to store the boxes in anticipation of his arrival—not unpack them. And sure as *hell* not unpack them into this impersonal room.

His skin crawled at the invasion of his privacy. If he'd been willing to put up with people in his room—in his territory—he would've stayed at a hotel.

He crouched, resting a hand on Kaylee's back, as the world rocked around him. This was supposed to be his anchor, more than just somewhere to stay. More than just a house. He needed a *home*. Somewhere he could continue to nurture the fragile civilian identity he'd begun to construct back in DC, after he was discharged from the hospital.

Kaylee shuffled around so she could rest her muzzle on his shoulder, a comfort behavior that she'd developed on her own. Michael wrapped his arms around her and breathed deeply, pretending to be calm until he fooled his body into complying. He had a safe place to stay, even if it wasn't secure, and he had his meager belongings, even if someone else had fucked with them. This was nothing he couldn't work with. Nothing he couldn't overcome.

"Okay." Another deep breath, and he straightened, braced against Kaylee for balance. He looked at the house keys with their neat labels: front door, back door, kitchen door, garage door, barn. "Okay, Kaylee. Let's go scout out somewhere better to live."

She wagged her tail in answer.

"Will you look at that?" Michael asked Kaylee, slowly grinning as he took in what used to be a gaping space full of cobwebs and mold-rotted wood. Somewhere along the line, his dad must have pulled strings to get a building permit for the barn. It was nothing like what he remembered from the few memorable occasions he and Amanda had managed to pick the lock on the doors—usually it was Amanda, with her more dexterous fingers, who succeeded—and creep inside the deathtrap full of splintered beams, spiders, and garter snakes.

Now, though, the barn was a light and airy refuge, despite having only a few tiny windows. The space by the doors was a high-ceilinged living area with an antique wood-burning stove in the corner and a massive television on the front wall. Quilts covered a plush sofa and the armchairs. In the back, a rustic dining set divided the living area from a single-story kitchen with a loft bedroom overhead.

As he led Kaylee inside, the tension drained from his shoulders and back. He explored every inch of the rebuilt barn, thinking *this* was where he belonged—a place with one entrance, one lock that he'd change as soon as possible, so only he would have the key. A place where childhood memory and his need for sanctuary could comfortably, safely intersect. Very comfortably, in fact. The bathroom tucked behind the kitchen had an extra-deep claw-foot bathtub as well as a luxuriously modern steam shower, and the bed in the loft was king size, big enough for Kaylee to sprawl at his feet.

The refrigerator and cupboards were empty, but he took care of that in a half-dozen trips to the main house. By the end of the afternoon, he had his belongings stowed away upstairs and the kitchen stocked. Obviously someone had given the caretaker a very outdated list, because along with staples—bread, eggs, milk—he'd found two boxes of sugary cereal and canned pasta right out of his childhood diet. Those he left behind in favor of keeping only the basics on hand.

"What're the chances the truck's in the garage?" he asked Kaylee. The diner in town once had the best burgers on the planet.

Kaylee, sprawled on the colorful rag rug by the sink, wagged her tail.

"Yeah, probably. Come on," he said, and she jumped up to follow him to the front door. At the *click* of her nails, he added, "Remind me to find the toenail clippers later." One of these days, he'd take the time to dig into his phone and figure out how to set automatic reminders, but not now. He couldn't let the phone distract him into avoiding going out in public.

He'd hung Kaylee's leash and vest on the coat hooks made from horseshoes—surprisingly kitschy for any decorator his mom would hire—along with the messenger bag that he kept stocked with dog care and cleanup supplies. Kaylee sat while he got her geared up, then walked with him back to the main house, where he let himself inside. He'd have to ask for the garage code; for now, he unlocked the interior door, stepping in just enough for the automatic lights to trigger.

As he expected, his SUV had been parked on the far side of the garage, leaving room for whatever new cars his parents were driving this year. Michael stared at the SUV, clenching and unclenching his fists. He really hadn't considered the layout of the island. The drive would be short and quick, but the roads were curved and unlit for the most part.

Dark roads. Low visibility.

Bad idea, Baldwin.

After two days on the train and a sleepless night at a hotel in Boston, he was too tired to drive safely. But Hartsbridge Island was small enough that even tired—even dead-on-his-feet-exhausted—he could walk safely to town and back.

"You up for another walk, Kaylee?" he asked, backing up a step so he could close and lock the interior door. She was in her vest, so she didn't bounce happily in circles, but her tail wagged a little harder. He couldn't help but smile in response as he ducked his head under the strap of his messenger bag, settling it across his chest. If only he could be so cheerful all the time.

Rocky Shores Diner had never lost its one-step-above-a-trailer feel, even with the extended dining room the owners had tacked on a few years back. When the satellite college campus opened on the south side of the island, the menu had expanded to include wings and chili-cheese fries, but the locals all knew better than to stray from plain hand-cut steak fries.

Josh picked up one of those fries now and used it to point across the booth at his dad. "This is me reminding you"—he took a bite of the fry—"to call the meat delivery guy first thing tomorrow morning."

Dad groaned dramatically and snatched the other half of the fry right out of Josh's fingers. "You have to remind me *in the morning.* Otherwise, I'll just forget."

In retribution, Josh stole one of the fries off his dad's plate. "I'll leave you a voice mail. But really, if he doesn't get his shit together—"

"Josh," Dad scolded, dark brows drawing together.

Josh ignored the reprimand. "We can't keep putting up with late deliveries, Dad. Especially not when summer business really kicks off. What are we going to do? Tell people we don't have corned beef? We're the only supplier on the island."

Dad laughed and slurped some of his milk shake. "It's corned beef, not heroin."

"And you're not in Brooklyn anymore. Corned beef might as well be heroin, the way the tourists gobble it up." Josh tried to sound stern, but he was struggling to hide his grin. "You too. Don't think I don't know about your stash in the back of the walk-in."

"A guy's got to eat," Dad pointed out, though he didn't need to worry about his weight—not like Josh did. "Speaking of Brooklyn," Dad continued, refilling his milk shake from the frosty metal cup, "I might take a trip down there this weekend or next. See your aunt. We'll probably go to the cemetery to visit Bubbe."

"I'll have things covered," Josh said, looking up automatically when the bell over the door rang—a habit from running Bagel End.

His dad's answer was lost under the abrupt *thump* of Josh's heartbeat when he spotted that afternoon's customer—the one with the service dog. God, he was *nice* to look at in profile, expression soft and unguarded as he turned from one side to the other, taking in the scope of the diner. Josh couldn't see if he had the dog, but he assumed so.

"Sit anywhere you like, hon," Betty called from behind the counter, giving a friendly wave with the coffeepot that always seemed to be stuck in her hand. As the guy walked between the booths, Betty frowned, though it melted into a sappy smile almost immediately. "Aww, what a pretty boy!"

Wasn't the dog a girl? Josh couldn't remember, and the guy didn't answer her, at least not loudly enough for Josh to hear. He just walked to the corner booth, as Josh guessed he would, and sat where he could see the door—and Josh, who quickly slouched down and gave his dad a somewhat scrambled smile.

"Sorry, what?"

Dad's eyebrows did a slow creep toward his hairline. "I didn't say anything." He turned to look over his shoulder. "Someone you know?" he asked, which really meant *Someone you're dating?*

Josh snorted. His dad was more of an interfering matchmaker than any twelve yentas from Brooklyn. "A customer, that's all. He came in this afternoon. Stop staring." *Please*, he added mentally, sinking another inch. Too bad the booths low, not the super-high style popular in the seventies, making it easy for Dad to take a nice long look at the guy.

"Uh-huh." Dad finally turned back, a sly grin on his face. "Early in the season for a tourist, isn't it?"

Josh didn't roll his eyes, but it was a close call. "Mainlander, with a family house here, yeah. He'll be here for a while, I think." He was proud he didn't say, *I hope.*

"Uh-huh," Dad repeated, stealing another of Josh's fries. But then he got back to business, saying, "The meat delivery guy. Any other issues we need to deal with?"

Josh shook his head, trying to focus again—these dinnertime business meetings were crucial to keeping the shop running smoothly, as well as being the only real time he and his dad could relax and catch up with each other. But he kept stealing glances at the guy, who'd settled down to look over the menu.

While wearing glasses.

The sight made Josh's knees go a little weak. He *liked* glasses, even though he'd never needed them himself—and he wasn't hipster enough to get plain lenses just so he could try to look hot. It wouldn't work. He was about as far from "sexy librarian" as possible.

Remembering that his dad was expecting a coherent answer, he said, "Uh . . . no, I think we're good. Lizzie and I did the books, and the schedule's set for the next couple of weeks. Speaking of . . ." He glanced past his dad again before he could stop himself. *Glasses.* His voice wavered a bit as he said, "Why don't I open tomorrow? You can sleep in."

Dad let Josh's distraction pass, though not unnoticed, judging by the grin still plastered on his face as his eyebrows went up again. "Not that I'm arguing, but why?"

Because Hot Tourist Guy might be an early riser, and I don't want to miss the chance to see him, Josh thought. "To deal with the meat delivery guy."

Dad shrugged. "You got it." He slurped up the last of his milk shake and didn't bother stealing another fry, a sign that he was done for the night.

Damn. There went Josh's opportunity to maybe make first contact—second contact?—with his handsome customer. His gaze slid past Dad to Hot Tourist Guy, no longer obscured by his menu.

Unfortunately, he was also no longer wearing the glasses. He just needed them for reading, then, which was still hot as hell.

Their eyes met, and Josh quickly looked away, not wanting to be seen as a creepy stalker, even though he'd been in the diner first. God, he was terrible at making the first move. Or responding to one, for that matter. He was terrible with potential dating interests in general. His people skills were top-notch only in the bagel-pushing field. Otherwise, he got self-conscious with girls and nervous about triggering homophobic idiocy with guys, and there wasn't even a hint of a queer community on the island.

Well, maybe there was something at the college, but Josh wasn't one of *them*.

Defeat made his shoulders slump. The hot guy with the dog would fit in great with the college crowd, even if he looked to be a few years older than them. He would have no trouble turning heads no matter where he went. A dumpy, boring, dropout-turned-bagel-guy didn't stand a damn chance with someone like him.

In three bites, he wolfed down the rest of his burger and fries. His dad put a twenty on the table, and Josh added a five for the tip. They left together, and he heroically refrained from throwing one last look at the corner booth. Hot or not, the guy was a customer, and it wasn't as if Bagel End could afford to have Josh scaring away anyone. Besides, if the guy came back or called for a delivery—as he'd implied he would—maybe they could at least become friends. That wouldn't be so bad, would it?

CHAPTER
THREE

S ix a.m., and Hartsbridge was a ghost town. Michael stood next to the deer statue on the green, wrapped in a windbreaker that was fine for DC but insufficient for the chilly wind blowing in off the Atlantic, and stared out at the emptiness. Only the twenty-four-hour diner was open, and even that looked ominous, almost dystopian. With the sun rising behind the low building, the front was in shadow, lit by the red neon sign over the door. The extended dining room was night-dark; the lights were on over the long counter and booths, though they were deserted.

Kaylee's leash twisted in Michael's grasp. Free of her vest, she dove headfirst into the grass and writhed over onto her back, kicking her legs, tail wagging madly. He smiled down at her—at the reminder that he wasn't alone in a postapocalyptic world—and made a mental note to look into local dog ordinances. Growing up, he'd never had a dog, so he wasn't sure if it was legal to have one off-leash or not.

The tinkle of a bell, too faint to really startle him, made him turn to the other side of the green. All the shops there were still dark, except for Bagel End. The door was propped open, and someone had sneaked out long enough to set up a sandwich board outside.

"Diner or bagel place?" Michael asked Kaylee, though he'd already made his decision. Yesterday's lunch bagel had been a little wheel of heaven—not to mention the cashier.

What were the chances that the blond guy from yesterday was on the opening shift? Six a.m. was an unholy hour for most civilians, but the guy seemed to be a manager type, so . . . maybe.

Recognizing Michael's tone of voice, Kaylee got to her feet, giving a good whole-body shake. A cloud of grass poofed around her, only to be swept away by the sea-salt breeze. She stood still while Michael took her vest down from his shoulder, and as he fastened it around her body, he could see her brain kicking into high gear. Her ears perked forward, eyes going sharp and alert. Much as she loved to play, she was a working dog, happiest when she had a task to perform.

When he said, "Let's go," she paced beside him, no longer sniffing everywhere, and paused at the curb to get his okay to cross the deserted street. Growing up in the city had given her good street manners.

The wind went briefly still, filling the air outside the shop with the warm scent of fresh baking. Michael's stomach growled, and Kaylee's nostrils flared as she sniffed. She didn't surge ahead, but her steps went springy and light until they reached the open door, where training kept her from rushing inside.

At this hour, it was a formality to check for anyone coming through the doorway, but the key to training was consistency. After verifying no one was in the way, he told her, "Go through," then followed her in.

"Be right—" The blond guy from yesterday popped into sight behind the glass case half-full of bagels; his smile was breathtakingly sincere. "Hey, be right with you." He turned to take a wire basket of bagels from a rolling rack taller than he was.

"No rush." Michael hung back, not wanting to seem like he was demanding immediate service. Six months ago, he might've slipped out and come back later, but his DC therapist had worked with him on that. Not that he still didn't wish for the ability to turn invisible, to disappear and avoid confrontation of any kind. He was just conscious of the desire and able to push past it most of the time.

Besides, this was what he'd wanted, right? A chance to see the blond guy again, maybe figure out if his smile was friendly or genuinely interested.

So he stood his ground and petted Kaylee, who sat at his left side and leaned against his leg with just enough pressure to reassure him without pushing him off-balance. But instead of focusing entirely on her, he kept sneaking glances at the guy behind the counter. *Cute* was the first word that came to mind, with messy blond curls and the little smile playing around his mouth. *Awake*, too, judging by how quick he was at setting up the baskets, smoothly sliding each one into place until the bagel case was full. His eyes—hazel, Michael guessed, though he didn't want to stare—were bright and free of dark circles and drooping lids. Most civilians didn't have half this much energy at six in the morning. Hell, most *soldiers* didn't.

"Okay, there," the guy said, straightening up to rest one arm on top of the counter. "Didn't want you to have only a partial selection. They're all fresh. What can I get you?"

Your number, Michael thought, but there was no way in hell he'd say it, much as he wanted some of that warm, cheerful energy for himself. He stared unseeing at the display, finally asking, "What's good? I mean, besides everything? Breakfast special, maybe?"

The guy pointed up and over one shoulder, and Michael belatedly remembered the menu board. Before he could stammer an apology, though, the guy said, "If you're wanting something bagel-based, we do a killer breakfast sandwich combo. Comes with coffee or tea, and I can cook up some extra bacon for your friend . . ." The way he trailed off felt expectant without pushing Michael for any information he didn't want to share. He was grateful for that. Growing up in the political fishbowl meant he wasn't the sharing type.

So he was surprised to find himself saying, "Kaylee. And sure."

The sunny smile brightened a notch. "I'm Josh. Sorry I didn't introduce myself yesterday. I always forget my name tag, which is my way of setting a bad example, I guess. Bagel preference?"

Thrown off guard—Michael had expected to be asked for his name—he said, "Uh. Whichever? You pick."

Josh narrowed his eyes—definitely hazel—but his smile didn't fade. "Everything," he said after a moment. "Everything bagel, eggs scrambled with cheese, sausage patty, bacon on the side. Sound good?" He pulled a piece of waxed paper out of a box and rested a hand on the basket of everything bagels.

Michael would've probably ordered something plainer, but his stomach's approving growl had him nodding. "Perfect. Thanks."

Beaming, Josh used the waxed paper to take out one of the bagels and asked, "One last question, and then I can get started. Bold or mild coffee? Both pots are fresh."

Bold would've been Michael's choice, prehospital. Now, grateful for the option, he said, "Mild, black."

"Five minutes. Go have a seat. I'll bring everything out to you. Did"—Josh hesitated, eyeing the dog—"Kaylee? Did she want water?"

"No, thanks. She's good," Michael said truthfully. He'd slept poorly as usual and gotten out of bed around four, which gave him plenty of time to water and brush Kaylee this morning, though he'd forgotten entirely about her nails. Again.

He wandered toward the front of the store, thinking he should have paid first. But Josh seemed to be the only one working, and he'd disappeared into the kitchen. At least that saved Michael from the temptation of staring, though he did take the same front corner table as yesterday. From there, he could see straight back behind the counter, just by turning his head. When he did, he saw Josh pulling a bright-green apron over his blue polo shirt, then ruffling one hand through his already-messy hair, making Michael wonder what those curls felt like.

So much for resisting temptation.

Josh couldn't stop grinning as he washed his hands and prepped the first order of the day. Hot Tourist Guy was back, which made switching shifts with Dad absolutely worth the morning's caffeine jitters. It had been a long time since Josh had been on opening shift, but maybe he could get his sleep cycle turned around. Seeing Hot Tourist Guy was definitely incentive to try.

Hoping to entice Hot Tourist Guy into coming in again tomorrow morning, Josh took a little extra care assembling the sandwich and cooked up enough bacon to win any dog's heart. *Kaylee.* Pretty name. He'd have to figure out her human's name somehow. He should've asked, but the words hadn't quite made it out of his brain. Now, as he plated the sandwich and tucked the bacon in a to-go box for the dog, it felt too late.

Maybe the guy would pay with a credit card, Josh hoped, carrying the breakfast sandwich out. Hot Tourist Guy was back at the table in the corner—developing a regular's habits already? Hopefully.

Josh filled a cup with mild coffee, arranged everything nicely on the tray, then carried the tray out front. The dog was lying comfortably on the floor under the table, though she sat up at Josh's approach. She probably smelled the bacon.

"Here you go," Josh said, sliding the tray onto the table. The guy had taken off his jacket, revealing arms that were thin but solid with muscle. *Don't stare.* "If you need anything else, just give a yell."

Brown eyes met Josh's for long enough to scramble his brain—at least a full second. "The check?"

Josh made an indistinct gesture in the direction of the cash register. "Whenever you're done." He smiled reassuringly before realizing the guy might want to skip out at a moment's notice. "Or do you want me to ring you up now?"

"No rush." The guy smiled. "Thanks."

That was a clear dismissal. Too bad. "Enjoy," Josh said as he turned away, just in time. A familiar car had pulled up to the curb in front of the shop. Dr. Miller was usually the shop's first customer, stopping by on her way to the civic center. This morning, she'd brought her wife, the other Dr. Miller.

Josh headed back to the pass-through and took out a couple of plastic gloves, ready to take the Millers' orders. There'd be time enough to chat with Hot Tourist Guy later—and maybe figure out how to ask the new morning regular's name.

Apparently the island had changed more than Michael expected. The way the two women were holding hands, bumping shoulders and smiling at each other, spoke of something more than friendship. He couldn't remember seeing any same-sex couples back when he'd vacationed here. And they weren't tourists either, judging by Josh's cheerful, "Good morning, Millers!"

Maybe that was why Michael's parents wouldn't need the summer house anytime soon. Diversity was precisely the sort of thing to drive them to hide in their country refuge of mansions and genteel farms. But this boded well for Michael's future social life. It'd be nice to have a shot at meeting an interested guy without having to hide their relationship behind closed doors.

Assuming anyone would *want* a relationship with him.

The thought made him sigh and sip at his coffee, only to put the mug back down when Kaylee sat up for the second time. The first had warned Michael of Josh's approach. Now, Michael glanced up and saw the shorter Miller heading for his table.

"Sorry to bother you," the woman said politely, barely giving Michael a glance, eyes fixed on Kaylee instead. She pushed a lock of thick graying hair behind one ear and asked, "Service dog, right?"

Michael nodded, taking a deep breath of coffee-scented steam. Having a service dog was at odds with his desire to go unnoticed, but he'd practiced standard answers to all the questions strangers might ask, from intrusive—*What's your disability?*—to obvious—*Is that a German shepherd?*

He was completely unprepared when she smiled and said, "If any of the businesses give you a problem, have them give me a call." She felt around her pockets, then finally pulled a wallet out of her jacket. "I'm . . . Doctor—aha"—she offered Michael a business card—"Arielle Miller, with Hartsbridge General Hospital. No relation to the soap opera. I can help straighten out any questions of access. He's very well trained. She?"

Michael took the card and nodded again, feeling like he'd been run over by a very friendly truck. "She—"

"She's beautiful. Just beautiful. Oh, Dr. Mason's the island vet, if you need to see her." She patted her pockets again. "I don't think I have her number in my phone, but her office is just across the street from the elementary school. You can't miss it."

When the rush of words stopped, Michael had to take a moment to gather his wits, then said, "Thanks."

Dr. Miller smiled at Michael, beamed at Kaylee, and hurried back to where her wife—presumably, going by their shared last name—was waiting at the register. The other Miller gave Arielle a curious look, and the shop was quiet enough that Michael heard Arielle say, in more subdued tones, "Remember the ADA seminar last November? It covered service animals versus therapy animals. And with the mainlanders and all their dogs . . ."

"Which reminds me," the other Miller said in a rich British accent, "we need to do something about the pets people leave behind after the summer."

"Bastards," Josh said with a huff, winning Michael's heart forever. There was a special place in hell reserved for anyone who'd abandon a family pet. "Sorry. It's just—"

"I quite agree," she answered, taking one of the cups he offered; Arielle took the other one. "Would you be interested in attending a town hall meeting to address the issue?"

"Me?" When the British Miller nodded, Josh said, "Uh, sure. I'll tell my dad too. Want us to bring bagels and coffee?"

Her smile lit up her whole face. With her rich contralto voice, high cheekbones and deep brown eyes, she was beautiful enough to catch anyone's attention—even Michael's, and his preferences were firmly on the masculine side of the spectrum. She took the bag Josh offered her and said, "That would be lovely. As soon as I have a time and date, I'll send someone over with the information."

As Josh rang them up, Michael turned his attention back to his excellent breakfast. Kaylee was too well trained to focus on the bacon, but she knew she'd get a reward once they left the restaurant. The bacon was cooked but not so crunchy it would fall apart at the first bite, so he could feed it to her neatly on the sidewalk right outside, if he wanted. Maybe that would coax Josh into coming out from behind the counter? Even though Kaylee was a service dog, Michael had taught her a few tricks that might impress Josh.

Stupid idea, Baldwin. Josh was apparently running the shop on his own this morning. He wasn't going to abandon his job to watch dog tricks and talk with someone too shy to even offer his name.

Time to go, Michael decided, before he could do anything stupid. He wolfed down the rest of his food, picked up the to-go box, and brought his tray to the register. Josh had disappeared into the back, but he'd apparently been keeping an eye on the counter. He headed over and asked, "How was everything?"

"Great." It came out barely above a mumble and had him instantly feeling guilty. He forced himself to look Josh in the eye and add, "It really was. You can't get bagels like that in DC."

"And this is why I don't regret never going farther south than Brooklyn," Josh said, eyes bright with the force of his grin. His fingers danced over the cash register buttons. "I'd be lost without good food."

The blunt words, spoken so cheerfully and matter-of-factly, startled Michael. In the Air Force, everyone worried about physical fitness checks, to the point where he'd known people to get liposuction so they wouldn't get a letter of reprimand and possibly miss out on a promotion.

"I— Yeah." Sensing an impending ridiculous grin, Michael looked down at Kaylee. "I think we'll both be back for breakfast tomorrow." If not lunch later today, though he didn't say that. There was a difference between being a good customer and a creepy one.

"The door opens at six," Josh said, his voice warm. Inviting. And Michael wanted to accept that invitation, but . . .

He's just being a good businessman, Baldwin. The voice of caution was too loud for Michael to do anything more than pay his bill and slip out with a soft "Thanks."

But when Josh called after him, "See you tomorrow!" it sounded genuinely hopeful, not just polite, and Michael left the shop with a smile.

By the fifth "What a beautiful dog!" that interrupted the trip to the hardware store, Michael was actually relieved to hear his phone ring. Unless it was his dog trainer back in DC, the call probably *wasn't* from someone wanting to talk about Kaylee. He stopped the shopping cart, made sure Kaylee sat out of the way, and checked the caller ID.

Unlisted. Never a good sign.

He was tempted to let the call go to voice mail, but that was avoidance behavior, and he couldn't let himself fall back into the habit of self-isolation. Reluctantly, he swiped the screen and put the phone to his ear.

"Yeah?" he asked gruffly. Only a dozen or so people had his number, and fully half of them didn't warrant a friendly hello.

"Mr. Baldwin?" The voice was unfamiliar.

He switched hands so he could dig his fingers into the fur between Kaylee's ears. She leaned heavily against his leg in response, tail wagging. "Who's this?" he asked, conscious that he wasn't alone in the aisle of hand tools.

"Lee Wilkins, chief of staff for Governor Baldwin. How are you doing?"

Wishing I hadn't answered. A lifetime of etiquette lessons urged him to mind his words; his instincts screamed at him to rip out the phone's battery and throw it away. The end result was a gruff, "What?"

The chief of staff was too polite—or, more likely, too well trained—to sound offended. Instead, he asked, "All settled in? Governor Baldwin told me you'd returned to New Hampshire." He obviously didn't expect a response, because he forged ahead, adding, "Which is why I'm calling. There's a fund-raiser barbecue at the Knox family farm tomorrow, and you're invited."

Michael bit back a laugh. *Invited* was political code for *required*, in his experience. "I don't—"

"Your father specifically asked me to contact you," Wilkins interrupted. "As I understand it, one of the guests of honor served in the New Hampshire Air National Guard during the Vietnam War."

Michael's chest went tight. This was worse than the usual dog and pony show. He'd *known* this would happen, Dad wanting to use Michael's Air Force service as a political tool. It was one of the biggest hazards of moving back to New Hampshire instead of, say, California, but he hadn't expected it to happen this soon.

"Would you like me to check the governor's schedule, see if he can call you to talk about the agenda?" Wilkins offered into the silence, smoothly as a knife slipping between Michael's ribs.

"No. I'll—" Michael stared down at Kaylee, who'd practically melted against his leg. At least he wouldn't be doing this alone. "Send me the information. Location, time, all that."

"Fantastic. I'm sending . . . now," Wilkins said as Michael's phone buzzed with an incoming text. He must have had it ready. "See you tomorrow. It's great that you're back." He hung up before Michael could say good-bye. Or possibly, *Fuck off.*

Well, shit. Michael scrubbed a hand over his face, staring blankly into the cart. He had a new lock for the barn door, a couple of screwdrivers, and some graphite spray. For the life of him, he couldn't remember what else was on his shopping list.

"Let's go," he muttered to Kaylee, who stood and looked up at him, still leaning against his leg until he gave the cart a push, heading for the register. There was no sense in shopping for anything else. Apparently, he'd be away from home tomorrow.

CHAPTER
FOUR

Josh's day started with two strikes: an overcast sky and no Hot Tourist Guy in the first three hours Bagel End was open. For the second morning in a row, Josh had traded shifts with his dad, only to be left in isolation for a good hour after Dr. Miller stopped in for her usual morning coffee.

But then Charlie showed up for his shift, just in time for the morning rush. Josh took over the coffee machine and cash register, leaving Charlie to scramble eggs and fry bacon, and they were both too busy to think about anything but the next customer. It took longer than usual for the rush to taper off, and Josh was dead on his feet by the time he could take a breath and pour himself a cup of coffee. He'd never been much of a morning person, and two opening shifts in a row were killing him.

He'd just lifted the steaming mug to his lips when the bell over the door rang. Biting back a groan, Josh turned—

This is becoming a trend, he thought when he spotted Hot Tourist Guy, and he had to tell himself not to grin like an idiot. Or not like a complete idiot. He was pretty sure he'd hit levels of mild idiocy yesterday or the day before—ever since the guy first walked into Bagel End, in fact.

"Morning!" he called with appropriate cheer, swiping two gloves out of the box. "Breakfast sandwich, bacon for your dog, or both?"

Hot Tourist Guy met Josh's eyes for all of a second before turning his attention to the dog. "Just a bagel and coffee," he muttered, and Josh's heart sank. "To go."

"Sure thing," Josh said more gently, eyeing the display case. There'd been a run on sesame and blueberry bagels, but all the other baskets were at least half-full. Good selection. "What kind of bagel?"

The guy's tense shrug left his shoulders hunched. "Whatever's fine."

Kicked puppy. Josh resisted the urge to offer a hug along with the bagel and coffee. "How about a plain bagel, toasted, with cream cheese?" he suggested. "It'll just take a couple minutes—long enough for me to brew a fresh pot of coffee."

Another quick glance up, though this one looked hopeful, maybe even relieved. "Yeah? Okay." One corner of the guy's mouth twitched, the start of a smile. Josh counted that as a win and turned to brew the coffee.

He was tempted to fill the silence with friendly chatter, but when he sneaked a glance over one shoulder, he saw Hot Tourist Guy had moved down the counter to lurk near the cash register, attention focused on his dog.

If Josh hadn't caught the guy's shy smile for the last two days, he would've written him off as withdrawn, even sullen. He busied himself with toasting the bagel and opening a new tub of cream cheese—anything to keep from looking over at his only customer. The last thing he needed was to get caught staring and drive the guy away.

No, better to make this a safe space for him. As Josh spread cream cheese on the bagel, he got the mental image of trying to coax a stray dog out of the cold using bits of food and a soft, kind voice. And that set off alarm bells. Josh hadn't been Mr. Popular during his short stint in high school, which meant his only real chance of finding dates had been with other outcasts, something that hadn't worked out well for him.

But Hot Tourist Guy—really, *what was his name?*—didn't give off any other warning vibes. He'd been friendly to Dr. Miller yesterday morning, and watching him with his dog was just about the sweetest thing Josh had seen in ages.

Besides, everyone had bad days.

So Josh finished putting together the order and brought everything to the register with a warm smile. "How about that bacon for your dog?" he offered, racking his brain for the dog's name. "Kylie?"

"Kaylee," the guy corrected, meeting Josh's eyes—and smiling, which Josh counted as a win. "I fed— *Shit.*"

"What? What's wrong?"

Sighing, the guy gestured at the dog. "Forgot to clip her nails. Again."

Josh couldn't help but laugh as he leaned against the counter and followed Hot Tourist Guy's eyes. "She's still gorgeous, even without a manicure." *Like you*, he added silently, letting his gaze take the long way back up to the guy's face. It was more blatant than Josh's usual near-invisible brand of flirting, but he needed cheering up, and it was fifty-fifty that he'd smile at being found attractive—or he'd take offense and storm out.

But the guy's feet stayed rooted to the spot, and his eyes widened just a touch before he turned away. "Thanks. Maybe yesterday."

Josh paused, hand over the cash register buttons. "Huh?"

The guy met Josh's eyes. Blinked a couple of times. "Maybe yesterday morning."

"*Tomorrow* morning?" Josh blurted, realizing it might be rude only after the words were out. The guy looked even more like a kicked puppy, and now Josh sounded like he was mocking him or something.

Frowning, the guy reached down to scratch at Kaylee's pointy ears for a couple of tense seconds. Then he hunched his shoulders even more and scowled down at his feet, mumbling, "Tomorrow morning. Yeah."

Damn it. Hating himself for having said anything, Josh rang up the transaction. "We'll be open at six, like usual," he said as cheerfully as he could manage.

That got a faint smile in response, though it disappeared just seconds later. With a quiet sigh, the guy slowly said, "I don't even know when I'll be back." Again, he offered cash instead of a credit card, so Josh had no chance of finding out the guy's name. This didn't seem like the right time to ask.

Josh opened his mouth to ask where he was going, then caught himself. It was none of his business. "I'll be here," he said, though he probably should've said *we*, not *I*. Damn. Why was he making this all personal and awkward?

Probably because the guy looked like he was in desperate need of a hug.

But the best Josh could do was food, so he handed over the change and breakfast with an encouraging, "I hope your day gets better."

The guy's smile was practically a wince. "Not a chance, but thanks."

Two hours later, Michael slowed his truck outside a white fence splashed with blue and red from the light bar on the sheriff department's truck guarding the driveway. Was it legal to have deputies guarding a campaign event for a political party? Maybe Michael's father had skirted the law by hiring off-duty law enforcement to provide security.

No, more likely he'd gotten the Knox family to do the hiring. He wasn't stupid enough to leave a paper trail back to the governor's office.

Already, Michael had the beginnings of a migraine just from thinking about the machinations—but that was how everything went with his family. Layered motives, hidden agendas, backstabbing deals, and buried secrets. The Baldwin family legacy.

Michael showed his DC driver's license to the security guard, who studied it as if he couldn't read English. He scraped the license down his clipboard, then stopped near the bottom and tapped the license against the page. With a quick, skeptical glance, he moved away, mumbling into his radio. Michael sighed, and Kaylee stuck her muzzle between the front seats, nosing at his elbow.

"Yeah, I know," he muttered, grateful that she, at least, picked up on his frustration. Apparently his father's staff hadn't notified security that Michael would be attending.

It was another minute or two before the oblivious guard warily returned Michael's license and waved him through. Michael resisted the urge to spin the tires and kick up gravel, and instead eased through the gate and up the long, winding driveway.

He vaguely recognized the Knox farm from events ten years ago, "intimate" gatherings of a hundred of then-Senator Baldwin's best contributors and their families. The farm had a small orchard to one side of the driveway and pastures to the other, though the only livestock were horses and a few well-groomed cows suitable for winning ribbons at the county fair and providing photo ops for politically connected kids. The huge white farmhouse sat atop a low hill, surrounded by grass and neatly trimmed hedges. It was idyllic, peaceful, and perfect for exploitation.

And today was all about exploitation, with bunting and balloons in red, white, and blue. The New Hampshire state flag—a detailed gold seal on a blue background—was also prominently displayed, just in case any of the out-of-state guests forgot where they were. Not that any of them could probably recognize the flag of any state, much less a tiny one like New Hampshire. Judging by the rental cars parked on the square of dirt, about half of the guests were from somewhere else, which meant a big press presence.

Shit. Michael wasn't surprised, but still . . . "Shit," he told Kaylee as he steered slowly toward a kid waving two tiny flags to catch his attention. He might've made a joke about semaphore signals, but the sight of a dozen *Support Baldwin!* and *Baldwin for New Hampshire!* buttons rattling on the boy's T-shirt made him freeze up.

The boy bounced up to the driver's side. Michael rolled the window down in time to hear the kid cheerfully direct, "Left side, all the way to the end of the row!"

There were four rows of parked cars so far, and it was just past ten in the morning. Just how many people were going to be at this "friendly little barbecue" anyway? Michael considered ignoring the kid and parking all the way at the back of the cleared ground, before deciding his balance couldn't handle it. On a good day, he and Kaylee could walk for miles. Today was *not* a good day.

He flipped open the center console and pulled out the blue tag he rarely bothered to hang from his rearview mirror. "I've got this"—he brandished the tag, racking his brain for the right word—"thing."

That got him a blank look, followed by a shouted, "One sec!" before the kid ran off.

"Like a vampire running from a . . ." Michael's thoughts stuttered and glitched again. *Church. Stained glass.* He shook his head and twisted his right arm so he could scratch at Kaylee's muzzle. She didn't care if he couldn't finish a sentence. But twice in a row . . . That wasn't good. And hadn't he misspoken this morning, when he got breakfast from Josh the Cute Bagel Guy?

He made sure the truck was in park, relaxed into his seat, and took a deep breath, then another. By the third, Kaylee had slithered halfway onto the console so she could rest her muzzle on his forearm. She pressed down hard, and he focused all of his attention on the feel of her soft fur and bristly whiskers, the warmth of her breath puffing over the back of his hand, her gentle gaze as she watched him, attentive but not judging. Not demanding.

He made it to nineteen breaths before his heart stopped racing, then another twelve before the kid came running back, kicking up clouds of dirt. He skidded around the front of the truck and stopped by the door, saying, "You can park by the garage, over there." He used a flag to point the way.

"Thanks." Michael hung the handicap tag from the rearview mirror, just in case someone decided to challenge him, and put the truck in drive. Gravel crunched until, with a double *thump*, the truck rolled onto the smooth asphalt in front of two wide garage doors. He spun the wheel and backed onto the lawn, where nobody could block him in without trying. Clear escape routes helped him to relax, whether he was sleeping or forward deployed—or at a political fund-raiser, which was almost as bad.

Still, it took him a good five minutes to go from turning off the engine to opening the truck door. Some of that time he spent readying his messenger bag of dog gear—cleaning supplies in case of an accident, treats, a mat so Kaylee could lie down comfortably, and so on—but the rest was just him staring out the windshield, wishing he'd said no to the chief of staff.

He'd always had trouble saying no to his parents. Hell, he'd been *trained* not to, because the consequences were usually worse than conceding. But not being able to say no to his dad's flunky? That was just depressing.

Kaylee's worried nudge finally got him moving. He slung the messenger bag across his chest, got out of the truck, and opened the back door for her to jump out. Bracing a hand on her back, above her front legs, he bent to take the leash she was holding in her mouth. The world swam, but that was more anxiety than a relapse of his balance issues.

He stood up just in time to see a wonderfully familiar woman jogging toward him, denim jacket flapping open with each step. In a disorienting reverse-mirror of how his own hair was growing out from a buzz cut, her hair was even shorter than in her online pictures.

Years ago, she would've thrown herself bodily at him for a hug. Now, she skidded to a halt two feet away when Kaylee surged in front of Michael, preserving his personal space.

"Heel," he told Kaylee, who backed up to his left side. With a genuine smile, he held out his arms, saying, "Hey, sis."

Amanda was four years younger than Michael (or three for half the year, as she'd reminded him all through their childhood) and his closest ally in the war against politics. While he'd openly rebelled at eighteen, dropping out of college so he could enlist in the Air Force, she'd gone away to Mount Holyoke, where she'd majored in gender studies and minored in . . . something. Michael couldn't remember, but that wasn't important. She was *here*, which meant he and Kaylee weren't alone.

"I didn't think you were back," she mumbled against his shoulder. "Or did you come up from DC?"

"They didn't tell you?" Michael asked as she let go. "I'm staying at the island hou— Ow!" He made a show of rubbing his arm where she'd punched him. "What was that for?"

"For not telling me, asshole!" She pouted down at Kaylee, her voice going a half-octave higher as she asked, "Is he always like this?"

Michael rolled his eyes and said, "Kaylee, say hello." She broke position and nosed at Amanda's hip until she got the ear scratches she so loved. "I finished physical therapy, and Kaylee's almost done with training. I figure a summer on the island will be good for both of us."

"Uh-huh," Amanda said, crouching to better love on the dog. The last time they saw each other, Kaylee had been a gangly puppy, barely into her first month of obedience training. "And *after* the summer?"

Michael took a deep breath, dropping his hand so he could scratch Kaylee's back, just above her vest. "I'll probably stay. I'd rather not go up to . . . wherever they're living when they're not at the governor's mansion."

"I've got room in my town house. Two bedrooms."

"In Concord?" he asked suspiciously.

Amanda looked up with a weak smile. "Yeah."

"Where Bridges House is located."

"And the family shelter where I work," she protested as she stood up. "I can put you on my lease—"

"And when they're not at Bridges House, they're living . . ." he prompted.

"They've still got the farm."

"Which is all of an hour away from Concord." He shook his head.

Amanda sighed. "It's New Hampshire, Mike. *Everything* is like an hour away."

"Uh-huh. And that's why I'm glad to stay on the island, with a crappy two-lane bridge between me and the rest of the world," he said bluntly.

"Ouch." She clutched at her chest and staggered back. "Fine, be that way."

"Jealous?" Michael grinned. Amanda had always gotten along with their parents better than him, but that didn't mean her relationship with them was anything like ideal. "Want to quit your job and come stay with me?"

That got him another punch in the arm.

The habits of childhood weren't easily broken. "We are *way* the hell early," Michael muttered to Kaylee and Amanda. All around them, people were rushing about, taping down kitschy red-and-white checkered tablecloths, setting up chairs and tables, testing the speakers around the low stage off to one side. Reporters were wandering everywhere, marked more by their sharp eyes and coffee cups than their cameras or assistants.

"Yep," Amanda agreed grimly, bumping her shoulder against Michael's. "Want to go see Mom and Dad?"

Michael snorted. "No."

She raised an eyebrow at him. "Want to hang out here and wait for the reporters to put two and two together? The war hero veteran son—"

"Fuck that."

She shot him a dry smile. "You do know that's why you were invited, right?"

Michael rubbed at his forehead, trying to will away his impending migraine. "Why the hell did I say yes?"

"Because you're an idiot," Amanda said, tugging him toward the farmhouse where two security guards in matching black off-the-rack suits were lurking ominously on the porch. One stepped into sight, frowning at Kaylee. Typical breed prejudice, ignoring the way the big, scary dog walked calmly at his side. Tension crawled up Michael's spine and across his shoulders.

As he reached the stairs, he raised his voice and said, "Did you know the first guide dogs ever were German shepherds, in World War I?" It was a convenient truth, one he'd practiced saying until it came out smoothly no matter how anxious or glitchy he felt.

"Guide dogs?" Amanda asked, obviously baffled. "You're not blind."

The sight of the security guard backing away made Michael grin. "You figured that out all by yourself, sis?"

She shook her head and crossed the porch. One of the security guards opened the door for her, but she stepped aside to let Michael in first. He had to stop himself from instinctively sending Kaylee in to check the house's security. The guards would keep out physical threats, and . . . well, there was no way to manage the familial threat, short of moving to California.

A booming laugh rang out down the hall, surrounded by lighter, more decorous laughter. Michael's steps faltered, and Kaylee stopped, ready to brace him if he lost his balance. "Keep going," he murmured, trying—and failing—to ignore the ball of ice forming in his gut.

It had been eight months since he last saw his parents, when they came to DC before the winter holiday recess sent all of their political contacts home for the holidays. Michael had been walking with a cane, spending his days in physical therapy and counseling. He'd gone out to two dinners with them and seen them in passing when they made a "thank the veterans" visit to Walter Reed.

They'd treated him like glass, but underneath it, Michael's father had projected a deep sense of *You brought this on yourself.* Dad had been instrumental in Michael's admission to Dartmouth College as the next step in their thirty-year plan to turn Michael into the next political powerhouse of the Baldwins. Nowhere in that plan had there been room for Michael to drop out and enlist in the Air Force. In *supply*, rather than something politically useful, like flying a fighter jet or pararescue.

Their relationship was contentious, strained, full of barely hidden resentment on both sides—and that was *without* Dad finding out that Michael was gay.

"Think of it like a trip to the dentist," Amanda muttered, taking Michael's arm as they approached the open doorway, beyond which their dad was waiting, presumably with their hosts, their mom, and assorted hangers-on. "Get it over with, then get the hell out as soon as you can."

"Yeah." Michael took a deep breath, fist clenching around Kaylee's leash. "Okay."

They took the last few steps, and Michael froze in the doorway. His dad was holding court from an armchair by an unlit fireplace, Mom sitting nearby. The people on the couches were vaguely familiar—the Knoxes, Michael assumed. Everyone had steaming cups and saucers in hand. The early hour meant that the serving tray on the sideboard held coffee, though Dad's was doubtless spiked to give it a little kick.

". . . been the heart of American politics—" Dad spotted Michael and Amanda and cut off in midsentence. A heartbeat later, he put aside his coffee and rose with a falsely warm grin, holding out a hand to them. "There he is!" he announced, and Michael braced himself.

"Dad—"

There was no hope of stopping him, though, once he got started. The governor rolled right on as heads turned. "My son, the war hero!"

CHAPTER

FIVE

"Hey, Dad," Josh said, sinking into the empty chair. The cramped office was dominated by a secondhand desk—a monstrosity of scarred wood and tarnished brass—with barely enough room for two chairs and a file cabinet. Upgrading the office was on Josh's list of business improvements, though near the bottom.

"You look exhausted," his dad observed unhelpfully, closing the laptop lid partway.

Josh's derisive huff turned into a yawn halfway through. "Your morning schedule sucks," slipped out before he could stop himself.

"Yeah, it does." Dad's grin went sly. "Nice of you to volunteer, though. Care to tell me why?"

Josh groaned and looked out the door, through the kitchen, and into the main part of the shop. The lunch rush was just starting, but the three people working the counter—two on sandwich prep, one on register—were capable of handling things without him for five minutes. The ache in his feet had reached critical levels.

"Think I should make a fresh pot of coffee?" he asked, fumbling to change the subject. Not that it would work.

It didn't. Dad just asked, "So, you're dating a schoolteacher?"

"*What?*"

Dad shrugged. "You open the shop, you get out around two, after the lunch rush and cleanup. The elementary school lets out at three, which means—"

"No!" Josh shook his head, blinking against the too-long hair that got in his eyes. He kept forgetting to get a haircut. "No, Dad. I'm not dating a schoolteacher. I'm not dating *anyone*."

And saying that was a tactical mistake.

Dad jumped on the opening. "But you should be. You're bisexual, Josh. Men *and* women. Surely you can find *someone*."

"Oh my God," Josh muttered, bracing his elbows on the desk so he could hide his face in his hands. "Why did I ever tell you that?"

"I'm just saying, I'd like grandkids one day, and there's always adoption." Dad beamed. "You were adopted, and you turned out okay, right?"

That coffee was becoming more of a medical necessity than resting tired feet. "Come on, Dad. Really? I'm *not dating anyone*."

"Then what's so important that you've gotten out of bed at three in the morning for the last couple of days?"

Josh opened his mouth, but all that came to mind was Hot Tourist Guy. And even *hinting* at Hot Tourist Guy would be enough to set off Dad's bloodhound instincts, which meant he would be lurking at the shop first thing tomorrow morning and for every hour they were open until he ferreted out the object of Josh's crush.

Josh needed a diversion.

"I've been running numbers," he said, and was rewarded with his dad's faint wince. "Lizzie helped. The shop's making a nice profit—really nice—since we started the catering thing."

"Good," Dad said automatically, dark brows drawn together. "That's good, right?"

"Of course." Relieved that Dad had taken the bait, Josh tried to keep his grin to a minimum. "So maybe we can meet later tonight? Have a talk about what to do with the money?"

"We save it," Dad said at once, frowning even more. "What else would we do with it?"

Josh took a deep breath, steeling himself. He hadn't intended to have *this* talk, but it was better than discussing his unrequited crush on a guy whose name he didn't even know.

"Put it into the business."

Dad leaned back in his chair, still unsmiling. "We could put it in the business emergency fund. Stash it away in case some of our equipment breaks. If we need a new catering van. That sort of thing."

Josh hid a sigh of resignation. With the money already in the business emergency fund, they could reprovision, buy a brand-new van, and have enough left over to repaint and redo the flooring, all while paying their staff a decent wage. But now wasn't the time to get into the details.

"Let's talk about it later," he said, standing up despite how his feet protested. "I'm going to the store after shift for new gel insoles. Need anything?"

Dad looked at Josh, and—*shit*—that sly light came back into his eyes. "Does your girlfriend work at the store?"

Josh threw up his hands and headed for the door.

"Boyfriend?" Dad called after him.

"We'll talk more after closing, Dad," Josh yelled back.

"You can tell me anything! You know that!"

"Thanks, Dad," Josh muttered, though he was smiling. For a pain in the ass, Dad had his heart in the right place.

The best part of being a politician's son—possibly the *only* good part—was the food. Politicians who served lousy food, at least at the state level or higher, were doomed to failure. Today's barbecue was the best Michael had eaten in . . . Well, he couldn't remember better, and he went back for seconds. When it was time for thirds, the smiling server passed him a plated sandwich stacked on top of a bowl of plain shredded brisket, no sauce. "For your puppy," she said, as if Michael couldn't figure it out.

Fuck the rules, Michael thought, taking the plate and bowl. They were eating on the grass, under a cloudy sky, not in a restaurant, and the food really was top-notch. Kaylee deserved a reward for not even drooling as Michael had gorged.

"She says thanks," Michael said, then led Kaylee to a table on the other side of the field, away from all the action.

So far, he'd gone unnoticed, speaking to no one of consequence after the stilted initial meeting with his parents and the Knox family. Amanda, sensing a fund-raising opportunity for her shelter, had gone off to network, leaving Michael to eat his lunch in peace. Kaylee helped preserve Michael's privacy, thanks to absurd prejudice against German shepherds, no matter how silly she looked licking at her fur to get the last bits of brisket and rubbing her muzzle on the grass.

"You ridiculous goofball," he told her before taking another bite of his sandwich. Her tail wagged once before she abruptly stopped, raising her head, ears perked forward. Chest going tight, Michael followed the direction of her gaze, then relaxed in his seat when he spotted Amanda.

She took the empty seat beside Michael, Kaylee sprawled in the grass between them, and said, "God, I love taking money from rich assholes. Especially when they'd hate the cause if they only read the fine print."

Michael put down his half-eaten sandwich and swallowed. "What fine print?"

"We help *all* victims of domestic violence." Amanda's grin went sharp. "Married, unmarried, het, gay, lesbian, trans, you name it."

She was the only family member who knew he was gay. He'd come out to her years ago, when he called her from Misawa Air Base in Japan to wish her a happy eighteenth birthday. She hadn't come out to him in return, but she'd declared that she was changing her major from politics to gender studies, which was almost as radical, as far as their parents were concerned.

"Good for you," Michael said, and they shared a conspiratorial grin. Subverting their parents' political machinations was one of the few pleasures their strange childhood had offered.

"So what are you up to?" Amanda glanced down at Kaylee, hands twitching in a familiar way, though she didn't try to pet. "Tell me a Frisbee is involved."

"Only a little. We just got there," he reminded her between bites. "It took two days to get up here from DC."

Amanda deliberately looked away from him and down at Kaylee. "Don't like flying anymore?"

He pushed his plate away. "Too . . . confined. A train, it's easier to think I could get out if I needed," he said honestly. "I just had to overnight in Boston so I could switch lines."

She gave him a quick glance. "You drove here, though, didn't you?"

"It's night driving that I can't handle." Michael turned his wrist, watching Kaylee's leash swing back and forth. "That's like when it happened. The convoy attack. A late-afternoon dust storm. Even less visibility than at night."

"Mike . . ." She put a hand on his shoulder and caught his eye. "Are you . . . okay? Really okay?"

Define "okay." He shrugged and nodded down at Kaylee. "She helps. We do a lot of training." He smiled. "I think she's smarter than you and me put together."

"You were in a dog training school in DC, right?" When he nodded, she asked, "Do you have one here too?"

"No, but I can call the trainers if I have questions. And we're mostly polishing behaviors."

"That's not—" She cut off with a sigh. "Your school had a whole class of students. You were with people. Not at home . . ."

Alone. She didn't say it, but Michael heard it. He sat back in his chair and gave her a smile that he hoped was reassuring. "We're going out every day. Lots of walks—not just so she can do her business. My trainer even said it: having a service dog means you'll make excuses to get out of the house."

She grinned. "And go where? Isn't the island kind of dead compared to DC?"

"Yeah, but I like the quiet." Michael smiled at the thought of going back there in just a few hours. Maybe sooner. Maybe in time to stop at the bagel place and pick up dinner. "We can go into town to shop or go to restaurants. It's good. We both need the exercise."

Amanda snorted and looked him up and down. "Another twenty pounds is what you need."

"I just ate," he protested, pointing at the empty plate. "And I got a bagel and coffee this morning before driving up here."

"Mike . . ."

"Come on." He kicked at her shin. "You should be glad. First time in our lives you're in better shape than me. Are you working out?"

Amanda was practically glowing from the praise, though her shrug was casual. "Yeah. I kept up with cross-country, but I added in weight training last fall. I have a personal trainer and everything."

Smirking, Michael nudged her again. "Great. At least our father's probably happy with you."

"Yeah, right." She rolled her eyes. "They wanted a son. *Two* sons would've been better."

"You were the one into sports and fast cars. Me, he never understood. I was a nerd." It didn't come out bitter. The only thing Michael had liked about boarding school was his advanced placement in most classes. Well, that and the library. "I wouldn't have even played soccer if not for the tight shorts."

"And the bathing suits on our summer vacations, huh?"

Michael snickered. "Of course."

"Speaking of sons . . ." Amanda trailed off for a couple of seconds—long enough that Michael almost spoke up—before she said, "Are you going back to Dartmouth? You know they're going to want you to at least start working for the family law firm."

"As a stepping-stone to a political career. Fuck that," Michael said bluntly. "I don't want to be a lawyer any more than you did."

Amanda gave an exaggerated sigh. "You should've heard the absolute shit I got for changing my major. Though I guess it wasn't *that* bad, compared to you. They're more interested in me marrying into the 'right' family than getting a law degree."

"And the whole marriage-grandchildren thing?"

"Not happening. Ever," she said, her voice so frosty, Michael shivered. "But that reminds me . . . I'd come visit you this summer, but I'm leaving for a while. On my birthday, in fact."

"You are?" Michael did the mental math and realized she was turning twenty-five, which meant— "The trust fund? Taking advantage of your windfall?"

Her mouth twitched. "Sort of. I'm going overseas for a year. It's all part of my gender studies degree."

"Which you completed, didn't you? Or did I send you a graduation present you didn't earn?"

She smacked his arm. "I graduated, you jerk. But, you know, some stuff I learned . . . It's, um . . . Things that are multicultural and all . . ."

Michael stared at his usually eloquent sister, for a moment worried that his own aphasia was taking a new turn, making him perceive someone else as stumbling and losing their words. But no, this was all her. "What—"

Kaylee surged to her feet in warning, and Michael snapped his mouth shut. Amanda frowned at them both, then looked over her shoulder. The man heading toward them was dressed in a carefully casual way, with a sport jacket hanging open over a button-down, top two buttons undone. He had a practiced smile that was as artificial as his hairline.

"Shit," Amanda muttered, barely moving her lips as she turned back to Michael. "That's Wilkins, Dad's—"

"Chief of staff," Michael finished. Time to pay for those barbecue sandwiches he'd eaten.

"Mr. Baldwin! And Miss Baldwin," Wilkins called cheerfully, earning a thunderous scowl from Amanda, who'd once treated Michael to a twenty-minute rant on the inherent sexism in gendered courtesy titles. Especially "miss."

"What?" Michael asked sharply, just as he'd done on the phone, though this time it was intentional—a way to head off Amanda's imminent explosion.

Wilkins was easier to ruffle in person than over the phone. He blinked once, then rallied and flashed his smile again, focusing on Michael. "Glad I found you. The governor wants to see you. Just a quick private chat."

Everything inside Michael's head screamed *No!* He glanced down at his plate, but all that was left of sandwich number three was a bit of crust. No help there. If he tried to stick with Amanda, that would just drag her into whatever his father wanted. And nice as it would be to have an ally other than Kaylee, Amanda didn't deserve that. She was already too close to their parents.

So Michael stood and said, "Sure. I have a couple of minutes."

Wilkins's frown was baffled. "A crate of . . . what?"

Amanda shot Michael a quick, alarmed look before turning to Wilkins. "He has a couple of minutes," she said sharply, as if daring Wilkins to ask.

Shit. Had Michael glitched? His heart kicked hard against his ribs. He could've *sworn* he said it right.

Kaylee leaned against Michael's leg, never turning her attention from Wilkins. Michael scratched between her ears and told her, "Kaylee, leash." She ducked and picked up the leash to offer him the handle.

"Aw, that's such a cute little doggie," Wilkins said in a baby voice. "Does it do any other tricks?"

"*She* doesn't do tricks," Michael snapped. Amanda did a half-assed job of hiding her laugh with a cough. Wilkins's face flushed, and he turned to head to the house.

Michael had to take a couple of breaths to calm himself. His father was hard enough to handle without piling anger and disorientation and aphasia on top of everything else. He was tempted to slip away—three cheers for strategic parking—but that would just make things worse. His parents might well demand he move from the island to the family farm "for his health" or some bullshit.

Amanda reached out to him, but Kaylee body-blocked her by turning to face Michael, smacking her tail into Amanda's arm. Michael waved Kaylee off with a quiet, "Good girl," and took hold of Amanda's hand.

She looked up into his eyes, her face grave. "Remember," she said in a solemn voice, "no biting."

"Kaylee doesn't bite," he protested automatically.

One corner of Amanda's mouth twitched up. "I was talking to you."

Michael rolled his eyes, but her humor, bad as it was, shattered the tension choking his breath. He laughed roughly and said, "Actually, yeah, you were. What were you saying?"

Her smile turned regretful. "Don't worry about it. Are you going to try to get out of here?"

She knew him too well. "Yeah," he said, leaning down to kiss her cheek. "Sorry to abandon you—"

"Go," she insisted. "I'll send you a postcard from Thailand or something."

"Be safe," he said, wondering what was so interesting in Thailand, though only for a moment. He picked up his bag and told Kaylee, "Let's go," then hurried after Wilkins, feeling like he was headed for a firing squad.

Two o'clock in the afternoon was early for social drinks in any sphere but business or politics. Michael wasn't surprised to find his father had a Scotch in hand. Liquid sloshed when he waved the glass at the bar in the corner of the Knoxes' sitting room, playing host. "Something to drink, son?"

"No. Thanks." Michael flinched at a loud *thump* and twisted to glare at the door Wilkins had pulled closed, leaving his father and him alone in the sitting room. "What'd you want?"

The governor leaned back in his chair and crossed one leg over the other, the very picture of casual, competent power. "You're walking without your cane."

So it was going to be an interrogation. Carefully, Michael said, "For the last month."

"Settled into the house all right?"

Michael shrugged. "The barn."

A flicker of irritation appeared on his father's face, then disappeared. "Uh-huh. Did you get a chance to meet Elijah Knox? The veteran from the Vietnam War?"

Michael nodded. They'd been introduced by one of the older Knox children, though Elijah—who answered exclusively to Captain Knox or Grandpa—probably couldn't remember. The captain seemed to think it was the late seventies, when he had been a pilot for a local airline that had gone out of business ten or fifteen years later. A nurse had been in close attendance through Michael's whole meeting, probably to keep Captain Knox from getting out of his wheelchair and wandering off in search of his plane.

"Good," his father approved. He took a sip of his drink, and Michael could feel his stare. "And what are you doing with yourself these days?"

Michael had seen *that* question coming six months ago. It had taken him three months of role-play with his therapist to be able to meet his father's eyes and say, "I'm continuing my recovery, as my doctors directed. Just because I'm out of the hospital and on my feet doesn't mean I'm fully healed."

His father could spot a memorized speech at fifty yards. His eyes narrowed, and Michael looked down at Kaylee, trying to hide the way his chest went tight again. He wanted out. He *needed* to get out.

"But what are you *doing*?" his father asked. "There's nothing on that island outside tourist season. None of the other families are there yet, are they?"

Michael clenched Kaylee's leash hard, focusing on his memory of Josh's warm smile just this morning. It was no surprise his father dismissed the town's full-time residents as if they didn't exist—and Michael had no desire to correct that impression.

"I've been working with Kaylee," he said. "I have to keep up her training."

His father frowned in that "baffled and unhappy about being confused" way of his; he didn't like not being in the know. "And?" he finally pressed. "What about your . . . What was it? Those movies you used to always watch."

Leather creaked under Michael's fingers. He'd spent his childhood immersed in sci-fi movies and comic books, but when he awakened in the hospital, he had . . . lost his love for most everything. Shows he once enjoyed were remade into shadows of what they'd been. Comics were regurgitated storylines or bizarre crossovers. He didn't have the mental energy to get invested anymore.

"I work with Kaylee," he said, the words coming slow and hard, like pushing a boulder uphill. Fighting the weight of his father's disappointment.

"Well, you're up on your feet. That's something," his father finally said. "Any scheduled doctor's appointments? Physical therapy? A *psychiatrist*?"

Michael flinched again at the subtly scathing emphasis on that last word. His father had made his feelings on psychological therapy crystal clear back in DC. "No. Nothing yet. I need to wait for VA paperwork to catch up." That was a blatant lie, thanks to his medical retirement from the Air Force, but his father didn't know the intricacies of the military's health care program. After two years of recovery in DC, with his parents interfering at every turn, he wasn't willing to get into the details of his health care with *anyone*, much less his father.

He glanced up in time to see his father nod in a satisfied sort of way. "Then you've got plenty of time," his father said, now one hundred percent in political mode. "We could use you on the campaign trail. VFW halls, a few hospitals, the state veterans' cemetery in November."

Panic seized Michael's voice. He'd suspected this would happen—he'd *expected* it—but the blunt statement was enough to paralyze him.

Kaylee's soft weight pressed against his leg, and she nosed at his hand a heartbeat before the door clicked open. He still jumped and backed away, heart racing, as his mother swept in. Hair dye, Pilates, and a carefully chosen wardrobe made her look ten years younger than her actual age.

A bit crazily, Michael thought that he actually had no idea what his mother looked like without the touch of her personal assistant, who doubled as a stylist and wardrobe consultant.

His breathing kicked in at the wrong time—just as she leaned close to give him a perfumed, impersonal kiss on the cheek. Muffling his cough with one fist, he tried to stop breathing again.

"Sorry I'm late," she said, bestowing an equally impersonal kiss on her husband's cheek, a brief stop on the way to the bar. "We'll have updated donation figures in twenty minutes. Don't let me interrupt."

"I was just talking about Michael's role in the upcoming campaign," his father said, not even looking in Michael's direction—as if his compliance were a foregone conclusion. "We'll stay local through the new year. Then he can take charge of getting the military vote."

"Military and women, eighteen to thirty-five," his mother put in, mixing herself a gin and tonic. "Look at him. They'll be lining up around the block to take pictures with him."

Michael's rising panic hit critical mass. "No!"

Not that it stopped his parents. His mother said, "Don't be ridiculous," while his father shot him a disappointed look.

"My policies have consistently supported a stronger, better-equipped military," he said, his voice taking on a rough growl. "Do you suddenly have an issue with that? You were pro-military enough to abandon your enrollment at one of the nation's finest universities..."

Roaring filled Michael's ears, one-tenth anger and nine-tenths dread that his father had pulled strings and arranged for Michael to go back to Dartmouth. To get his life back on the family railroad, next stop a soul-crushing career in politics.

"No!" he repeated, drowning out his father's voice. Kaylee was leaning against his legs, a warm weight that wasn't quite enough to ground him against the combined force of his parents. He gripped her leash so tightly, his knuckles cracked.

His shout cut off whatever they were saying. They stared at him with identical affronted expressions until his mother shrugged and asked, "No? What do you mean, no?"

"This is important," his father continued as he got up to refill his drink. He was two inches taller than Michael, with broad shoulders left over from his college football days. His presence sucked all the air out of the room. "This isn't some local campaign. We're going *national*. And to succeed, we're going to need everyone in the family onboard."

"Our staff is working on the last details of our strategy. We're finalizing the itineraries for you and your sister next week," his mother said over the sound of Scotch splashing into his father's glass.

So they didn't know about Amanda's plans to spend the next year abroad. Did her timing have less to do with getting her hands on her trust fund and more to do with their parents' campaign strategy?

He went cold inside when he realized that she was going to sneak off to another continent and abandon him to their parents. *Alone.*

"Absolutely not," he said, shaking his head a little too hard, enough to risk a dizzy spell. "I'm not getting involved in *any* campaign. Not national, not statewide, not a local campaign for the school board!" The words surged out in a rush, carried on a wave of anger that slammed into his parents with the force of a tsunami—

Or *should* have.

They were staring at him, his father with a thunderous scowl, his mother in absolute bafflement.

"Well," his father said flatly. "He can't go out in public like *that*."

She waved her glass and gave Michael an insincere smile. "We'll find you a speech therapist. Just speak more slowly and *think* about what you're saying."

What the hell had he said? The ice in his gut expanded, driving the air from his lungs as he struggled to remember. He thought he'd taken a stand against his parents' control, for the first time in his life, but apparently the words had gotten scrambled on the way to his mouth from his brain. His *broken* brain.

Get out.

He thought it. Might've said it, because Kaylee spun and went for the door to scratch it with her too-long toenails. She could open lever-operated doors, but not doorknobs. Michael automatically turned it until it unlatched—something he'd taught himself to do even in a fugue state.

And then they were in the hall, through the foyer, out the front door, and down the steps. Trained to find the most direct route in emergencies, Kaylee cut across soft grass, next to a bed of late-spring flowers. When they reached the truck, she quietly barked and nudged at his hip.

He let out a breath in a dizzying rush of air. He could hear his mother's sharp, angry voice calling his name, and that spurred him to unlock the truck. As soon as he had the driver's-side door open, Kaylee leaped in, holding the leash in her mouth, and squirmed between the front seats to get in back. Michael followed, right on her tail, and slammed the door.

Wonderful silence.

He dragged in another breath and jabbed at the start button until the engine roared. As soon as he had the SUV in gear, he drove straight down the driveway, tires kicking up gravel. He swerved halfway onto the grass to avoid a train of three cars packed with late arrivals, and accelerated to get through the gate before the sheriff's car could block it.

Freedom. Shaking with relief, he spun the wheel, turning onto the main road. In his rearview mirror, he saw the sheriff watching him, probably assessing his erratic driving. The thought of being pulled over, subjected to an interrogation and possibly a test of his balance, cut through the chaos in his head enough to steady his hands on the wheel. He eased up on the gas and drove more sedately down the road, heading southeast. Heading home.

CHAPTER
SIX

Raimo's Pizza had started life as a narrow hole-in-the-wall pizza joint, tucked awkwardly into a corner storefront between a salon and a defunct real estate agency. They'd since expanded into the real estate agency's office space, adding round bistro-style tables that were too small for students to occupy for hours at a shot, enabling them to do a brisk business in by-the-slice lunch specials and pies to go. The tiny tables meant Raimo's was off-limits for Josh and Dad's wrap-up dinners, except on nights like tonight—nights when they were both too exhausted to do anything more than eat in front of the TV and then drag themselves upstairs to collapse.

As soon as Josh opened the pizzeria door and got a whiff of oregano and garlic, his neglected stomach let out a roar. "Three hours repairing that mixer," he grumbled, holding the door for his dad. "Three hours!"

"And you did great," Dad said, patting Josh's shoulder in passing. "Three hours of work was a whole lot better than waiting three *days* for the repairman."

"Yeah, but three hours." Josh fell in line behind the other customers. "That's me being three hours late for both food and a nap."

Dad's grin was offensively cheerful. Offensively *awake*. "On the bright side, pizza."

Scrubbing at his eyes, Josh playfully complained, "I swear, you're twelve years old."

Dad threw an arm around Josh's shoulders and pulled him into a quick, rough hug. "The joys of parenthood—when your kid's old enough to take the opening shift for a whole week in a row."

"Oh, no." Josh held up his hands. "I may not be awake, but I'm not sleepy enough to fall for that. Tomorrow morning, the keys are all yours."

Dad sighed theatrically and released him, stepping aside for a customer carrying an immense pizza box. Josh caught the distinct smell of bacon and regretted, not for the first time, that he and his dad kept sort of kosher in their house. The occasional cheeseburger was fine, and pepperoni didn't count, because no one actually knew what went into pepperoni, but bacon was off-limits at home. Maybe he'd sneak over here tomorrow for the lunch special, if Bagel End wasn't too busy.

"So hey, you wanted to talk earlier," Dad said as the line moved up a couple of feet. "And you're not going to be awake in an hour."

"I did?" Josh frowned up at the menu board, trying to push his sluggish brain into working again. He remembered a lot of teasing about girlfriends—and boyfriends—followed by the metal-on-metal grind of a dough hook that had slipped out of alignment. Before all that, everything was a blur.

"You, Lizzie, the books? Investing profits?" Dad prompted.

Shit. Now was *not* the right time for this talk. Josh rubbed at his eyes again and nodded. "Yeah, but it's not . . ." Important? It was. "There's no rush."

Dad nudged him with an elbow. "Come on. Talk to me."

Josh sighed. This was a terrible idea—even worse than discussing his love life—but he was too tired to fight off his dad's tenacity. Best to get it over with quickly.

Actually, no. Best to start with small steps.

"A new product line. Not too much of a risk," he said confidently.

"New products?" Dad frowned at him. "We're a bagel place."

"But that's not all we are," Josh said. "When you opened the store, it was bagels, deli meat, and cheese. Now we do breakfasts, paninis, soup—"

"Okay, okay. What new product?" Dad asked skeptically.

"Dog treats." Josh's heart skipped a beat. He'd been thinking of bagel chips, because everyone loved crunchy, salty snacks, but he'd seen bagel-style dog treats online. Somehow, his brain had made the jump.

No, not somehow. It was all because of Hot Tourist Guy.

"Dog treats?" Dad's frown turned baffled. "What kind of dog treats? Can we even? The health department—"

"No, no. Not like dog-only biscuits. Just crunchy minibagels for dogs. Flavored stuff like"—Josh racked his brain—"peanut butter, bacon, cheese, that sort of thing. People could even eat them, since they'll be just like normal bagels, only crunchy."

"Huh. You know," Dad said thoughtfully, "that might work. Lots of tourists have dogs."

Hope blossomed in Josh's chest. "And locals. We could give out samples at the vet's office."

Dad slowly smiled. "Yeah. Yeah, okay. But we'll need a recipe. A cost analysis. Packaging. A *name*."

"I'll take care of it," Josh promised, wondering if Tolkien's books included any dogs. His dad was a huge Tolkien geek—hence the shop name—and he'd want something thematic for the dog bagels.

"That's a really good idea, you know. Good thought, son," Dad said, pulling him in for another hug.

Josh laughed and playfully twisted free. He nearly let the subject drop there, but he was on a roll. His dad was finally looking at him like a *partner*, not an apprentice. "I had another idea too."

"Yeah?" Dad asked, still smiling, which meant this was a good time.

"The shop's great. The catering business is phenomenal. I want to expand into supplying bagels and baked goods to restaurants and hotels."

He didn't need to look to know Dad was frowning. "I thought we were going to bulk up the emergency fund. Expansion is risky."

"Risky?" Josh nodded, glancing over at the frown for a second. "I know. But it's *managed* risk."

"How can you *manage* risk?" Dad scoffed. "By definition, if risk can be 'managed,' it's not a risk. When it comes to betting, there are—"

"No sure things," Josh finished with his dad. He lowered his voice, aware that they were surrounded by people who were sometimes their customers, and said, "I know. But we already have a solid emergency fund. We own the shop, so we're not at risk for a rent hike, and we own our house, so we're not at risk of being homeless. We have an *opportunity*, Dad."

"An opportunity? What opportunity?" Dad challenged, just above a whisper.

"The Ludwigs, at Breakwater Cove B&B. They've got a standing catering order for brunch every Sunday and Thursday, with a dozen extra bagels to carry them through to the next delivery day."

"I don't know . . ."

Josh rubbed at the back of his neck, wishing he had stopped at the dog bagels. He let out a frustrated breath and took a couple of steps forward when the line moved. He wasn't prepared for this discussion. He had none of his notes, the business plan outline was on his laptop, and he was dead on his feet.

"Okay, no," he said when his dad caught up with him. "Can we just . . . *not*? Not now, okay?"

Dad opened his mouth, then closed it, looking into Josh's eyes. Slowly, Dad smiled and said, "Yeah. We'll talk about it when I'm back from Brooklyn. How's that sound?"

Gratefully, Josh nodded, bumping his shoulder against his dad's. "Good. That's good."

"In that case," Dad said, giving Josh a bump of his own, "what do you say we get double pepperoni?"

"And extra cheese?" Josh proposed, awake enough to take advantage of his dad's goodwill.

Dad laughed. "And extra cheese."

It took two hours at a rest stop, surrounded by trees and exhaust fumes, for Michael's thoughts to stop racing. He sat on a picnic bench behind the amenities building, Kaylee sleeping on his feet, his phone a dead weight in his pocket—minus its battery, because it was likely his parents had sicced Wilkins on him and he wasn't taking any chances.

How could he have lost control so badly? He knew better. He *knew* that when emotions ran hot and stress levels soared, he was more likely to lose his words. For seven horrible months after his surgery, he'd tripped over his own brain, struggling to find even the simplest words, substituting rhymes or concepts connected by only the most bizarre associations, though he *heard* himself speaking correctly. Hell, he hadn't even believed no one could understand him until a speech pathologist had come to his hospital room to explain the new twist in his recovery—aphasia—and discuss his treatment.

He braced his elbows on the picnic table and dropped his face into his hands. His fingertips automatically sought the scar under his bangs, above his left eyebrow. The combat medics and trauma surgeons had done a phenomenal job keeping him alive, getting him back on his feet, helping him relearn how to talk and function and get on with his life, now as a civilian.

When he sighed, Kaylee pushed herself upright so she could rest her muzzle heavily against his knee. Automatically, he scratched at her fur, letting her settle his thoughts. "Okay," he muttered, leaning back to look under the table at her.

She tipped her head without breaking physical contact and fixed him with one deep-brown eye. No judgment. No recrimination. Just love and loyalty and absolute willingness to support him, however he needed.

He smiled and ruffled between her ears. "Let's go." Together, they walked back to the truck.

The eastern sky was a deepening turquoise by the time he drove onto the bridge to Hartsbridge Island. He ended up behind a delivery truck going a steady forty miles per hour, but the slower speed gave him a chance to plan ahead. Wilkins had interrupted yesterday's plans for grocery shopping, and for the life of him, he couldn't remember what he had in his kitchen. He was too stressed to even think about walking back into town for dinner.

"Takeout?" he asked Kaylee, who'd been dozing on the backseat.

She twisted around, front paws braced in the footwell, and nosed at his arm where it rested on the center console. He decided to take that as agreement.

Most of the town hadn't transitioned to summer's late hours, so he drove past dark shops until he spotted a pool of light spilling out onto a corner, hinting at the possible presence of food and to-go boxes. He slowed, looking through the windows, noting the ceiling-high stack of prefolded pizza boxes against the wall.

And at the counter, he saw a now-familiar head of dark-blond curls and a stocky body not quite hidden by jeans and a bright-blue polo shirt. His heart gave a quick *thump* of excitement. *Josh.*

Maybe this was a sign—a hint that Michael should get up the courage to speak to Josh about more than bagels and bacon. He'd started the day with Josh's smile. What better way to end it?

"How's pizza sound?" he asked Kaylee, who knew *pizza* as well as she knew any of her commands. She answered with an enthusiastic bark. She had no food allergies, so a couple of slices wouldn't do her any harm. They could get her back onto her regular diet tomorrow.

The handicap parking tag was still hanging from the rearview mirror, so he took a spot in front of the doors and got out as quickly as he could without falling flat on his face. Kaylee's jump to the pavement was significantly more graceful, and Michael muttered, "Showoff."

Energized by a day of tension-filled highs and lazy lows, she pranced at his side like her AKC champion mother, pausing alertly so he could open the door.

As soon as he told her, "Go through," Josh's head whipped around, and he gave Michael a wide-eyed stare. After a blink, he smiled warmly and waved, turning back only at a nudge from the older man at his side. When the older man turned to say something to Josh, showing a sharp profile with a hooked nose, Michael recognized him from the diner.

A relative? They didn't look at all alike, so maybe a coworker. Or a boyfriend, though that'd be one hell of an age difference—at least fifteen, twenty years.

When Josh looked back again, Michael got his head out of his ass and remembered to actually *smile back*. Josh's smile turned into a grin—and God, this silent communication was so much easier than using words.

Michael's confidence lasted until the older man turned and followed Josh's gaze. Sharp, dark eyes seemed to bore right into Michael's skull. Unaccountably guilty at being caught staring at Josh, Michael glanced down at Kaylee, who looked up at him with a happy canine grin.

Then she pushed up to all four feet, body angled to one side, blocking—

Josh.

Michael's ability to form coherent sentences vanished like a flock of startled birds. He smiled—at least, he hoped it was a smile and not a grimace—and gave a jerky nod. Without the barrier of a counter between them, Josh was . . . well, obviously, closer. Accessible. Within reach as a person, not just as the facilitator of a commercial transaction.

"Hey." Josh's smile left his mouth higher at one corner than the other, and he looked down at Kaylee as if intentionally showing off long, light-brown lashes.

This was high school all over again.

Michael said, "Hey." That was as far as he could go until he remembered to wave Kaylee out of the way.

Say something, you idiot, he told himself, but nothing came to mind. Back in DC, he hadn't had any difficulty picking up one-night stands in nightclubs, but now he was in a damned pizza place, for God's sake.

"So, uh," Josh said, capturing Michael's gaze once more, "pizza? Or are you stalking me for more bagels?"

Michael laughed, letting the leash go slack so he could shove his hands in his pockets. It was that or reach out to casually touch Josh's arm. "Pizza. Though we'll probably have bagels for breakfast. *A* bagel, at least. Kaylee gets a snack for breakfast before we leave."

"Tell me what kind you want, and I'll keep one in reserve," Josh promised.

Was he flirting, or was this just really, *really* good customer service? It had to be flirting. That or Michael was being an optimist, which never happened.

And Josh had asked a question. Michael scrambled for an answer and blurted out, "Everything," which had nothing to do with bagels and everything to do with his uncharacteristic optimism.

Josh's smile made his eyes squint. The hint of crow's feet briefly made him look older. "You got it." He tipped his head, studying Michael's face, and asked, "What name should I put on the bag?"

Had Michael not given his name? Josh had introduced himself ages ago. Well, yesterday, anyway. Quickly, he said, "Michael. Michael Baldwin." Then, before Josh could think about connecting him to the governor, he said, "Just Michael."

"Michael." Josh's smile went warm, his eyes soft. "One everything bagel, and I'll throw in a couple pieces of crispy bacon for your girl there."

Michael nearly said, *You don't have to*, before he realized that'd be both stupid and rude. Instead, he said, "Thanks, Josh."

"Anytime."

For a few slow, simmering seconds, they stood there, staring at one another, before Michael realized that he had to come up with a reason for Josh to stick around. The line had moved up, so Michael took a step, glancing from the menu board back to Josh again, and quickly asked, "What's good here?"

Josh gave a wistful sigh. "Spinach, onion, and bacon Sicilian. That's the, uh, square pizza."

"They do Sicilian here?" Michael looked at the menu board, and there it was, printed large enough for him to read without his glasses: round, deep dish, Sicilian. Oops.

"It's the best."

"Is that what you're getting?"

Josh shot a mournful look at the older man who was lurking by the counter, failing to hide his amusement. "Dad prefers New York–style pizza, and we keep kosher at home, so we're doing double pepperoni."

Michael almost missed that, in his inappropriate happiness at the confirmation that the older man wasn't a boyfriend. "Wait," he said, replaying Josh's words in his head. Had he misheard? "Is pepperoni kosher?"

Josh shrugged. "Probably not, but it's not bacon, and bacon's *definitely* not kosher. Pepperoni's sort of a gray area, as long as we don't know the ingredients."

That was just . . . adorable. Laughing, Michael asked, "Isn't that cheating?"

"Well, yeah." Josh's grin was unrepentant. "But it's pepperoni."

Michael, Josh decided, had the best laugh of anyone he'd met in ages. There was something surprised about it, as if Michael hadn't really had a reason to for a while. *New mission: make him laugh more.*

"It makes perfect religious sense," Josh pointed out. "Jews are practical that way. Reform Jews, anyway. It's kind of like cheeseburgers."

Michael gave Josh a confused look that was almost identical to a dog's curious head tilt. "Cheeseburgers?" he asked.

"A cheeseburger made with actual cheese, like cheddar, isn't kosher. Obviously, right?" When Michael nodded, Josh continued, "But with American cheese—as in, 'processed cheese food'—the law gets a little fuzzy."

"I'm pretty sure that's not how it works," Michael said.

"Really, it is," Josh protested, his voice going high-pitched with his own repressed laughter. "It's like ice cream. You're supposed to wait X hours after eating meat before you can eat ice cream, but a restaurant would kick you out for waiting that long for dessert. Which means that ice cream, even after burgers or steaks, is good for the economy."

Michael snorted, his whole face lighting up. "Oh my God. Have you actually tried this logic on an authority? A rabbi, maybe?" he suggested.

"Nah. No sense bothering him with silly"—Josh hesitated when Michael's grin faded a couple of notches and the dog pushed between them—"questions . . . What?"

The answer came not from Michael but from Josh's dad, who poked at Josh's arm with one corner of the pizza box. "You ready, or did you want to stick around and hang out with your *friend* here?" he asked, all but spelling out *boyfriend*.

Josh sputtered, "Oh, I'll—"

"We're just—" Michael snapped his mouth shut, looking between the two of them before he locked his attention on the dog.

"Dad." It didn't quite come out as a growl, but it was close. "This is Michael. He's—" A customer? Too impersonal. Hot as hell? Both rude and obvious. "He's a friend," Josh said, even though it was presumptuous. But they *were* friends, right? Or acquaintances, anyway.

Michael offered Dad a shy nod, then his hand. "Hi. Michael Baldwin."

Dad grinned and switched the pizza box to his left hand so he could shake. "Oren Goldberg. Nice to meet you, Michael." He turned to Josh and asked again, "You sticking around?"

Yes. Josh shot Michael a look, but before either of them could say anything, a new voice pointedly asked, "Can I help you, sir?"

The line between Michael and the counter had vanished. No one was behind Michael, which was why they hadn't noticed. Michael gestured toward the counter, saying, "I should— We haven't eaten since lunch."

And that was practically an invitation for Josh's dad to suggest Michael and Kaylee join them for dinner, which was a disaster waiting to happen. "I'll have that bagel for you tomorrow," Josh promised, waving Michael toward the counter. "Enjoy your pizza."

Michael's smile was subtle and shy and felt like it was just for Josh. "You too, Josh. Nice to meet you," he added with a quick nod for Dad.

"We'll see you around, Michael," Dad said. It came out ominous.

Josh took the pizza box from his father. "Come *on*, Dad. Night, Michael," Josh said, herding his father away.

"G'night," Michael called after them.

Before they'd even hit the door, Dad stage-whispered to Josh, "Is *that* the boyfriend you claim you don't have?"

Josh groaned and nudged his dad to get him moving. Only when they were outside—door closed—did Josh say, "Really, Dad. He's a customer, not my boyfriend."

"*Yet?*"

Josh sighed.

Dad smiled reassuringly. "The way you two were looking at each other? It's 'yet,' Josh. Trust me."

CHAPTER

SEVEN

"Sure you want to go in?"

Stupid o'clock was no time for Josh to be conscious, much less having a conversation. It took him a few long seconds to turn away from the front door and blink up at the patch of darkness that slowly resolved into his dad. In pajamas and a bathrobe. Unlike Josh, who'd put on his shirt three times—once backward, once inside out, before getting it right.

"Huh?" Josh asked. He was still running on caffeine-free autopilot. The coffeepot at home sucked compared to the industrial machine at the shop.

Snickering, Dad came to the bottom of the stairs. "Sure you want to switch shifts?"

Switch shifts? That was a terrible idea. Except . . .

Michael. Hot Tourist Guy, whose name Josh now knew, who was coming to the shop for a reserved everything bagel and bacon.

"Yeah. You . . ." Josh shook his head, marginally more awake now that he was thinking of Michael. "You go back to bed."

"Okay." Dad was still grinning, because even stupid o'clock wasn't too early for his sense of humor. "Have fun, Josh."

All Josh could manage in return was a grunt. He took his keys from the hook by the door, then hung them back up so he could put on his windbreaker. And when he opened the door, he almost forgot the keys again.

Mornings *sucked.*

But he walked the two blocks to work, where he spent the next couple of hours drinking coffee, making bagels, and generally regaining consciousness. He had no idea when Michael would be in. Six a.m.?

After the breakfast rush? Late in the day, after Josh went home and collapsed? God, he hoped not. The thought of his dad—who was on the afternoon shift—having free rein to regale Michael with stories from Josh's childhood was horrifying.

At least the morning's baking was easy. Years ago, Dad—and Mom, before she died—had worked out a rotating schedule to maintain a supply of fresh bagels, in various flavors, without needing to triple their kitchen equipment. They'd made adjustments over the years, and their catering business had thrown a wrench into the schedule for six months, but eventually things had smoothed out again. Today's morning baking wasn't supposed to include everything bagels, but it was easy for Josh to make an extra batch.

Maybe he'd send Michael home with a free baker's dozen. Or was it too soon for things like that? Could be. Plus it might cost Josh in terms of visits, if Michael had the option to stay home and toast up a frozen bagel each morning. Of course, then Josh could actually get a decent night's sleep.

He was being ridiculous. A free baker's dozen was just nice—a "welcome back to the island" gift box, as it were. Instead of sleep, he'd drink more coffee so he'd stay awake even if Michael didn't show up before shift change.

Having a plan helped, as did his usual six o'clock customer, Dr. Miller—alone, today. "This is becoming a habit, Josh," she said when he came out of the kitchen to greet her. Her British accent was heavier first thing in the morning, one of the few reasons he enjoyed the early shift—second only to seeing Michael, in fact. "Have you and your father switched permanently?"

"Temporarily permanently," Josh explained with a grin. She'd left her long gray hair loose today, a wealth of thick waves hanging past her shoulders. "Nice hair," he complimented.

She winked. "You too, love. And do I smell everything bagels?"

"Fresh out of the oven. Want one?" He'd made a whole batch in case some of them bubbled or burned—it happened under the best of circumstances—but they'd all come out perfect.

"Mmm. My wife will regret missing out." She tapped her nails on the glass bagel counter. "You know what? Give me two. I'll run by the hospital."

"Is she still eating vending machine food?" Josh dropped two everything bagels in the slicer.

She sighed dramatically. "Medical doctors have the *worst* health habits. Next time I take her home to London, I'm setting my mum on her. Perhaps I'll get the twins to help—they're relatively health-conscious."

"Isn't one of the twins in the army?"

"Keith is."

"Keith . . . He's the taller one?" Josh asked, before realizing how stalkery that sounded. He'd had an on-off crush on the twins for years, back when their parents were summer visitors, not full-time residents. He filled a large Styrofoam cup with coffee and two sugars, no cream. "Regular or decaf for your wife?"

"Decaf. And the light cream cheese for us both, please. It'll be our little secret." As Josh unwrapped the cream cheese, Dr. Miller said, "Oh, I won't be around next Monday. I'm going up to Concord to meet with Governor Baldwin."

"Yeah? That's—" Josh cut off, remembering Michael's introduction last night. "*Baldwin?*" he blurted, instantly feeling like an idiot for forgetting the name of his state's governor.

Dr. Miller arched one eyebrow, a skill Josh had always envied. "Yes . . . Governor Samuel Baldwin. He's asking for endorsements."

"And what are you asking for?"

Dr. Miller's smile went sharp. "Funding for an engineering study of the structural integrity of the bridge."

Momentarily derailed from the possible Baldwin connection, Josh asked, "What's wrong with the bridge?"

"It's almost a hundred years old. We have *no idea* what's wrong with it," she said bluntly. "My wife compared it to a hundred-year-old patient who's never gone to the doctor. Yes, he might still be alive, but who knows what's going on inside there without an X-ray or MRI or what have you?"

Josh wrapped each bagel in waxed paper, admitting, "That's . . . slightly terrifying. If the bridge just"—he waved a hand—"*boom,* do we have a backup plan? Pontoon bridges? A ferry?"

She gave an exasperated sigh. "The state *says* it has a plan, but . . ."

"Shit. Uh, excuse me," he said automatically, distracted by the thought of the bridge collapsing right before tourist season.

"Precisely," she agreed, sliding a wallet out of her jacket pocket. Josh had never seen her carrying a purse.

He bagged the wrapped bagels, put the coffees in a carrier, and went to the register, trying—and failing—to sound casual as he asked, "Do you know Governor Baldwin? Is he one of the summer tourists?"

She hummed thoughtfully and handed over a twenty-dollar bill. "I believe the Baldwins have a family house on the island, yes, though can't recall seeing them here. In passing, perhaps."

"The whole family? Kids?" Josh asked, looking down to count out her change, conveniently avoiding eye contact.

"A daughter? Perhaps?" She shrugged and said, "I can't actually recall. I tend to focus more on the issues than ephemera, I'm afraid."

And Josh was prying. Guiltily, he passed over her change and said, "We should all follow your example, Doc."

She pocketed the change and gave him a brilliant smile. "I haven't forgotten the town hall meeting. I expect you to be there—you and your father both."

"Just say when. And have a good day," he added, waving her out of the store. He watched her walk through the fog and get into her car. Once she drove off, he took out his phone—and then put it back. It'd be creepy to cyberstalk the governor just to see if he had a son or nephew named Michael. Wouldn't it?

Michael was *not* going to show up at Bagel End at one minute after six in the morning. He wasn't. That'd be desperate and pathetic and a sad snapshot of what his life had become. In fact, he didn't even set an alarm on his phone—as in, the phone that still didn't have its battery installed, which was how he ended up wide-awake in bed while it was barely light outside the round barn window that faced the ocean. He had an hour, maybe two, before Bagel End opened. Josh was probably still in bed, like any normal human being. Even Kaylee was deeply asleep, her muzzle buried under a pillow, feet hanging off the edge of the mattress.

But Michael wasn't going to fall back asleep, so he sat up, closing his eyes while the world rocked and swam around him, until his perception stabilized. Kaylee snuffled and jerked awake, lifting her head to give him an eloquently sleepy look.

"Yeah, yeah," he told her, twisting around to sit on the edge of the bed. When nothing disastrous happened, he got to his feet, one hand braced on the headboard. Kaylee bounded across the bed and dropped to the floor beside his leg with a huff, as if scolding him for standing without her help. First thing in the morning, he was always a little off.

Thankfully, today was a good day. He took a few tentative steps, all the way to the railing that overlooked the living room, and the only problem was that his feet were cold. He didn't have slippers or a bathrobe. He'd never bothered, living in a shoebox apartment in DC, but now he wondered if he should do some shopping. Own more stuff than could fit into a couple of duffel bags and boxes. That was part of his transition to civilian living, wasn't it?

Not that he was awake enough to justify this introspection. He pushed away from the railing and looked down at Kaylee, whose tail was *whooshing* across the floor in a lazy, happy way. "Okay, let's go," he said, heading for the stairs. On the way down, he hung on to the banister, with Kaylee close to his other side, ready to brace him if he lost his balance.

He nearly went into the kitchen to make coffee before remembering two important things: he had a date—sort of—at Bagel End, and he hated the pod coffee machine that was the only source of caffeine he'd found in either the main house or the barn. One more thing for the shopping list.

So he cut through the living room to the front of the barn, shoved his feet into his sneakers, and let Kaylee out. She was too well trained to run away, and without her service dog vest, she was free to do as she liked. She promptly disappeared into the fog, and Michael knew she was rolling around on the wet grass.

The morning was chilly and damp. The dark-blue sky was streaked with gray clouds. Rain later today? Maybe. Which meant he should make sure he had rain jackets for himself and Kaylee in his bag, a small towel, maybe an umbrella—and he'd need to bring Kaylee's boots, because nobody liked muddy paws.

"Kaylee! Better go now!" he yelled into the fog. Sometimes she got too distracted by grass to remember to visit a convenient tree, and he wanted to get into the shower, then change into actual clothes. If it wasn't six o'clock yet, it would be once he got to town.

Michael had no idea what time it was when he walked into Bagel End. All he knew was that it was after six, which was good enough. On the fog-obscured walk into town, he'd started to worry that he would end up lurking outside the shop like a bagel-obsessed stalker. His sense of time had been off since moving up north.

As soon as Michael sent Kaylee through the door, the now-familiar smell of fresh bagels hit. The tension in his chest and shoulders eased.

The bell brought Josh out of the kitchen at a fast walk. Michael went tense all over again until he saw Josh's smile, bright enough to burn through the fog outside.

"Morning, Michael," Josh said when he made it to the near end of the counter, by the cash register. He leaned over and said, "Hi, Kaylee. Or should I not say hi to her?"

Michael had snapped at people for distracting Kaylee when she was working, but not Josh. He shrugged and brought Kaylee over to the counter—too far away for Josh to actually touch her, but Michael pointed to Josh and told her, "Say hi," anyway. She sat and looked up at Josh, mouth hanging open in a doggie grin.

"She's just gorgeous, isn't she?" Josh said, shaking his head.

Michael scratched at her ears, sneaking a couple of quick looks at Josh's profile. Cute. Definitely cute. From his curved lips to his round cheeks to the faint crinkles around his eyes . . . and his curls, natural and a little messy, without a hint of product to make them crunchy or sticky to the touch.

When the silence stretched on too long—at least three full seconds—Michael asked, "Am I early? The door was unlocked."

Josh laughed and pushed himself upright again to meet Michael's eyes. "It's six fifteen. You're good."

That was a relief. Fifteen minutes after opening was respectable. "Good. Okay."

"You didn't set an alarm this morning?" Josh put on a suspicious look, eyes narrowed, but his mouth was twitching. "Are you always up at this hour?"

I was up two hours ago, Michael thought, though he didn't say it. "Yeah, old habits and everything. It was barely starting to get light when I got out of bed."

"Same." When Josh frowned, his nose crinkled up, and Michael had to look away or risk giving him another stupid grin. "I've been up for *hours*, but I have the excuse of making bagels. Speaking of which . . ." He gestured back to the kitchen. "Want to come back with me? Your breakfast will be a good twenty seconds fresher, and seconds count."

Michael's heart skipped. There it was, his first hint that this might be more than just a friendly attempt at making him into a regular customer. There was interest in that offer, maybe even playful flirtation. But tempted as he was to say yes, he looked down at Kaylee and shook his head. "We can't. She's not allowed in a food-prep area." And while he was positive that Kaylee would lie down on her blanket under a table and not move from her spot, he wasn't ready to be away from her. Cute and friendly and, yeah, hot as Josh was, he was also a stranger.

One who wasn't about to let a little thing like health codes get in the way, judging by how his smile didn't fade. "Then I'll just have to bring it out nice and quick. Go sit down. You want coffee? Water?"

This felt halfway like a date, halfway like a transaction, leaving Michael feeling awkward. He nodded, glancing a bit longingly at the coffeepot. "Coffee, yeah. Please. But you don't have to do anything—"

"Uh-uh," Josh interrupted, pointing at him in warning before turning to fill a large Styrofoam cup with life-giving coffee. "Bubbe would claw out of her grave if I let someone go hungry, and going without caffeine counts."

Struggling not to laugh, Michael asked, "'Bubbe'?"

"Yiddish for my dad's grandma." Josh handed over the coffee with a grin, then headed for the kitchen, saying over his shoulder,

"Four feet tall, three feet wide, a terror in the kitchen. Didn't speak a word of English! Taught my dad everything he knows about cooking. Sit!"

Unable to hold back, Michael laughed and called back, "Yes, sir!"

For a breakfast bagel sandwich, Josh just had to fry or scramble an egg, add cheese, cook up some meat, and then assemble, but that was simple. Too simple? He wasn't great at making exotic dinners—and the less said about his roasts or skill with a barbecue, the better—but he could do breakfasts. French toast, omelets, the perfect scramble, pancakes, feather-light crepes, quiches that didn't collapse, even frittatas.

But Michael was expecting a breakfast bagel sandwich. Josh couldn't just surprise him, right?

He could improvise, though. After all, half of running a restaurant—even a bagel place—was presentation. Okay, maybe a quarter.

Josh rattled through the cupboards to find one of the small frying pans he used to use back when they'd had a gas burner cooktop instead of a flattop grill. He gave it a rinse, dried it, then set some butter to melting. He'd scramble the eggs in that, add some cheese and chopped scallions to make a quasi-omelet, then bring the eggs out so Michael could assemble the sandwich himself, or eat the eggs separately. And instead of toasting the bagel in the toaster, he'd use the flattop and fry it with butter. No way was Michael counting calories.

Humming now that he had a plan, Josh got to cooking, glad for the two cups of coffee he'd had before he started chopping and frying. Bacon sizzled and butter hissed, and Josh's stomach growled.

The six-to-seven hour was all but dead. He'd finished the morning's baking, and while there were things he could do, there were *always* things to be done. He was a manager and co-owner. Nothing was stopping *him* from having breakfast—though his food was about three minutes behind schedule, even if he went with something simple.

Two more eggs hit the flattop, along with a sausage patty and another everything bagel. He flipped and scraped, then shoved his eggs and sausage over to the cooler side to cook slowly while he assembled Michael's breakfast on a tray, the still-hot frying pan resting on a folded kitchen towel to keep it from melting the plastic. He added a napkin and plasticware, kind of wishing he and his dad had splurged on a bigger dishwasher to handle actual ceramics and silverware.

Ah, well. If this morning went well, maybe Josh could suggest a proper restaurant for a date.

Is this a date?

He froze in the kitchen doorway, hoping to hell that he wasn't reading too much into last night and this morning. Then he spotted the empty table in the corner by the front window. The one he was already thinking of as Michael's table.

Why wasn't he there? Had he run off? Had he intentionally come in just to get Josh's hopes up, knowing he'd crush them by walking out?

No. No, he was *nice*. Maybe there'd been an emergency with his dog or—

"Josh?"

The scrape of a chair from a back table, right beside the counter pass-through door, startled Josh into nearly dropping the tray. Michael was standing there, his dog lying in a *C* shape around the center post of the table.

Josh's laugh bubbled with relief. "Hey. Need more coffee? Let me get you a refill. Here. I didn't know if you'd want to put it together yourself, so—skillet." He hooked a foot under the pass-through door and pulled it open, giving a twist to catch it behind his leg; navigating the store with his hands full had been one of the first things he'd mastered, back in elementary school, when he helped out on weekends.

Michael intercepted him on the other side of the counter. He took the tray, and for a few breathless seconds, they had their hands an inch apart, eyes locked, standing so close that Josh could practically feel his body heat.

"Thanks," they both said at the same instant. Then they laughed, and Josh relinquished the tray.

"Want me to get you that refill?" he offered, following Michael to the table. He was pleased to see the cup was half-empty already.

"Please." Michael's hand shook as he put down the tray. Josh had to stop himself from reaching out to help. He'd tried that with his father once, during chemo, and had gotten his head bitten off.

Did that tremor have to do with whatever Michael needed the service dog for? He didn't seem to have difficulty walking, and Josh hadn't seen him drive a car. Nothing was parked on the foggy street outside.

Distracted, Josh took the Styrofoam cup behind the counter, only to catch the smell of burning dough from the kitchen. He swore, abandoned the cup, and ran into the kitchen, where he spotted smoke curling up from under his bagel. He flipped the bagel halves, revealing charred dough. Another flip sent the burnt former bagel over to the side to cool so it wouldn't scorch through the trash bag.

He did a quick count of the remaining everything bagels, verifying that he wouldn't be cutting into Michael's baker's dozen. He wouldn't, but there was no time for toasting. And shit! He'd forgotten Michael's coffee.

He took one of the bagels with him and dropped it into the automatic slicer on the way to the coffeepot. What the hell was wrong with him? He could keep a dozen orders straight in his head without writing a single note, but two breakfasts—one of them his!—had him completely scatterbrained.

No, not the breakfasts. Michael. Hot Tourist Guy, who was actually Hot *Nice* Tourist Guy, who was actually showing an interest in Josh.

Okay. Deep breath, Josh told himself, pausing for a few critical, calming seconds. Well, not so calming. Not while Michael was waiting for his coffee refill. Josh went back out to the coffeepot, where he dumped the old cup and poured Michael a fresh one.

He brought it over to the table, saying, "Sorry. I was making myself breakfast. House rules: you can burn your own food, but not a customer's. Or a guest's." He put down the coffee with a smile.

"You haven't eaten?" Michael glanced from Josh to the tray and back. "Do you want . . ." He pointed at the opposite seat.

Yes! Trying not to grin in triumph, Josh said, "Sure. Thank you. Let me just go rescue my eggs. And should I put up that extra bacon for Kaylee now or later? You said you don't feed her in restaurants, right?"

"Yeah. I mean, no. But you should eat before you get busy. Kaylee can wait. We're actually not . . ." A curious expression crossed Michael's face. When Josh just looked at him, Michael shook his head and said, "Go, get your food. We have time."

"Okay. Be right back." Josh let some of his happiness show in his smile as he added, "Don't go anywhere."

CHAPTER
EIGHT

"Okay, nothing caught fire," Josh said as he settled across the table from Michael. He'd been in a rush to get back, so he hadn't bothered putting his sandwich together. He started now, both to have something to do with his hands and so he wouldn't stare at Michael like a lovestruck teenager.

Michael laughed quietly. "Was that a possibility?" he asked, picking up his coffee cup.

"Not usually, no, but mornings kind of suck." Josh hadn't ripped the soft insides out of his bagel to make room for the eggs, sausage, and cheese, so he had to crush the sandwich under his palm to make it manageable. It was habit, the type of thing he did whenever he had lunch at the shop instead of going out, and only when he actually lifted the sandwich did he realize how it looked. Here he was, stuffing his face as if he didn't already have enough padding around his middle, sitting across from a skinny, hot, well-muscled, *really* hot guy who probably usually lived on wheatgrass and flaxseed smoothies.

Then the voice of reason asserted itself, reminding Josh that Michael *also* ate bagel sandwiches for breakfast and pizza for dinner. Josh took his first bite, feeling better about the whole thing, even if his bagel wasn't properly toasted.

Michael sipped his coffee, closing his eyes for a moment. The sight of his long, dark lashes made Josh forget his self-consciousness, especially when Michael's eyes opened again. "For a guy who thinks mornings suck, you're pretty awake."

Josh made a show of looking over his shoulder at the deserted shop and the foggy, empty sidewalk beyond the window. Then, lowering his voice, he admitted, "The first pot I make, at 4 a.m.?

I've got a stash of beans hidden in the office. Double the normal caffeine. It tastes disgusting, even with those flavored syrups, but it sure as hell wakes you up."

"Sounds like rocket fuel. And you drink that stuff every day?" Michael shook his head. "That could kill you."

Was it time for some awkward truths? No, too soon. Josh temporized, swallowing a huge bite of his bagel before saying, "My dad usually opens. Most days, I come in for the eleven to closing shift, unless he needs a day off or goes down to see his relatives in Brooklyn."

Thank God, Michael didn't latch on to Josh's unusual recent behavior. "Brooklyn, huh? I don't hear an accent . . ."

"I don't go there very much, but Dad grew up there." Josh almost mentioned his mom, but he didn't want to wreck the happy mood. "He goes back every few months to see his sister and their kids. They have a deli too, so I think they have bake-offs after hours. He always comes back with refinements to his recipes."

Michael's smile turned wistful, then vanished. "That must be nice." He picked up his sandwich and took a bite.

What? Josh wondered. The family connection? Michael had said he was staying here alone . . . Where was the rest of his family? The Baldwins.

Before he could be tempted to ask about the governor, he said, "In fact, I'm going to be working on a new recipe myself in the next few days. Maybe you could help with the taste tests? It's your fault."

"Huh?" Michael blinked and swallowed. "My fault?"

Josh grinned. "You introduced me to Kaylee. I've seen these crunchy bagel treats for dogs. I was going to start experimenting, maybe make some flavored ones, see which ones she likes best. Then we can start a whole new product line."

"Oh." A hint of color showed on Michael's cheeks as he leaned back, looking under the table. Kaylee hadn't moved, except for her tail, which was thumping against Josh's leg. "Okay, yeah. She doesn't have any food allergies. Some dogs are allergic to wheat or other stuff."

"Good to know." Josh eyed the bagel counter, with its wire baskets full of today's and yesterday's baking. "Wonder if I can make bagels with oat flour. I think that's one of the gluten-free substitutes. Think they'd taste okay?"

"For us or for them?" Michael sat back up and picked up his coffee. "You wouldn't *believe* what she used to eat as a puppy."

Josh laughed. "More for them than for us. Though I was also thinking of doing bagel chips. Kind of like pretzels, only with bagels instead."

"Those sound good. If you need a taste tester, I'll"—Michael hesitated, looking past Josh, smile vanishing—"volunteer."

Josh turned back just as the bell rang and a customer walked in. Candace something, a teacher at the elementary school, usually in twice a week around seven. "Be right back," he told Michael, snatching one last sip of coffee before he headed around the counter with a wave for Candace. She didn't usually have a complicated order—bagel, cream cheese, coffee—but her arrival signaled the start of the morning rush, which also meant whoever was on the schedule for mornings would be in soon. Hopefully very soon, so Josh would have a chance to get back to Michael and their maybe-date.

"We should go," Michael muttered to Kaylee, though she caught the inflection in his voice and didn't move from where she'd sprawled. She must have picked up on his relaxed mood, because her only reaction to approaching customers was to lift her head. Most of them didn't even notice her.

The shop wasn't crowded, but business was brisk, with a handful of customers at the counter at any given time. Josh's staff seemed efficient, dispensing bagels and coffee and the occasional deli order without delay, and they knew most customers by name. Josh trusted them enough to sneak back to the table whenever there was a free moment, so he could take a bite of his surely cold sandwich or offer Michael a refill of coffee.

"You really don't have to," Michael said the fifth time Josh asked. "This is— I mean, you're *working*."

"It's okay," Josh assured him. "This should taper off around seven thirty, then pick up again around ten to eight. Unless you had something to do? You don't have to sit around here waiting—"

"No," Michael cut in, all but gripping the table to keep from getting thrown out, which was ridiculous. But the thought of going back to the empty, lonely barn filled him with dread, and it wasn't as if he had anything else to do. At all. Ever. "I was thinking... When do you get off work?"

"Technically, any time after the lunch rush, but I usually end up staying late. If you tell me you have an idea that's more exciting than doing inventory, I'll—" Color tinted Josh's cheeks and ears. "I'll be grateful."

Not what he was going to say, Michael thought, struggling not to grin—or blush, for that matter. Josh was interested. He had to be interested. Michael's first foray into civilian dating that didn't involve a gay nightclub was, so far, a success.

So far. Since the morning rush started, he'd been racking his brain to think of what else he and Josh could do. Hartsbridge Island was full of tourist attractions—Birchwhite House, a handful of old churches, the museum, the marina, and so on—but Josh lived here. He had to have seen everything. And while Michael knew of some nice places on the mainland, he didn't think he could handle another extended drive, even as a passenger. Not after yesterday.

"How about a park?" he suggested, looking hopefully across the table at Josh. "Or a beach, somewhere deserted? Kaylee worked all day yesterday, so she could use a break. I've got a Frisbee, some tennis balls..." He gestured to the bag hanging over the back of his chair.

"She can do that?" Josh asked, glancing under the table. Then he blinked and flushed, saying, "Sorry. I mean— Just—"

This was another familiar topic for Michael. He shrugged, saying, "She needs time off, just like people. And she's great at catching..." Only then did it occur to him that *normal* first dates probably didn't involve playing fetch with a four-legged third wheel. Not everyone liked dogs, after all. "Or we could go somewhere else. The"—*think, think*—"breakwater?" he finally tried, having vague memories of climbing the boulders in search of crabs and starfish.

When Josh laughed, his eyes lit up over his rounded cheeks. "You said you've got a Frisbee?"

Michael nodded. "A soft one. Easier for her to catch."

"Perfect." Josh leaned back and said, with exaggerated pride, "I'm a champ with Frisbees. It's genetic. Well, culturally genetic."

"Huh?" Michael didn't know if he'd heard that right or if his brain was playing tricks on him.

"I'm adopted, but I was adopted at birth, so . . ."

That explained the lack of similarity between Josh and his father. "Okay, but . . . the culture part?"

Josh gestured at the bagel counter. "Bagels, Frisbees . . . You know. Round things you can throw."

Michael snorted. "And yet your father lets you work around ammunition like that? Sounds dangerous."

"Nobody would dare rob us. Like I said, expert." Josh's cocky smile made Michael's breath catch, and he nearly missed Josh asking, " So, maybe we should exchange numbers? Coordinate when and where we meet up?"

"Oh. Yeah," Michael said, silently chiding himself. He was supposed to be the logistics and planning expert. He opened the outer pocket of his gear bag and pulled out his phone, only to feel the empty battery compartment rather than the smooth back plate. *Shit.*

"Uh . . . Did it break?" Josh asked, eyeing the phone.

I'm an idiot. Michael just shook his head. "I— The battery . . . fell out," he said, avoiding Josh's eyes. He hated lying, especially about something so stupid, but the truth was even more stupid. He dug out one of the ADA information cards he carried in case a business challenged Kaylee's right to enter, flipped it over, and wrote his number on the back. "I haven't switched to a local cell yet. Haven't done *anything* local yet. I need to change my driver's license, all that . . . Here." He offered Josh the card.

When Josh took it, their fingers brushed, and he seemed to intentionally draw out the contact. "I'll call you when I'm free?"

"Yeah. And, uh, I'll find the battery," Michael promised, though he couldn't for the life of him remember where it was. Hopefully he hadn't dropped it at the rest stop where he'd zoned out for hours yesterday. Maybe he should just go get a new phone. Yeah, that was a better idea. And he'd only give the number to Amanda, not the rest of his family. He held out his pen, saying, "How about you give me yours? Your number, I mean. There's a cellular place somewhere on the island, right?"

"Actually, no." Josh smiled wryly. "And our movie theater still only has one screen. But here." Instead of reaching for the pen, he took a phone out of his pocket and unlocked it. After a few quick presses, he slid it across the table. An info screen was up, including the phone's number.

It was strange that Josh didn't write it down himself, but Michael didn't ask. He took out another card and quickly wrote down Josh's number. "If I can't find the battery, I'll call you from the house phone. I think there's still a landline there. If not, I'll just come back here?" It turned into a question as his confidence faltered. "If that's okay?"

Josh shoved the phone back into his pocket. "More than okay. I can make you lunch, if you're not sick of bagels. Soup and a panini sandwich, maybe?"

Michael laughed and ducked his head, safely tucking the card with Josh's number into his bag, along with the useless phone. "You don't have to keep feeding me."

"I run a bagel shop. It's my job to feed people, remember?"

Their whole relationship couldn't be built around Josh feeding Michael. That was ridiculous—not to mention unfair. "Maybe you'll let me take you out to lunch instead? Or dinner. After we find a park or somewhere? Whatever you want to do."

"A park sounds great." The front bell rang, and Josh twisted around as four people came in.

Michael bit back a sigh. "Should you . . ." He gestured to the counter.

"Yeah. I'm sorry." Josh sounded sincere, which was something. He stood, picked up his tray, and reached for Michael's.

"You don't have to," Michael protested, holding on to his tray.

Josh gave a little tug. "Actually, it's my job, remember?" he said, amused. He gently slid the tray out of Michael's grasp and stacked both trays. "You can hang out as long as you want, but it's going to get more crowded."

Was that a subtle hint that Michael should vacate the table? Or had Josh picked up on Michael's dislike of most crowds? Either way, it was Michael's cue to leave. "That's okay. We have stuff to do." It wasn't even a lie, now that he thought about it. "I'll call you or stop by later."

It was too early for him to hope for a kiss, but the smile he got in return was almost as good. "Later, then," Josh said warmly.

Michael watched Josh hurry over to the counter pass-through, stacked trays balanced in one hand. The bell up front rang again, signaling more customers. Time to go. He did a last check for anything he'd forgotten, made sure his bag was closed up, and told Kaylee, "Let's go."

Home to find the phone battery and pick up the car, then the vet's office, and then maybe a quick trip to the mainland to pick up a new phone. Or maybe he'd just scope out the island to find a nice, quiet park where he and Josh could be alone. Yeah, that sounded like a better idea. He didn't have it in him to face a crowded store and high-pressure salespeople when he could be thinking about Josh instead.

CHAPTER

NINE

Michael sprawled in the back footwell of the SUV, trying to see into the blurry, shadowy space under the seat. *Modern convenience, my ass*, he thought, slowly easing his arm into the darkness, wary of sharp edges. Smartphones were great, with their flashlight apps. No need to carry a separate flashlight.

Unless you were looking for the damned battery.

Kaylee nudged at Michael's calf, distressed that he was acting strangely. "It's okay. Kaylee, go play," he grunted as his fingertips brushed against something that moved. *Aha.* He stretched a little more, catching one corner, then the edges. Sighing in relief, he grabbed the battery and shifted onto his side, freeing his arm without any damage worse than red indents on his forearms from the seat supports.

He sat up, and the world went fuzzy. Swearing under his breath, he braced his arm on the backseat and rested his head, breathing deeply until the dizziness faded. Six months ago, he would've had to lie down for an hour; now the spell passed in minutes. Maybe he wasn't healing as quickly as he would've liked, but he was making *some* progress.

Once the front yard was no longer a blur, he pushed himself to the edge of the footwell, legs hanging out the doorway. Kaylee trotted across the driveway to sniff at his sneakers. He scratched one shoe along her side and fitted the battery into the phone, then snapped the back cover into place. His stomach gave a nervous flip as the phone booted up.

"What do you think, baby? Ten messages? More?" He didn't even want to look, but if nothing else, he needed to program Josh's number in before he lost the card. At least he could read the number, since he'd written it with care. Maybe that was why Josh hadn't written it himself? Maybe they had bad handwriting in common, along with an appreciation for good bagels and pepperoni pizza. They could send each other birthday cards with incoherent scribbles. That'd be fun.

The phone's buzz made Michael jump. His heart lodged somewhere in his throat, cutting off his air. He patted his knee, and Kaylee braced her paws against the truck's running boards so she could lean on his lap, muzzle shoved under his arm. He concentrated on her warm weight, reminding himself that he was away from his parents and capable of getting farther away—*much* farther if he dipped into his trust fund.

Thank God for Grandma and Grandpa Hanson. He barely remembered them—they'd died the year after Amanda was born—but they'd left their estate in trust to their only grandchildren. Amanda was apparently spending her share on a trip to the other side of the world. For Michael, that money was at the heart of his backup plan, an essential tool for his escape if living in New Hampshire became too politically charged.

That security net gave him the reassurance he needed to check his phone. Only seven messages—three from his father's chief of staff, three from Amanda, and one from a private number that was surely his father's personal cell. He went right for Amanda's, ignoring the rest.

"Hey, what happened? Wilkins is having a shit fit. Call me," was the first message. The second was, "Okay, now I'm worried. Text me if you don't want to talk. Just let me know you're okay." Number three was the kicker: "You have to stop letting them get to you, Mike. You're an adult. They can't do anything to you anymore."

She was right, of course, but it was easy for her to be right. For all their father's speeches about equality between the sexes and races and social classes, they'd been raised in an old-fashioned, sexist family. Amanda's job was to look pretty and go to a good college so she could catch herself a well-connected husband—preferably a lawyer or politician. Michael, though . . . He was supposed to be his father's heir, whether he wanted to be or not. Growing up, his father had made damned sure that the alternative was unpleasant, to say the least.

He deleted Wilkins's messages without bothering to play them. He wanted to do the same to his father's, but he hesitated and decided to call Amanda instead. She didn't live with their parents, but she was close enough that she'd be able to give him a heads-up if their father was genuinely angry and not just irritated with Michael, which was his baseline.

"Michael. Are you okay?" Amanda asked before the phone rang twice. Her voice was low and gruff, as if she were trying to be quiet.

"I'm fine." He got out of the truck and closed the door. Free of her vest, Kaylee bounced around at his feet.

Amanda grunted. "Fine. You sure about that?"

Michael waved a hand at Kaylee, sending her off across the lawn at a run. "Yeah. My phone was dead. I just got the battery working." It wasn't quite a lie.

She took a deep breath, then released it. He couldn't hear any background noise. "What happened? You disappeared."

Off in the distance, Kaylee was sniffing at the grass. He was tempted to find a ball, but he didn't want to tire her out before his maybe-date with Josh. And he was trying to avoid discussing what happened yesterday.

"Dad was . . ." He kicked at the grass edging the driveway. "You know how he is. With me."

Gently, Amanda said, "Yeah. I kind of figured that's why he wanted you there."

"He wanted me to play nice with an old veteran. I'm surprised there weren't cameras there, but the poor guy was in his pajamas." Michael shrugged. "It would've been more dramatic if he'd been in uniform, I guess. Pj's aren't exactly newsworthy." He couldn't keep the sneer off his face or out of his voice. His father was all for military heroism, as long as it was packaged in a way that would lure more voters to his side.

Which was why Michael had made a point of being as unphotogenic as possible while he was at Walter Reed, at least once he awoke from his coma.

"*Everything's* about politics." Amanda's groan sounded harsh, full of disgust. "If they weren't so damned useful for fund-raising and visibility, I would've banned them from the charity's home office."

Michael winced. For years he'd been overseas, shuffled from one base to another, and then safe behind restricted access at the hospital.

Yeah, his parents had insinuated themselves into his life when he was an outpatient living in DC, but that had been incidental—the result of his proximity to useful political connections.

Amanda, though, had been within their reach her whole life. No wonder she wanted to spread her wings and fly away the instant she turned twenty-five.

"I know you have plans," he said thoughtfully, "but if you want to come down here for a little while before you go away—even just a weekend—you can."

"I won't be interrupting anything?"

"Huh?"

She laughed, light and quick, a contrast to how low and rough her voice had been. "I thought you had a new boy at least two or three times a week when you were in DC."

Michael's face went hot. He walked briskly out onto the lawn, trying to distract himself by finding a stick to throw for Kaylee. "I— The clubs—"

"How'd that work, anyway?" Amanda interrupted. "Did you bring your dog with you?"

The yard was distressingly devoid of sticks. The caretaker must have arranged for the landscaper to visit recently. Kaylee was sniffing around the hedges. It looked like she was oblivious to him, but if he said her name or snapped his fingers, she'd be at his side in a heartbeat. "She was in training," he said, remembering how gangly she'd been, with legs too long for her body and huge feet; she was still a juvenile, growing into her body. "I left her at home."

"You were okay without— Didn't you *need* her?"

Michael kicked at the grass again, and Kaylee trotted over to investigate. "Things were different," he said evasively. It had taken three months for his therapist to help him recognize the uncomfortable truths about how he was using strangers for meaningless sex—how picking up one-night stands wasn't actually healthy socializing. He wasn't going to have that discussion with his sister.

The silence stretched out for long, awkward seconds before Amanda finally said, "I just want you to be happy. Not alone."

Braced for a lecture, Michael had no defense against her genuine concern. "I did meet someone here," he said before he could catch himself. Quickly he added, "It might be nothing. I don't even know for sure if he's interested in guys."

"One of these days, you'll have to explain how exactly you figure out who's gay and who's not."

Michael grinned. His sister was so weird. "Why? Since when do *you* have trouble finding guys?"

"It's not finding guys-plural that's the problem. It's finding *the one* guy." She laughed wickedly. "Or maybe two, in case the first one gets tired."

"Maybe you should be giving *me* tips." He leaned down to ruffle Kaylee's ears, then waved her away again. "What's this really about? Are you having relationship trouble?"

It took Amanda a few seconds to answer, "Ask me in a year."

That was worrying, but if Michael pried, she'd pry right back. "Okay. Think you'll make it out here to visit?"

"We'll see," she said in a way that sounded more like *no*. "Email's the best way to get in touch with me once I'm gone. Send me pics."

Relieved to have escaped the interrogation about Josh, Michael said, "You got it. I'll send you my new phone number too, so you can call me whenever you have a chance."

"You'd better. Love you, Mike."

"You too." Michael disconnected the call and didn't bother listening to the one remaining voice mail. He had enough to do without getting distracted by family politics, starting with programming Josh's number into the phone.

The lunch rush was still going at quarter after one, when Josh's phone buzzed twice in quick succession. It was another ten minutes before he could step back from the counter, take off his gloves, and check.

He had two texts from a private number: *How's your day going?* and *It's Michael.*

Going okay. You? he typed back carefully, double-checking autocorrect before he hit Send. Then he pulled on fresh gloves and picked up the pastrami.

He was in the middle of slicing off tissue-thin pieces when the response came. After he built and wrapped the sandwich, he checked his phone again. Michael had sent: *Got lots done. We're on the green by the statue whenever you're done for the day.*

Josh looked up at the solid wall of customers along the counter, from the register all the way back to the pass-through. Dee was bagging and ringing up orders, Josh and his dad were working the deli section, and Charlie was taking orders and prepping bagels and sandwich breads. And Heather wasn't scheduled to start until two.

"Can you cover me for two minutes?" Josh quietly asked his dad.

Dad scanned the customers, then jerked his head toward the back room. "Go. You've been here long enough."

Josh wanted to nod—he wanted to rip off his apron and run across the street like the star in a bad rom-com—but he couldn't abandon his crew. "I can hold off until Heather gets here. I just want to let Michael know."

He must've spoken too loudly, because Dee piped up, "Michael? Who's Michael?"

Dad's sudden grin was all the warning Josh needed to preemptively say, "A friend. And he can wait, Dad."

Dad frowned at Josh, reaching past him to take hold of the next plate. Charlie said, "Lox deluxe. What kind of friend?"

Josh sighed. "Not you too."

"Got it, Charlie," Dad said, grin never fading. He took the salmon out of the deli case. "Josh, go."

Despite wanting nothing more than to do just that, he had to ask, "Are you *sure*?"

Dee leaned back to look past Dad, asking, "Are *you* sure he's just a friend?"

"Okay, going." Josh retreated before they could gang up on him. He threw out his gloves on the way to the office, where he took out his phone. *Be there in a few minutes*, he sent to Michael.

The Bagel End uniform was almost subtle enough to pass for normal clothing, if not for the eye-searing yellow logo, but Josh was sick of the bright-blue polo shirt. Besides, he smelled like bagels. He had a couple of T-shirts in the office, though, along with an emergency toiletries kit. Five minutes in the bathroom, and he'd changed his shirt, splashed water on his face, and brushed his teeth. That was as close to presentable as he'd get without a shower and a shave.

But when he was done, he froze up, leaning against the sink to stare in the mirror. What he saw there was discouraging. With his round baby face, he looked five years younger than he actually was, except for the dark circles under his eyes, thanks to his stupidly early schedule these past few days. He was in desperate need of a haircut, not that there was any style on the planet that would make his floppy curls look fashionable. His body's idea of five-o'clock shadow was a dirty-blond patch on his chin that made him look like a high school hipster.

What the *hell* was he doing getting ready for what might be a date with what had to be the hottest guy to walk into Bagel End in the last year? Here in his home territory, where being customer and server gave them the excuse to associate, he felt somewhat comfortable. Out there, though, in the wild? They were such a mismatched pair, they'd be laughed out of wherever they went, including the green.

Then he looked at his phone, where there were two more texts from Michael. *See you soon*, followed by a smiley face. Mismatched or not, Michael was putting an effort into this.

He's interested in me, Josh thought as he slid the phone into his pocket. Then he looked in the mirror and mustered up a smile for his reflection. Apparently, they were interested in each other, which was good enough for him.

CHAPTER

TEN

The triangular town green was lined with benches, giving Michael his choice of a dozen exposed positions for his wait. Shivers crawled up his spine despite the unseasonable warmth of the sun that had burned through the morning's fog. No matter where he sat, his back was to a street or a building. The island was so different from DC—so different from the places where he'd been deployed—that every noise felt unfamiliar. Threatening.

After coming here from the veterinarian's office, he'd taken off Kaylee's vest to let her roll around in the grass in front of the bench, which was probably a mistake. Every time a car rumbled past, his chest went a little tighter, until he was struggling to breathe, time skittering from moment to moment in snapshots. Kaylee sniffing for bugs. A car braking sharply. Two cyclists on the sidewalk right behind Michael's bench. A delivery truck roaring by.

He had nothing to distract him. Even the statue looming nearby, with its sharp antlers and dead bronze eyes, had him spooked.

"Kaylee, vest," he finally said, needing *something* to ground him before his nerve broke. He wasn't going to run and miss out on seeing Josh so he could hide in his parents' barn.

Despite playtime being cut short, Kaylee stood quietly for Michael to put on her vest and rearrange her leash. At a quick hand signal, she jumped onto the bench and slithered across his lap, leaning heavily against his body, a warm weight keeping him present, reminding him that he was safe. He let go of the leash and buried both hands in her fur. When she went limp with contentment, he actually managed to smile.

And when she lifted her head, looking behind Michael, he tensed but didn't get lost in a rush of adrenaline. *Safe.* He just looked around, holding Kaylee to keep her from falling, and spotted Josh stepping up onto the curb nearby.

Josh, *not* in the blue polo that had been the only shirt Michael had seen him in so far. His T-shirt was red and looked soft, stretched at the collar, casual and comfortable and inviting. Michael gave Kaylee's fur one last ruffle and told her, "Off." She jumped down, and Michael hastily brushed at the coat of dog fur he was now wearing.

"Hey. Sorry that took so long," Josh said as he hurried around the bench. When Kaylee moved to block him, he smiled down at her. "You didn't say if you wanted me to bring anything, but—"

"What? No." Michael quickly got to his feet, or tried to. He made it halfway, then sat back down hard as the world went briefly fuzzy. Trying to cover his stumble, he said, "Kaylee, back. Have a seat. Or did you want to go somewhere?"

Kaylee made room for Josh to sit down. He did, though he twisted and stuck out one leg so he could shove a hand in his pocket. "Whatever. We, um, had some extra bacon, though . . ." He pulled out a folded, somewhat crumpled bundle of waxed paper and offered it to Michael. "For your girl there. Or you, if you want a snack, I guess."

Michael took the bundle, fingers tingling as they brushed against Josh's. "Thanks," he said, unfolding the paper to reveal a few broken strips of bacon, cooked crunchy and now cool. He grinned, thinking this was both unnecessary and adorable.

"I didn't know if it'd be okay. I don't want to spoil her." Josh gave a shy little shrug. "Okay, I do, but only because she's cute. But I know she's working—"

"No, it's okay. She can say hi to you," Michael interrupted before Josh could talk himself out of liking Kaylee. He held out the waxed paper, asking, "Did you want to . . .?"

"Yeah. I love dogs." Josh's grin was warm and light, banishing the last of the tension knotted in Michael's chest.

Michael found the end of the leash and caught Kaylee's eye. "Kaylee, say hi," he said, and she wagged her tail, jaw dropping in a grin. He gestured for her to focus on Josh, who happily held out a piece of bacon resting on his palm, as if he were feeding a horse. "She won't bite," Michael assured him.

Josh nodded, cheeks darkening. "I didn't think—" He twitched his hand toward Kaylee, then frowned. "Doesn't she want it? She likes bacon, right?"

"Oh. Tell her, 'Take it.' She's very polite."

"Take it," Josh said, and Kaylee made the bacon disappear in an instant.

"Good girl," Michael said encouragingly. "You can give her the rest, if you want. Part of the public access test is she has to ignore a plate of food put on the floor in front of her for a full minute. That's why she's trained for 'Leave it' and 'Take it.'"

"Damn. That's just mean. Take it," Josh said, giving her two pieces of bacon this time, as if to make up for her past trials. "What's the test for? So she can legally go out in public?"

"Legally, all she needs is to be trained to mitigate a disability and be housebroken, under control, and not disruptive or a health hazard." The memorized speech flowed easily. Kaylee was a comfortable topic of conversation, even with strangers. There wasn't a hint of judgment or selfishness anywhere in Josh, as far as Michael could tell. "She's been going out since she was a puppy, but this was to prove she could do stuff like ignore food dropped in front of her and not go sniffing everything at the grocery store or restaurants."

"Aww. I hope you spoil her when she's off duty." Josh did his part, offering her the rest of the bacon, instead of taking the unintentional opening to ask for specifics about Michael's disability. "Take it. That's a good girl."

"Yeah, I do. She's a big help." Michael rested his elbows on his knees so he could scratch her back. She wiggled without breaking her sit, head tipped to look at him with brown eyes full of affection and happiness. "It's not required."

"What?" Josh crumpled the paper and shoved it into his pocket, then dusted his hands off on his jeans.

"The test. There's no government certification for service dogs or anything. We did the tests because training for them made sure Kaylee was ready for anything she might encounter." He smiled down at her as Josh ran his fingers through the fur between her ears.

It felt intimate, something Michael wouldn't allow with anyone else. Wanting to prolong the moment, he added, "Shopping carts, forklifts, idiot drivers in parking lots, whatever."

"Sounds like you're lucky to have each other."

Michael frowned, thinking he'd misheard. "Huh?" Josh had to be saying Michael was lucky to have Kaylee, in that way that some well-meaning dog-lovers did, forgetting entirely about the "disability" part. All they saw was the cute ability to have a dog go everywhere.

Josh grinned at him. "It couldn't have been easy, all that training, right?"

"Well, no. It took a year and a half from when I got her as a puppy, just eight weeks old. We're still working on some stuff."

Josh nodded. "She's lucky to have someone willing to put in all that effort to teach her to be comfortable in public."

Oh. Michael hadn't misheard. Josh *understood.* "It's . . . We're partners."

"I've always loved dogs. We couldn't have one. My mom was allergic, and then it wouldn't have been fair, with the schedule Dad and I keep." Josh sat back with a soft sigh. "We get a lot of asshole tourists who bring dogs, then abandon them, like they're . . . I don't know. Fashion accessories or something." He glanced over at Michael. "There's going to be a town hall meeting about it, if you want to come."

"Dr. Mason mentioned something about that." When Josh frowned, Michael explained, "The town vet? We went there today to transfer Kaylee's health records. And we finally got her toenails clipped."

"Spa day, huh?" Josh reached out to ruffle her ears again.

The affection in Josh's voice warmed Michael down to his toes, even if it was directed at Kaylee, not him. "But no bath, even though she's due. We were—" Michael nearly said, *at a farm yesterday,* but that would lead to questions about his family. His father. He looked down at the grass clinging to her fur and quickly said, "We've been playing outside a lot. She likes sniffing around the bushes and trees."

Josh nodded as if he hadn't noticed the hesitation, or maybe he was too polite to mention it. "What about the beach?"

"We haven't gone yet."

"Well, have you had lunch? There's a pretty good hot dog stand there. I'm not sure if it's open—it's a tourist-season thing—but we can check."

"Yeah. That sounds good," Michael said, hoping that Josh wasn't looking at this as just two guys hanging out. If he was, Michael would learn to live with it—his therapist had said friends were more important than casual hookups—but he hoped this was something more. "Did you want to walk or drive?"

Josh darted a look at him. "I, uh . . . I only have keys to the shop truck. I like to leave the car for my dad, so he doesn't have to walk."

So Josh shared a car with his dad. Did that mean he lived with his dad? Not that Michael was in any position to judge, except that it could make dating awkward.

Michael took a moment to check in with himself. Kaylee had helped calm him down, and being with Josh left him feeling . . . *better*. It wasn't quite like how he remembered feeling before he'd been deployed—before he'd been wounded—but he felt better now than he had in years.

"I can drive," he offered, gesturing at his SUV. "Or we can walk."

Josh winced and looked down, lifting his feet off the grass, flexing his ankles back and forth. "If you don't mind driving . . . We got hit with a rush at like eleven, and it probably still hasn't let up. This is the first chance I've had to sit in a week, it feels like."

"I can run to"—Michael hesitated, glancing around at the nearby restaurants; there were only two, one of which was Bagel End—"the diner, pick up something to go, if you want to just sit here."

Josh laughed and kicked lightly at Michael's shoe; the momentary contact sent a thrill through Michael, a ridiculous overreaction to a casual, friendly touch. "Let's take our chances on hot dogs," Josh said. "Kaylee deserves another treat, and I think I can manage the walk from the parking lot."

This early in the season, the beach was deserted, the kiosks all shuttered. The isolation suited Josh just fine, even though they wouldn't be having lunch here after all. The problem with a small town was nothing was ever private. The last thing he wanted was to run into someone who remembered him from school—especially one of the teachers who'd nearly failed him before he'd dropped out.

Instead of taking a handicap spot by the short boardwalk, Michael parked a row back. There was no handicap tag hanging from the rearview mirror. What exactly was his disability? Did it have anything to do with how he sometimes got his words confused? Or how it looked like he'd almost fallen when Josh found him at the park?

Josh wouldn't ask, but he couldn't deny his curiosity, especially when Michael got out of the SUV and went around to the backseat so he could take off Kaylee's service vest. When Josh turned to get out, he spotted the parking meter in front of the SUV. He took out his wallet and dug through the various cards to find his residential parking pass. He and his dad renewed their passes every January like clockwork, though they rarely had a reason to use them. Josh slid it across the dashboard to the driver's side, making sure the info was visible, then hopped down and circled around the SUV.

"I put up my parking pass," he told Michael. "If you're going to be living here for more than six months, you can register for it at the police department. It's ten bucks a year, lets you park in any metered spot for free. You just need a driver's license with an address on the island."

"That's on my list." Michael called Kaylee out of the SUV, then closed the door. "It feels like I've only been back a few hours, not a few days. I have way too much to do."

"Anything I can help with?" Josh asked. "I can't do your paperwork, but I'm pretty good at moving boxes and assembling furniture."

"Thanks, but it's all paperwork. Change of address, voter registration, car registration, insurance, finding a doctor . . ." Michael sighed, shoulders slumped.

Josh smiled reassuringly. "Then I can offer bagels, caffeine, and bacon, since it looks like we won't be having hot dogs."

Michael grinned. "That I can accept. Thanks." He started for the beach, cutting diagonally across the parking lot. The hairs on his arms were standing up, making Josh wish he had a jacket to offer. This was a balmy day for the locals, but Michael's blood had apparently thinned.

And that made Josh think about the old fireplace in his living room. He and his dad rarely bothered lighting it except on the coldest winter nights, but Josh could all too easily picture Michael sitting on the awful floral-print couch, the glow of the fire bringing out highlights in his deep-brown hair. The two of them could wrap up in a quilt this winter and watch the snow fall while Kaylee slept on the warm hearth.

Stop getting ahead of yourself. Josh shook his head, focusing on the present instead. He was off work and in great company, with the rest of the day to himself. If he could convince Michael to come to Bagel End for lunch instead of breakfast, maybe he could even sleep in tomorrow morning.

When they reached the sand-dusted boardwalk, Michael stopped and looked around. "Think anyone else is going to be here?"

"Probably not. It's a weekday, too early in the season for tourists," Josh said with a shrug. The beach had recently been cleaned and raked, and about half the usual number of oil drums had been set along the boardwalk as trash barrels. None of the kiosks had For Rent signs on them, which was a good omen for a busy summer. The dark-blue waves smashing into the breakwaters to either side of the beach looked icy. Not that Josh gave a damn about scenery. Michael's sly grin was captivating.

"If I take off Kaylee's leash, will you call the cops on me, or do I get some slack as a fellow local?"

For that smile, Josh would drive the getaway car in a bank robbery. "I can be bribed into silence," he said, adrenaline singing through him in a sudden spike of nervousness. "Maybe with dinner?"

"You got it." Michael unclipped Kaylee's leash, then hung it around his neck. "We'll make it an early dinner, since we're not getting hot dogs. Sound good?"

That was actually a relief, since "early dinner" didn't imply "fancy dinner," which meant Josh didn't have to panic about not having anything nice to wear. His one dress shirt was three years out of date and probably didn't fit anymore.

"Sounds great . . ." Josh was going to say something about the meager choice of restaurants on the island, but Kaylee was standing at the very edge of the boardwalk, prodding at the sand with one front paw, head tilted almost sideways.

Michael lifted a hand and coughed, not quite hiding a laugh. "She's, ah, never seen sand. We worked on all sorts of surfaces—pavement, rocks, grass, but not sand."

Josh tried to hold back his own laughter as Kaylee got a second paw on the sand. "She'll manage. Maybe you should show—" He cut off with a yelp as Kaylee discovered that while sand wasn't for walking, it was definitely for digging.

Backing away from the waves of sand flying in all directions, Michael yelled, "Kaylee, sit!" The sand-based assault stopped instantly, except for the small cloud raised by her wagging tail. He looked down at himself, then at Josh. "Shit. I'm sorry," he said, brushing his hand down Josh's chest, sprinkling sand everywhere.

"Hey, it's fine. She's having fun," Josh said, staring at Michael's hand. Long, elegant fingers. No sign of a tan or calluses. "Want to show her the water?"

"She learned how to swim in a pool." Michael gave one last brush, slow and gentle enough to make Josh's breath catch. "The waves might make her head explode."

She's not the only one. Josh looked over at the dog, glad for the distraction. "Yeah," he said, though he had no idea what he was agreeing to.

Michael just nodded—at least *someone* knew what was going on—and stepped out onto the sand. "C'mon, Kaylee," he called, heading for the waves. Despite her misgivings, Kaylee followed loyally, prancing with her feet held high.

Josh trailed along after them, indulging in a quick up-and-down look at Michael's body. Definitely out of Josh's league.

But here they were, and it was about damned time Josh stopped questioning his luck and started enjoying it. He took two running steps and caught up with Michael, keeping his distance when Kaylee slipped between them. Michael smiled at him, warm and welcoming and friendly, and Josh met his eyes and smiled back. The air between them sparked.

"Think about where you want to go for dinner," Michael said, breaking eye contact after a few steps. "I don't know what's good here anymore."

"No problem." Josh reached down to scratch Kaylee's ears instead of touching Michael's arm. Baby steps. "I'll take care of you."

ELEVEN

As soon as Josh opened the door to the Rocky Shores Diner, Betty called out, "Hey, Josh! How's it going? How's—" She cut off, going wide-eyed a heartbeat later when she spotted Michael at Josh's back.

Josh held the door for Michael and Kaylee. "Things are good. It's just the two of us. Dad's still at the shop."

"Sit where you like." Betty crossed behind the counter, stopping only to pick up two menus.

Josh stepped out of the way to let Michael choose where they sat. Once again, Michael went for the corner, positioning himself so he could see the door. After he and Kaylee were settled, Josh sat down opposite, much as he wanted to share the same bench and sit pressed close to Michael.

When Betty hurried over, Josh took his menu, saying, "Thanks. But aren't you usually on night shift?"

"Technically I start in ten minutes," she said, making a show of checking her watch, "but for my favorite customer, I can clock in early." She clapped a hand on Josh's shoulder and turned her sharp gaze on Michael, offering him a menu. "You, I remember from the other night. Welcome back, hon. You sticking around for a while?"

Michael nodded, mumbling his thanks as he took the menu. Sensing his discomfort, Josh quickly asked, "Can I get a Coke? I'm dying without caffeine here. I've been up since before dawn."

Betty nodded without looking away from Michael. "And for you, hon?"

Michael darted a glance at her, then looked back down, fussing with his messenger bag. "Just water, no lemon, thanks."

Had Michael been that uncomfortable when he first came into Bagel End? Josh remembered him being reserved but friendly. Shy, not completely introverted.

As Betty left, Josh put his menu aside and folded his arms on the table, leaning forward. "As your local island guide, I can give you a few tips, if you want."

Michael's smile made a reappearance, thankfully. He took an eyeglass case out of the messenger bag and set it on the table, though he didn't put on the glasses. "Go for it."

Josh almost regretted the offer—Michael really had been hot as hell in those glasses—but hopefully he'd have another chance some other night. "The burgers are a solid choice. The dinner platters look fancy, but they can be iffy, depending on who's cooking tonight. But no matter what, you want the steak fries. No cheese, no chili, no Cajun seasoning. Plain, delicious steak fries." He grinned. "The after-dinner milk shake is optional. Or after-lunch, I guess."

Bemused, Michael put the eyeglass case back in the bag, then set his menu on top of Josh's. "How can I resist that sort of recommendation? I'll follow your lead."

"What about something for Kaylee?"

"She's good. I'll give her some leftovers once we're done, but she'll have dinner at home. I picked up some groceries before we hit the vet's office."

"Does this mean you won't be coming in tomorrow?" Josh asked before realizing how desperate that sounded. The last thing he wanted was to give Michael a heavy sales pitch. "And shit! I completely forgot."

Michael frowned, leaning closer. "Forgot what?"

"I made you extra everything bagels to take home, but with the morning rush . . ." Josh shook his head. "I'm sorry."

"No, you don't . . ." Michael laughed quietly and slid his hand across the table just far enough that his fingers brushed against Josh's. "You don't have to. And now I have an excuse to come in tomorrow."

Yes! That touch was intentional, direct, a clear signal that Michael's interest was more than friendly.

But before Josh could turn his hand over and reciprocate, Michael jerked away, looking past Josh to watch Betty come over with their drinks. She was too sharp-eyed to have missed what she interrupted, though she didn't say anything. Yet. Josh was positive the inquisition would start next time he came in, whether he was with his dad or not.

"Okay, boys," she said, taking out her order pad. "Decide what you want yet, or do you need more time?"

While Josh was trying to figure out what to say that didn't involve swearing, Michael said, "You can order for both of us. I'm having whatever you are."

And that made up for Betty's untimely interruption. Josh handed her the menus, saying, "Two bacon cheeseburgers, medium, and steak fries."

"You got it." She didn't wink at Josh, but her smirk was just for him, visible only when she turned away from Michael and walked off.

"So, what else do I need to know about living here on the island?" Michael asked when he and Josh were alone. Kaylee, once again wearing her vest, had fallen asleep almost as soon as she settled under the table. Her head was pillowed on his feet, and he could feel her warm breath puffing against his sock. "If I'm going to make this a permanent change, I may as well know everything."

"Okay. Let's see . . ." Josh slouched back, looking at the wall over Michael's head for a moment. "Avoid the bars on the south end year-round. They're packed with either tourists or college kids."

Michael winced, thinking of DC's dimly lit nightclubs. "Not a problem. I think my bar days are over."

Josh raised an eyebrow but let that pass. "We don't have much of a nightlife here at all. The bowling alley is kind of outdated, but it's got pool tables and an arcade. It's big with the high school crowd on weekends, but there's a bowling league, if that's your thing."

"Not really," Michael said before realizing Josh might be a bowler. He shook his head, explaining, "I have some balance problems. Bowling wouldn't work unless Kaylee could help."

Josh's eyes lit up with his smile. "Okay, now I kind of want to see her running a bowling ball down the lane."

Michael laughed and twitched his foot, though Kaylee didn't stir. "She'd give it a damn good try. She used to love playing with a soccer ball."

"We have to do that one day." Josh took a sip of his Coke. "Speaking of which, we've got soccer fields and a baseball diamond behind the elementary school, open to the public on weekends, I think. Bicycle and walking trails through the woods, and the greenbelt near some of the waterfront properties."

"That'll be nice for Kaylee. We did some walking down in DC, but it was always crowded." Michael repressed his shudder at the memory. Those walks around the National Mall were supposed to be healthy and relaxing, but they'd left him with frayed nerves and a pounding migraine every time.

"I know every inch of the island," Josh said confidently. "I can show you the best quiet trails for whatever time of year. The general rule for avoiding mainlanders and college kids is south during the summer, if you keep away from the bars, and north during the winter."

Again, he was calling them *kids*. Michael wanted to ask how old Josh was, but he didn't want to pry. "Easy enough."

"I, uh, assume you're set for a place to live?" Josh asked.

"For now. My family has a summer house. They redid the barn, so I've got my own place."

Josh snorted and took a quick drink that didn't hide his laugh.

"What?" Grinning, Michael extracted one foot from under Kaylee's head so he could kick at Josh's shin, though he was careful to keep it gentle. "It's a loft apartment. It's not like it's still a *barn*-barn."

"Oh, sure. Wreck my mental image of you and Kaylee curled up on a bed of hay."

"I have a perfectly good bed," Michael protested before he could stop himself. It was way too early to be discussing beds, wasn't it?

Smirking, Josh said, "I'm sure Kaylee appreciates it."

Michael rolled his eyes and kicked Josh again. "She does. She's very spoiled." It was also too early for Michael to mention that she helped him settle after nightmares. Time to change the subject. "You've lived here all your life?"

"Yeah. Well, I was born in Boston, I guess, but the adoption went through when I was a couple days old, so . . ." Josh shrugged, running a finger up and down the side of his glass. Then he grinned, adding, "Dad's from Brooklyn. He's got delis on both sides of the family, so Bagel End was sort of inevitable."

"That explains why your bagels are so good," Michael said, nodding. A couple of times on deployment, he'd had New York bagels that had been donated to the troops. Even after being packed in dry ice and shipped halfway around the world, they'd been delicious.

"I told you, it's genetic," Josh said proudly. "Anyway, Mom lived in Portsmouth, but she always loved it here. She and Dad met when she went to NYU for business, and then they moved up here to open the shop."

A family business that didn't involve power grabs and political machinations? Michael was enchanted. "Does your mom—"

"No." Josh's smile vanished, and he glanced down at the rings of condensation on the table. "She died when I was still young."

Shit, shit, shit. Michael scrambled to find a way to change the subject, but his mind had gone blank. All he could think of were random facts about his own parents—an offering, like for like—but that was the last place he wanted to go. And he was ten years out of practice for smoothly handling socially awkward situations, something not exactly needed since he'd run from the political fishbowl of his youth.

"Hey." A cold touch on Michael's hand startled him out of his building panic. Josh smiled across the table at him and shrugged. "It's okay. You didn't know."

"I'm sorry," Michael said, though it was too late.

"It's okay," Josh repeated. He drew his hand back and picked up his Coke. "How about you? What's your family like?"

A nightmare. Michael shook his head, seizing on the one bright spot in his family tree. "My sister's great. Amanda. She's working for a charity in Concord."

"That's good." Josh's smile looked a little strained. Had Michael scrambled his words again? "And she's not too far away, so you can see her whenever you want."

Michael let out a breath. "She's traveling soon." He nearly mentioned Amanda's plans for a yearlong overseas tour before realizing it was very possible Josh had never left the Northeast. How much money did a bagel shop make in a year?

Josh hummed thoughtfully and darted a glance Michael's way. "But *you're* staying, right?" he asked with an air of false casualness.

"Absolutely. I've always loved it here. This was . . ." *There was a boy*, he thought, remembering the summer when he was fifteen, when he met a boy at the beach and they climbed out onto the breakwater, going all the way to the end. His first real kiss—"real" as in not with a girl, not done because it was expected or because all his classmates were kissing girls—had been a thrill of feeling *right* and a black pit of terror at the thought of his father catching them.

"This was . . .?" Josh prompted.

Michael laughed and shook his head. "There was someone. Good memories. I mean, not someone I'll ever see again," he added quickly. The last thing he needed was Josh thinking this was a temporary measure until he could track down some long-lost love. "It's just . . . It's a good place, you know? I've always liked it here."

Josh's smile went soft. "Yeah. It's great here. Despite the mainlanders, tourists, and winter students."

Michael nudged him under the table. "Don't those tourists and students keep you in business?" he teased.

"Well, yeah." Josh leaned in, lowering his voice, eyes sparkling with amusement. "But if you're really going to be a local, you'll have to learn to love them in public and hate them in private. The traffic, the garbage, the noise, the crowd—"

A sudden, loud *crack* cut into Josh's words. Ceramic shattering. Glass shattering.

The windshield.

Adrenaline slammed into Michael's veins, sending electricity searing through his chest, leaving his fingers tingling. A voice was shouting, high-pitched and strained. He was shifting, just starting to duck, when a warm, soft, heavy body pushed against his legs and a cold nose nudged his arm.

"Kaylee." The name came out as a gasp. He blinked. Felt the padded booth under his legs, behind his back. Banged into the table when he tried to stand. *Restaurant.*

He had to get out. He could do that. He just had to leave money, or someone would stop him.

Wallet in hand. Cash on the table. Leash wrapped around his fist. Bag over his shoulder.

"Exit," he said, and followed the tug of Kaylee's leash as she started to move. Glass reflected sunlight into his eyes, making him flinch and hunch his shoulders. He grabbed a silver bar and pulled, then pushed. When the glass gave way, he staggered through.

Another shout behind him made him run, following Kaylee to a big black vehicle. He had keys in his hand—where had they come from?—and the door opened when he tugged the handle. Kaylee leaped in and scrambled over to the far side, leaving room for him behind the wheel.

Movement caught his eye. Someone rushing through the glass door, making it sparkle, momentarily blinding him. *Go!* a voice shouted in the back of his head, and the ignition screeched under the force of his turning key. He threw the vehicle into reverse and roared out onto the street, shifted gears, and tore away from the threat, heading for safety.

Josh stumbled to a halt on the sidewalk, staring after Michael's SUV, heart a lead weight in his chest. He'd barely had time to call Michael's name, much less try to call him back.

"What the hell?" Josh muttered, turning to go back inside because he didn't know what else to do.

"Everything okay, Josh?" Betty asked worriedly from where she was cleaning up the plates she'd dropped.

"Yeah." The lie came automatically. Josh had no idea what had happened, but it was nobody's business but Michael's. If he wanted to give Josh any details . . . Well, hopefully he would, and Josh would listen and try his hardest to be understanding.

Understanding of *what*? Betty had tripped and sent their lunch plates crashing to the floor. Yeah, it had been loud and startling, but that sort of thing happened in restaurants all the time.

But Michael had gone white, almost ashen. He'd stopped listening to Josh. Hadn't reacted at all to Josh saying his name. And then he and Kaylee were up, and he'd dumped all the bills in his wallet onto the table.

Josh went past Betty, knowing she wouldn't appreciate his offering to help clean up in her restaurant any more than he'd want her help in his, and returned to the table to see how much more he owed for lunch.

A five, two ones, a ten, *four* twenties . . . a *hundred*? Shit. Michael couldn't have been paying attention. Rich mainlander or not, he couldn't have intended to pay almost two hundred bucks for running out on lunch, right? He probably hadn't even known what he was doing. He'd been bumping into tables, and the door had completely stumped him. Josh gathered up the money, folded it, and tucked it into the pocket opposite his wallet. He'd pay out of his own pocket and give back all of Michael's cash.

Without the question of money to distract him, his thoughts turned back to the disastrous, unexpected end of this date. He'd had some pretty bad dates—a big reason he was still single—but this one was . . . Well, he'd never had someone run out on him like that.

He picked up his Coke and took a long drink, swallowing too fast. He coughed and had to put the glass down before he spilled it. The momentary tightness in his throat cleared the fog in his head.

And he realized Michael's abrupt departure had nothing to do with him.

Michael had been *terrified*. Just seconds after those plates hit the floor, he'd run out of the diner as if dinosaurs were chasing him. Everything he'd done, from grabbing his bag to "paying" the bill, had looked automatic, not controlled and thought out.

Fear of loud noises. Word replacement and misspeaking. His little stumble at the park when he'd tried to stand up. The way he sat with his back to a wall, where he could see everything around him. The way he'd told Kaylee, "Exit," and she'd all but dragged him straight to the door, like she'd been trained to find her way out of any room or building.

Was it all connected?

More to the point, did Josh want to deal with all that? He *liked* Michael a lot, but this was . . . also a lot to think about. Maybe it would've been easier to deal with if Michael had said something, but they were practically strangers. They'd only met a few days ago.

He needed more information. And while before he wouldn't have invaded Michael's privacy, now he needed to know *something*.

He was just taking out his phone when Betty came over and put down another Coke, saying, "I'm real sorry, Josh. Did you still want your burger?"

If this were a movie, Josh would be too caught up in the moment of drama to even think about food. But he'd been working since before sunrise and on his feet for hours, and the only food he'd eaten was sporadic bites between customers at breakfast.

"Please. And a milk shake," he told her, summoning a quick, fake smile.

She patted his shoulder and asked, more gently, "Is it just going to be you, hon?"

He nodded, swallowing around the lump in his throat. "Yeah. I guess so."

She gave his shoulder a squeeze. "I'll get that milk shake right out to you."

"Thanks." As she hurried off, he opened a search on his phone and turned on the mic instead of trying to spell everything correctly on the tiny keyboard. Then, one by one, he started making a list of everything he'd observed.

CHAPTER
TWELVE

A cold, wet nose pressed into Michael's palm. The engine's vibration was a low hum, not the bone-shaking roar part of his mind expected. He stared out the unbroken windshield at the white garage door and blinked a few times to soothe his burning eyes.

The driveway. Civilian vehicle. Kaylee, draped uncomfortably and awkwardly across the center console. Her forelegs were on his lap, neck stretched so she could reach his hand.

"I'm okay." His voice sounded like he'd been breathing sand and smoke. Memory made him cough. "Back, Kaylee. Off." He had no idea which command to use, because he'd never trained her to climb across the front seat and wedge herself between his legs and the steering wheel. Fuck, that was unsafe. Had she done that while he was driving? For that matter, how the hell had he gotten home without crashing? And where had he—

Shit. *Shit.* His date with Josh!

He had zero memory of anything that had happened between the diner and right now. He hadn't blacked out like this in months.

When he got out of the SUV, he nearly collapsed. He caught the door, wobbled, leaned his forehead against the cool driver's-side window.

Kaylee's quiet whine got him to straighten up. She was on the driver's seat, holding the leash in her mouth. He'd trained her to stay in the car until he commanded her out, to keep her from jumping into traffic or hurting herself if her leash got caught.

"Good girl." He let go of the door and turned carefully. His legs seemed to be working, so he took the leash and stepped back, beckoning her out. She stayed close as if understanding just how shaky he was.

Together, they walked slowly around the SUV so he could check for damage. Nothing. No dents, no scratches. So he hadn't done a hit and run—not a surprise. He'd had a couple of similar incidents in DC, before he cut back severely on how much driving he did, and he'd never even had a close call, as best he could tell. It was as if all of his defensive driving training, both from high school and the Air Force, took over his body when his brain went to hide under the bed.

Reassured that the cops wouldn't be coming to arrest him for a vehicular felony, he got his bag out of the passenger-side footwell—at least he hadn't left the bag behind—and headed for the barn. The big question now was, did Josh hate him? Should he call or text? He'd walked out on Josh and stiffed him for their lunch bill, and he had *no idea why*. What had triggered him? Some innocent thing Josh had done or said? Or something else, something entirely unrelated to their date?

By now, Michael was depressingly familiar with his list of known triggers: quick movement, anyone sneaking up behind him, breaking glass, loud noises, crowds, dark roads with low visibility, emotional stress . . . *Shit.* The list was way too long for him to be getting involved with anyone, especially a guy like Josh. He was nice. Innocent. Untouched by politics and money and all the shit that had overcomplicated Michael's life even before he enlisted.

He should call Josh and apologize. Or maybe text, so Josh didn't feel obliged to forgive him or say anything or even answer.

Yeah, he'd text. But not now. Now was too soon, and he had no idea what he'd say. He'd go have a hot bath and recover, maybe take something to help slow his racing thoughts, then lie on the couch and come up with a considerate, sincere apology text that he could send to Josh with no expectation of a response.

The thought made his chest go tight. He stopped in his tracks and swallowed against the lump in his throat. No matter what he said, Josh would think—*know*—he was damaged goods. Maybe if they'd known each other for years, Josh would be willing to take a chance, to look past all of Michael's issues and give a relationship a try. But they were strangers.

No, all Michael could do was explain his behavior as best he could, apologize, and bow out of Josh's life for good. Then they could each get on with their lives, separately. He owed Josh that much. Once he was a little more steady on his feet, he'd do that. Later tonight.

Much later tonight. Maybe tomorrow morning.

"Josh? You home?"

Josh sighed up at his bedroom ceiling and rubbed the headache centered between his eyes. "Yeah, Dad!" he shouted, rolling over to sit on the side of his bed. His closet door was propped open with a laundry basket full of jeans and Bagel End polo shirts. He had about twenty of the damned things so he'd never be caught without a uniform if he got called in to cover a shift. One corner of his Middle Earth map was curling up from the door; he couldn't remember when he'd lost the thumbtack, and he kept forgetting to replace it.

The sight was depressing. He was a grown man, half owner in the family business, and he'd lived away from home for a grand total of six months—one disastrous lease in a shithole apartment when he was nineteen and thought starving on his own was more grown-up than having food in the cupboards. Besides, living at home meant he could keep an eye on his dad's health, which was the real reason he lived here. At least, that was what he told himself.

The bedroom door was cracked open. When Dad knocked, it swung open the rest of the way. "Hey. You okay? I went to the diner . . ." he said, giving Josh a sympathetic smile.

Betty. She couldn't resist gossip, and Josh's date—both the fact of it and how abruptly it had ended—was a good month's worth of gossip in a small town like Hartsbridge Island. Dad must have gone there out of habit, expecting to meet Josh for their usual end-of-the-day wrap-up meeting, only to be entertained by Betty instead.

Josh sighed and got to his feet. "Yeah."

Dad tipped his head, beckoning Josh over. "I brought home a double order of fries. They should still be hot."

Josh managed a faint smile. "Thanks," he said, following Dad downstairs to the kitchen. The Styrofoam box of fries was there on the kitchen table. Dad had already taken the ketchup out of the fridge.

Stomach rumbling, Josh sat in his usual creaky old chair and opened the box. Dad sat down kitty-corner from him, in reach of the fries. As Josh squeezed ketchup into the box's lid, Dad asked, "So, you want to talk about it?"

Too much ketchup splashed out of the bottle. Josh cleaned the extra drips with one finger and capped the bottle. "I don't know, Dad. I mean, I *think* I know something, but . . ." He shook his head and picked up a fry. Swirling it through the ketchup was only a brief distraction.

"Uh-huh. Clear as mud." Dad snatched a fry and used it to point at Josh. "Want to try again? Or you can tell me to screw off. Up to you."

With a snap of teeth, Josh took out his frustration on his own fry. "Things were going really well, and then—*boom*!—they weren't."

Dad leaned over to open the fridge. There were some advantages to a kitchen the size of a postage stamp. He took out two diet sodas and set them on the table. The *pop-hiss* when he opened his can shattered the silence, but he didn't say anything.

That was his way of doing things. He'd sit there with Josh, all stoic and silent, offering his support without saying a single word. That tactic was how they'd survived the years after Mom died, when Dad got sick, when Josh dropped out of high school to help at the bagel shop. In the end, stuff that happened was just *stuff*. What mattered was that they loved each other, no matter what, and weren't alone.

Of course, Josh couldn't resist the urge to fill that silence. He lasted three fries before he asked, "What do you know about PTSD?"

Dad let out a slow breath and leaned back in his chair, taking a drink. "That explains it."

Josh's eyebrows shot up. "Did you skip a few parts there?"

"Betty said your 'boyfriend' rushed out when she dropped a tray." Dad put down his soda can. "'Left like a zombie, only fast,' she said. After a loud noise like that?" He nodded, his expression grave and full of sympathy. "It sounds like a couple of soldiers I once knew. Some of them, when they came back . . ."

Josh nodded, breaking a fry in half. He dipped the broken end in the ketchup. "I looked up some stuff on PTSD. It's not just soldiers. Any traumatic experience can cause it. Right?" he added uncertainly, glancing over at his father. Much as he'd tried to learn everything he could, he'd gotten lost in most of the articles, and his phone's screen was too small for him to read it for very long.

"True," Dad conceded. "But he's got a service dog, right? If he was wounded in combat—"

"He doesn't *seem* like a soldier," Josh interrupted. He couldn't picture Michael—so soft-spoken and gentle with Kaylee—carrying a gun.

"What's 'a soldier' seem like?" Dad asked, smiling wryly.

"Okay, that's fair." Josh shrugged and ate both halves of his fry together. "But he doesn't *act* like a soldier. And his hair's too long."

"So's yours." Dad reached out and tugged on Josh's curls. "You should stop at the barber's tomorrow, or we'll have the health department on our backs."

"Yeah, yeah. And *you* get to open tomorrow," Josh added a little bitterly. Michael had yet to text or phone. There wasn't a chance in hell that he'd show up at Bagel End tomorrow, so there was no point in Josh getting up at stupid o'clock.

"I figured." Dad folded his arms on the table, then extended one finger to push the fries closer to Josh. "Eat."

Obediently Josh picked up two fries. "If it *is* PTSD, what then?"

Dad let out a long sigh, eyes going distant. "Then you have to decide what you want. If he's worth it."

Josh's eyes narrowed. "Worth *what*?"

Dad held up one hand. "I'm not an expert."

"You know something, though," Josh pressed.

Dad nodded, though he didn't speak right away. He frowned as he drank his soda, staring absently at the table, brow furrowed. Josh wanted to press him but knew better. He'd speak when he was ready. Not before.

But instead of speaking—instead of imparting some great wisdom or helping to make sense of it all—Dad asked, "Do you like him?"

Instinctively, Josh hunched into his seat just a tiny bit. "I'm not twelve."

"Josh . . ."

Josh shrugged, focusing on eating his fries. "Yeah," he muttered between bites. Then he swallowed and glanced up at his dad, adding, "Or I *could* like him, if I got to know him better. I think."

"Okay." Dad leaned back in his seat again. "Back when I was first dating your mom . . . When your grandma and grandpa found out she'd been born with a bad heart, they brought me to see my uncle, Stuart. The cardiologist. He explained . . . everything. What could happen and might happen and probably would happen."

Josh swallowed, stomach churning. They rarely talked about Mom, and when they did, it was always about her life. Happy memories. Never about her illness or her death. "Dad—"

"Just—" Dad held up a hand and took a deep breath, gathering himself. "Just let me finish. Uncle Stu . . . He got almost everything right. I *knew* ahead of time—before I even asked her to marry me— about all of it. The doctors, the hospital, everything. I went into it with my eyes open. It was hard and painful and . . ." His voice went tight, and he shook his head, taking a drink.

"I know." Josh picked up his soda, but he hadn't opened it. He cringed at how loud it would be if he pulled up the tab, so he didn't. He just held the can, and the cold aluminum sent chills down his spine.

"But I did it. I asked her to marry me, and if . . . if I had the chance to do it again, I would." Dad blinked, eyes glassy. "But that's what I'm saying here, Josh. PTSD . . . it's not something you can magically *fix*. If it is PTSD, he's not going to spend a month with a therapist or get a prescription and be cured. Not even if he falls in love."

God, all Josh had wanted was a *date*. "That's moving a little fast, Dad."

"Is it?" Dad arched a brow. "The first time I saw your mom, it wasn't love at first sight. It was . . . it was 'hot date at first sight,' you could call it." He gave Josh a quick, embarrassed smile. "The rest of it—the love, the marriage—everything just snuck up on us. One day we were having fun, and the next, I was looking at rings, and to this day I couldn't tell you when we crossed the line between dating and forever."

"But this guy . . ." Josh let his dad's honesty bolster his courage and said, "I didn't even know his name until yesterday. He was just . . . Hot Tourist Guy."

Dad laughed. "'Hot Tourist Guy'? Really?"

Josh shrugged, torn between embarrassment and laughter of his own. "He paid in cash. Otherwise, I would've checked the name on his credit card. Not to be creepy," he added quickly. "Just, you know, out of curiosity. To be friendly."

"So, two days ago, you didn't know Hot Tourist Guy's name"—Dad smirked; he was having way too much fun with that nickname—"and today you went on a date with him."

"Or half a date," Josh corrected, finally opening his soda. "And you still haven't said if this is your way of saying I *shouldn't* try for another date. Or half of one."

Dad shook his head, his smile softening. "No, this is me saying that if he really has PTSD . . . well, you need to think about whether or not you want to be with him, knowing he has PTSD. If you want to make that commitment. Because that's what you'd have to live with for the rest of your life."

This felt too critical of Michael. Josh didn't even *know* Michael had PTSD, though he had to admit that was how it looked. He'd done a quick search of Michael's symptoms on his phone. The top two hits were PTSD and ghostly possession, and Josh flat-out didn't believe in ghosts. "That's not really fair, though. It's not his fault."

"I know. But you need to go into this with your eyes open."

"No. Dad, look. It was *half a date*. I'm not going to go . . . demanding his medical history and a background check—"

"Hang on," Dad interrupted, holding up both hands. "I'm just saying, educate yourself. That way, you can decide if you can live with being on this side of it. Mom's heart condition wasn't hers and hers alone. It affected every decision in our lives, from us getting married to our choosing to adopt you."

"Yeah, but you said she could've *died* from the stress of getting pregnant," Josh protested.

"And if I'd been set on a biological child? Because some people are, you know. For some people, that would've been a deal-breaker," Dad said bluntly. "If he does have PTSD—and that's going to require an honest talk between the two of you—then all I want is for you to understand what you *might* be getting into, to see if there are any deal-breakers. If there are any potential complications that you *can't* accept."

Josh's eyes narrowed. Stubbornly, he asked, "And if there aren't?"

Dad shrugged. "Then you should call him and see about the other half of that date." He took a quick drink of his soda.

"Huh?"

Dad blinked. "What?"

"You're not going to try to talk me out of it?" Josh asked, baffled. That was where this had all been going, right?

"Of course not." Dad leaned an arm on the table, earnestly meeting Josh's eyes. "I just want you to have all the facts first, before you make a decision either way."

Josh shook his head and picked up a few more fries. "Right. Okay." It still felt like a violation of Michael's privacy, but Dad was right. Josh needed to know. He stabbed the fries into the ketchup and said, "I'll look it up online or something."

"You could come to work first thing tomorrow morning. See if Arielle Miller shows up with her wife," Dad suggested. "She's a doctor. She's got to know something about PTSD, right?"

Josh snorted. "Or you're trying to get out of the opening shift for another day."

Dad's grin was bright and innocent, without a hint of embarrassment. "I'm just trying to help. Besides, I'm kind of enjoying sleeping in. Maybe we should make this shift change permanent."

Josh's only answer was to throw a french fry at him.

CHAPTER

THIRTEEN

It took Michael two days to empty the kitchen of everything picked up at the store and ransacked from the main house. Two days before he had the choice between going grocery shopping again or starvation. That didn't stop him from doing one last check of the fridge and one last search of the cupboards, because the thought of going out was so infuriating that he slammed the pantry door hard enough to make Kaylee yelp in surprise.

"Shit," he hissed, leaning back against the door so he could slide down to the floor. His head fell back, sadly not hard enough to knock him unconscious, and he snapped, "Shit!" again.

Kaylee crawled across his legs and rolled onto her side, pressing her back into his stomach. He sighed and buried both hands in her fur, taking the hint. Breathe through the anger. The anger just existed. Feel it, acknowledge it, release it. Just like his therapist had taught him.

It was all psychobabble bullshit, but it eventually worked. Well, Kaylee's heavy presence worked. The mental part was just a lousy way to kill time while his body followed his dog's example and calmed itself down.

This sort of irrational surge of anger was just one more new and exciting part of life after hospitalization. Honestly, Michael didn't know which was worse: the anger or the blackouts. He'd never *hurt* anyone—or himself, for that matter—during any of his episodes, but was that just a lack of opportunity?

No.

He could hear his therapist's voice in his head. *"Isolating yourself to protect others isn't a solution. It's an unhealthy coping mechanism."*

And he wasn't angry anymore. Just hungry, headachey, and lonely. So damned lonely, despite the dog draped over his legs, cutting off the circulation to his feet.

"Okay, okay. Up, mutt," he grunted, giving Kaylee a push. She got to her feet slowly, stretching one leg at a time, turning it into a full-body yawn that tempted him into tugging on her tongue. She went cross-eyed and jerked her head back, then gave him a disdainful look that made him smile.

Josh would've smiled too. He liked Kaylee. He *used* to like Michael, but there wasn't a chance in hell that he still did. Not after two days of radio silence.

"I should call him," Michael told Kaylee, who sat and stared up at him with hopeful interest. They were still in the kitchen, after all, and that was where the food lived. "I should at least text him, right?"

Kaylee's ears twitched. Her focus never wavered.

He sighed and ruffled her fur, then waved her away. It had been too long. He should've called or texted on day one. The next morning at the latest. Now . . . now, he couldn't call. At least not right now.

Had Josh called? Michael had turned off his phone . . . *Shit.* He couldn't remember when, except that it had been dark. Last night? The night before? For all he knew, Josh might have texted or called and left a message, and now he'd be thinking Michael was intentionally ignoring him.

There it was. Proof that Michael was an awful person. God, he had no right to contact someone as nice as Josh—not after leaving him hanging for days.

A hint of anger flickered through his consciousness, aimed solely at himself, but he didn't have the energy. He sighed down at Kaylee, who was still sitting by his feet, staring up at him, faithful and uncomplaining.

It was too late to do anything for Josh, but he had a responsibility to Kaylee. And to himself.

"Okay, come on, Kaylee," he said, heading out of the kitchen. He'd been wearing the same ratty sweats for a day and a half, which was a day too long to spend moping. He needed a shower, fresh clothes, and groceries, in that order. The sky outside was still light. If he hurried, he'd make it to the grocery store and back before it got too dark.

He'd think of something to do about Josh afterward, once he proved to himself that he was capable of being a functional adult.

"Okay, look. I know this seems like a lot, but it really isn't," Lizzie said, turning the laptop an inch more toward Josh. "First, you're not looking for outside funding, right? A bank loan, investors—"

"No." Josh and his dad shared that philosophy, at least. They each had the minimum amount of credit required to establish a credit rating, and that was it. "We'll handle it all ourselves."

"Right. So, skip this"—she tapped the part of the screen that discussed funding—"and you've only got these six parts to go."

Josh bit back the urge to tell her exactly what he thought of the word "only" when it came to writing a business plan. Executive summary? They sold bagels. They didn't have *executives*. And what exactly did "market analysis" mean? More to the point, how much did it cost to get one?

A little desperately, he said, "Company description. That should be easy enough. We sell bagels."

Lizzie twisted the laptop away so she could click the link, and Josh's heart sank when another wall of text appeared. "It's a bit more than that."

"Oh my God," Josh muttered, leaning back to look into the shop. Dee was almost done packing the deli case for the night. No help there. Maybe he could claim the floor was in dire need of a good mopping?

"No, Josh, it's fine," Lizzie said blithely, unconcerned with his need to escape. Then again, this meeting had been his idea. She had no reason to suspect he was regretting his decision. "We'll start here. Tonight, you write up the company description. We can meet in a day or two to go over it, and then we can look into doing a market analysis. We'll leave the executive summary for last. Once you've got everything else, the executive summary really writes itself."

Why won't it all write itself? Josh wondered morosely, eyeing the computer, suspicious of this whole mess. "Is this really necessary?" he asked. "We're selling bagels, not aircraft carriers."

Lizzie gave him a bright smile. "Trust me, you'll be thankful once you're done with it. It'll keep you on track. Make sure you and your dad are on the same page. Help with marketing later, since you need a whole new strategy, selling to businesses instead of walk-in customers—"

"Okay, okay," he interrupted, his own smile strained. "Business plan. You got it."

"Good!" Lizzie closed her laptop and slid it into her bag. "So you'll do the company description?"

"I'll"—*throw myself under a truck,* Josh thought—"get right on it. Just as soon as I lock up. In fact, I'll let you out."

He escorted Lizzie to the front door, which he unlocked and held open for her. She left cheerfully—probably because she wasn't stuck writing this stupid business plan. How had he ended up saddled with doing all the work? She was the expert.

Of course, she was the *unpaid* expert, at least for this. Expanding Bagel End was well outside the scope of her monthly fee for balancing the books. Josh had tried to hire her for this, but somehow he'd gone from bargaining to "convincing" her to shepherd him through the process instead.

Maybe she'd take a bribe.

For now, he put the idea of the business plan aside and went back to the kitchen. He'd already done most of the cleaning; all that was left was to put away the cleaning supplies and turn off the lights in back.

"I'm heading out, boss!" Dee called from up front.

Josh joined her so he could let her out and lock the door. It took him just a few minutes to close up the shop and get things ready for Dad tomorrow. They were back to their daily routine, with Dad opening the shop and Josh closing.

Back to the usual, lonely normal, Josh thought as he turned off the lights behind the counter. He'd opened yesterday, on the off chance that Michael would show up, but nothing. No visits, no phone calls, no texts. Josh hadn't even seen him on the street yesterday—and he'd been looking hard enough that he'd cut open his thumb while slicing lox.

The memory made the cut sting all over again. Rubbing a finger over the bandage, Josh did one last check of the shop, then set the alarm and let himself out. The wind off the ocean was cool but not cold, a reminder that the tourists would soon be flocking to the island. He'd have to remember to ask his dad if anyone had dropped off an application. If they didn't get extra summer help, they'd both end up dead on their feet.

As it was, Josh was so exhausted he made it halfway across the green, walking toward the diner on instinct, before remembering that Dad was at home. Flipping schedules had left them both scrambled and in need of a few good nights' sleep.

Josh groaned and took a couple more steps, thinking he could pick up two dinners to go, but no such luck. They needed general groceries at home, not just dinner. And while Josh could live with reheated french fries for breakfast, there were no good substitutes for toothpaste.

So he turned the other way and headed back to Bagel End, then past it and around the corner. The small grocery store was halfway down the street, where it shared a parking lot with a mechanic's station, the island's only dry cleaner, and the barber Josh still hadn't visited. It was too late now. Outside summer tourist season, most of the island's nonrestaurant businesses closed between five and six, like Bagel End. Even the grocery store would only be open until eight. After that, people would have to go down to the south side of the island, where a couple of convenience stores and the all-night laundromat stayed open to cater to college students.

On autopilot, Josh picked up a basket instead of grabbing a shopping cart. Using a cart would encourage him to overload with groceries, and then he'd have to phone Dad to get a ride to the house or pay for a taxi. Toothpaste was a priority, so he went for the health and beauty aisle first, tempted though he was by the freezer case. Maybe on the way out, if he had room in the basket for ice cream.

No. Room in the basket didn't equate to room in his waistband, and he was *not* going to turn to food to deal with how mopey he'd been over Michael's silence.

The buzz of his phone in his pocket distracted him from thoughts of both Michael and ice cream. He switched the basket to his other hand so he could check the caller ID—it was Dad—and answer, "Hey. Do we need any other bathroom stuff but toothpaste?"

"I don't think so, no. Are you picking up dinner?" Dad hinted. He sounded exhausted.

"Yeah. I'll get something quick. Maybe pasta." Josh's bandage scraped against his stubble, reminding him that he needed to shave tomorrow morning. "Do we have stuff to put on cuts?"

Instead of answering, Dad asked worriedly, "Does your thumb still hurt? Do you need to see the doctor?"

"It's fine, Dad. I used a packet of that antibiotic gel from the first aid kit at work."

Dad grumbled but let it pass, just saying, "Yeah, pick some up, then."

Josh nodded, absently searching his way down the row. Shampoo, bodywash, body spray . . . "Hey, do you have your old business plan?" he asked as he reached the toothpaste.

"What?"

"The business plan for Bagel End. Do you have it?" Josh figured it wouldn't be plagiarism to build on an existing business plan. Maybe he'd have half of it done already. That was a cheerful thought.

"No. What on earth . . ." Dad fell silent, and Josh could picture him frowning and shaking his head. "Why do you need a business plan?"

"Lizzie needs it," Josh answered before realizing the next logical question would lead to a discussion he wasn't prepared to have. He focused on scanning the shelves, trying to ignore the tooth-whitening, extended-breath-freshening stuff and find plain old toothpaste.

Sure enough, Dad asked, "What for?"

How the hell was Josh supposed to answer that? He didn't want to lie to his father, but other than their brief conversation about dog treats, his tentative forays into the "Hey Dad, let's expand the business" chat hadn't gone well to date. And now, when they were both tired and cranky, was definitely the wrong time to try again.

"Don't worry about it. What—"

"*Why*, Josh?" Dad asked sharply.

Josh closed his eyes for a couple of seconds and sighed. "She was asking to see it, that's all. No big deal." He picked up the first package of toothpaste that looked familiar, no longer trying to figure out the cheapest price per ounce, and headed for the far end of the aisle.

Suspicious now, Dad said, "She shouldn't need a business plan to do the books."

"Forget it," Josh snapped, rounding the corner, nearly running down a shopping cart. "Sorry—"

He cut off, the sound of his dad's voice falling away as his eyes locked with Michael's across the shopping cart. Michael looked like shit, his stubble inching close to a full beard, dark circles under his eyes. Josh had to glance away—to check for Kaylee, because he couldn't imagine anything short of losing Kaylee that would make Michael look this awful.

"Josh." It came out strangled, so different from Michael's usual, charming, sweet voice.

Fuck off. Not interested. Maybe we should take things slow, just be friends. For two days, Josh had been mentally rehearsing what he'd say to Michael, but what he actually said was, "Are you okay?"

Michael flinched and stared down into his cart. Josh stole a quick look, and his eyebrows shot up at the sight of about twenty pounds of ground beef, a huge package of paper towels, and a box of minibagel pizzas. This was Michael's idea of shopping?

"Yeah. I'm, uh . . . I feel"—Michael shook his head, still avoiding eye contact—"not good. The burger place . . ."

Josh winced at the utter lack of eloquence. Michael had misspoken a couple of times before, but this felt like he didn't even know what he was trying to say. "Hey, don't—" Josh put a hand on Michael's cart, saying, "It's okay. It's fine."

And to his surprise, it was. Josh had waffled about calling Michael for two days. It looked like Michael had gone right past wavering into full-blown disorganized panic. It was desperate and helpless, and Josh couldn't be angry about that.

Shoulders hunched, Michael met Josh's eyes and frowned. "I'm sorry," he said slowly, as though the words were in a foreign language.

"It's okay," Josh repeated, hand sliding along the shopping cart as he took a step closer. He wasn't ready to forget what had happened, but he couldn't stand seeing Michael in this sort of distress.

Kaylee apparently shared Josh's concern; she nosed at Michael's wrist until he let go of the cart and scratched between her ears. At the first touch, some of the tension melted out of his shoulders. *Thank God he's not alone*, Josh thought, watching them.

"Hey, if you . . ." Josh shrugged, trying to figure out a way to word an invitation without crossing over into pressuring Michael. The way he looked right now, one push might make him shatter into pieces. "You can call me sometime, if you want. We can meet up, give lunch another try or something."

Michael blinked at Josh. "Yeah?"

Josh wouldn't forget, but he sure as hell couldn't resist forgiving—not after hearing such hope in Michael's voice. "Yeah." But then, because he also had to take care of himself, he gently added, "Maybe we can talk about what happened last time."

"Yeah. Okay," Michael said guiltily, staring back down at the contents of his shopping cart.

Josh had to take a two-handed grip on his basket to keep from reaching for Michael's hand. "I've got to get home. Dad's waiting for dinner. But maybe pick up some actual food for yourself? You can't live on ground beef and paper towels."

Michael's laugh seemed to surprise him. This time, when he met Josh's eyes, he didn't seem like he was expecting to get kicked. "Frozen minipizzas don't count?"

"Remind me to teach you to cook," Josh said, rolling his eyes. He looked down at Kaylee and said, "Get him home safe. Okay, Kaylee?"

She ignored him until Michael said, "Kaylee, say hi." Then she stood—she'd been sitting on Michael's sneakers—and sniffed at Josh's hand. "Thanks, Josh."

Don't touch. Don't touch, Josh told himself. He scratched Kaylee's fur, keeping a good half inch between his fingers and Michael's, and said, "Talk to you soon."

Then he escaped down the pasta aisle before he could push for more, like a confirmation that Michael would call. Josh's minimal research on PTSD hadn't been enough—not by a long shot—but he knew that making demands, especially during a time of emotional stress, would make things worse, not better. Josh had to keep a light, almost delicate touch, as if he were coaxing a skittish deer out of the bushes, a comparison that he was sure Michael would hate. Best not to mention that.

"Josh? Josh?"

That wasn't Michael. Josh looked around, wondering why the hell he was hearing his dad's voice, and spotted his cell phone in the grocery basket. *Shit.* He'd been on a call.

He fumbled the phone up to his ear and asked, "Dad? You still there?"

"Uh-huh," Dad answered.

Josh winced. "So, uh . . . you heard all that?"

"Yeah," Dad said more softly. "That sounded tough. Are you okay?"

"Fine. I'm fine." It wasn't even a lie. Josh picked up a package of rigatoni and dropped it into the basket with a rustle of plastic. "Pasta okay for dinner tonight?"

"Sounds good."

"Is plain sauce okay? I don't feel like browning any ground beef." *If there's any left.*

"That's fine," Dad said absently. "Josh . . . was *he* okay? He didn't sound all that . . . I don't know."

Josh wasn't going to have this conversation with his dad. Not now, hopefully not ever, but definitely not without more facts. "Yeah. It's been a long day for everyone. Let me finish up here. I'll be home in twenty minutes. Heat up the water for me?"

Dad's pause was just long enough to let Josh know he'd seen through the casual dismissal. "Sure."

"Okay, then. See you in twenty," Josh said, and this time he made sure to disconnect the call before he dropped the phone in the basket. He'd made it halfway down the aisle, to the jars of sauce, when he remembered to check the battery. Twenty percent. He'd been less than diligent about charging the phone, but tonight he'd have to remember. He didn't want to miss out on talking to Michael again—assuming he called.

CHAPTER
FOURTEEN

What a difference a day makes, Josh thought when he spotted Michael's warm, easy smile through the locked front door. And wow, he cleaned up nicely. He'd shaved, for one thing, and his polo shirt and dark jeans were a far cry from the T-shirt and ratty jeans he'd worn to the grocery store last night. Even Kaylee looked better, or at least fluffier, as if she'd had a bath.

"You've got this, right? Got your keys?" Josh asked Dee as he looked himself over, self-conscious of how casually he was dressed. Sure, his T-shirt was clean, but Michael had some put-together quality that Josh lacked. Never had Josh been so aware of the chasm between townies and mainlanders—a chasm Josh had never even been tempted to bridge until now.

"I've got it." Dee snickered and elbowed him toward the pass-through. "Will you stop worrying? You're adorable," she scolded.

Josh's face went hot. *Adorable* wasn't what he was going for, but it was all he had going for him. "Sexual harassment! Hitting on your boss!" he teased, deflecting as he always did. He wasn't good with compliments.

"Your shift ended four minutes ago, so you're just some guy who's in the way. *Go.*" She shooed him away.

"Okay, okay. Good night. If there are any problems, call my dad."

Dee let out an exasperated huff. "I know. Good *night*, Josh."

Trying not to grin like an idiot, he came out from behind the counter, with Dee on his heels. He unlocked the door and opened it just enough to slip through. "Hey," he said to Michael, noting the way Michael waved Kaylee back rather than letting her move between them as she usually did.

Michael smiled, shifting his weight from foot to foot. "Hi. Sorry if I'm early."

"No, it's fine—"

"Yes, it is," Dee interrupted, startling Josh. How had he forgotten about her? "So go have fun, both of you."

Josh turned in time for Dee to close the door in his face. She grinned at him as she turned the lock, then waved at them both.

"Um. Should we have met somewhere else?" Michael asked as Josh turned back.

Probably, Josh thought, though he shook his head. "No, it's fine. She's just like that." He wanted to reach for Michael's hand, but not yet. Not now. He shoved his hands in his pockets instead. Michael had invited Josh to dinner, but he hadn't specified it was an actual *date*. "So, do you know where we're going, or do you need recommendations? Not that we have all that much of a selection . . ."

"Actually, uh, would you be okay with going into Portsmouth? There's a seafood place there that I used to love. It's still open—or at least its website is still up."

Portsmouth? Josh laughed softly and shrugged, looking over at Michael's SUV. If Michael had another . . . *incident*, Josh would be stranded. "I can't remember the last time I was on the mainland, honestly."

Michael's smile faded a notch. "Or we can stay here. We, uh, can give the diner another shot."

Josh weighed Michael's disappointment against the need for his dad to rescue him. Embarrassment was a small price to pay to put that excited light back in Michael's eyes. "No. No, if you don't mind the drive, I'm okay with it." Then he realized he had another potential cause for embarrassment and asked, "Er, am I dressed okay?"

"It's casual," Michael assured him, heading for the SUV. "And it's nice out. I figured maybe we could eat on the patio."

Josh hid a sigh of relief. Patio dining was hardly ever fancy. "Sounds great. As long as you won't be cold," he teased, pointedly looking at Michael's bare arms.

Michael laughed. "I have a jacket in the truck. And I was born here, you know. Well, not here-here, but up in Concord." He opened the rear driver's-side door and told Kaylee, "Car." She jumped up smoothly, vest brushing against the seat.

Josh circled around and got in the passenger side. The handicap parking tag hanging from the rearview mirror caught his eye. Had Michael been hiding it before, or was he just having a bad day now? He didn't seem to have any trouble getting into the car.

But seeing the tag reminded Josh that he and Michael needed to have a discussion if this thing between them was going to have a chance at becoming something more.

Not that he knew where to begin. He glanced at the darkening sky as Michael pulled the SUV out into what passed for rush-hour traffic on Hartsbridge Island. There was no delicate way to ask—to invade Michael's privacy—but their failed date had proven silence wasn't really an option.

Finally, Josh took a bracing breath, then asked, "What happened the other night? At the diner?"

He glanced over in time to see Michael's hands tighten on the steering wheel. Michael didn't look away from the road as he said, "I have PTSD. Loud noises . . . especially breaking glass."

Josh nodded, resting his arm on the side of the door, trying to be casual. He wasn't any good at it, but Michael was focused on driving. Gently, Josh said, "I kind of figured."

Michael moved one hand off the wheel and reached to the back of the center console, so Kaylee could nose at his fingers. "She's trained to help, if that happens. I don't . . . I don't always know where I am or what's going on. When it happens, she gets me somewhere quiet, where I can be alone, sort of . . . come down from it. The stress and all."

"Okay." So far, so good. Between research and common sense, Josh had figured all of this out already. "How'd it happen? I mean, if it's okay to ask, what—"

"I was in the Air Force," Michael interrupted. "I got shot."

"Shit," Josh blurted, twisting around in his seat. "Are you—are you okay now?" It was a stupid question, because obviously the answer wasn't an unconditional yes.

Michael shrugged. "Mostly? The last couple of years, I was in the hospital and in outpatient treatment. I wasn't able to move up here until a couple weeks ago."

"Shit," Josh repeated. He couldn't stop himself from reaching out to touch Michael's forearm. "I'm sorry."

"I survived." Michael glanced away from the road long enough to give Josh a quick smile. "I was shot in the head. Left side."

Josh's fingers twitched, but he didn't move his hand back. Michael was holding his arm very still, not even scratching at Kaylee's muzzle, as if he didn't want to accidentally pull away. "You don't have to talk about it," Josh offered quietly.

Michael shrugged. "It's okay. After the other night . . ." He sighed and glanced at Josh again. "I really am sorry."

"No. It's fine," Josh said firmly. "Completely not your fault." He caught himself rubbing up and down Michael's forearm, but he didn't want to stop. And Michael didn't seem to mind.

"I almost died," Michael said, his voice soft but firm, not asking for pity. "I *should* have died, but there were medics in the convoy. Really fucking fantastic medics. I don't even know how I got from the convoy to the hospital in Germany. I was in a coma for sixteen days."

"Oh my God." Josh's hand clenched around Michael's wrist. "Michael . . ."

"Yeah." Michael shot him a quick, humorless smile. "I had a bunch of surgeries, then almost two years of physical therapy. I still need it. I just have to figure out a local doctor so I don't have to drive to Boston."

"I don't . . . I don't even know what to say," Josh admitted.

Michael pulled his arm away, but only to turn his hand over and take hold of Josh's. "I'm here. I'm alive. Everything else . . ." He shrugged.

Josh nodded, spreading his fingers to interlace them with Michael's. "I'm . . . I'm glad you're okay. And here," he said softly.

This time, Michael's smile was genuine. "Me too."

The restaurant was almost exactly as Michael remembered it, a sprawling building with a patio overlooking the Piscataqua River. Growing up, it had been a family favorite; they'd eaten here at least twice a week whenever they came down to Hartsbridge Island for the summer. It had its share of good memories and bad, but Michael had always liked the food, and hopefully he and Josh could make some new good memories together.

Which was an incredibly sappy thought—one he didn't voice as he let go of Josh's hand and pulled into the only open handicap parking spot near the curving walkway up to the front doors. Josh was staring out the windshield, brows drawn together. "You're sure this is casual?"

Michael nodded. "I double-checked on the website, but yeah, it's always been casual." He shrugged and turned off the engine. "They've got great seafood. And other stuff—steaks and burgers—but what you really want is the fish. Or the shellfish, I guess. It's all fresh off the boats."

"Okay . . ." Josh unlatched his seatbelt and opened his door. "Sounds good."

It wasn't until Michael was letting Kaylee out of the SUV that he realized Josh might be worried about the cost of dinner. Even at the Maine–New Hampshire border, lobster wasn't exactly cheap.

He adjusted his bag over one shoulder, then led Kaylee around the front of the SUV and caught up with Josh. "And this is my treat," Michael offered. "It was my choice to come all the way here. And after the other night, it's—"

"You don't have to keep apologizing," Josh interrupted, stepping close, though he didn't reach for Michael's hand. Was he wary of being caught in public with another guy? Or was he thinking Michael was? Before Michael could figure out how to ask, Josh looked down at himself and took out his wallet, saying, "Oh. Hey. That reminds me . . ." He flipped open the wallet and took out a stack of bills, at least one of them a hundred. To Michael's utter confusion, Josh offered all the cash to him.

"What . . ." Michael frowned, trying to figure out why Josh was *paying* him outside a restaurant that was, yes, a little on the expensive side, but nothing extraordinary. Had he misunderstood Josh's words, or was this some new symptom of lingering brain trauma?

"You left this at the diner, when"—Josh hesitated—"when Kaylee led you out. You didn't even count it, but it was way, way too much."

Oh. Michael took the cash, feeling heat rise in his neck and cheeks. "Thanks. I . . . Yeah." He shook his head, trying to remember if he'd even given the money a second thought. He'd stopped at an ATM before going grocery shopping, and then again tonight before picking up Josh, but that was nothing unusual. Neither Michael nor Amanda used cards unless absolutely necessary, a habit since their teen years—all part of the wonderful paranoia that came from growing up in a political environment that left no room for privacy.

"Thanks." Michael tucked the cash into his pocket, telling himself it was no big deal. Josh wasn't freaked out about it. "But I'm definitely paying tonight."

Josh looked at him through narrowed eyes. "On one condition."

Michael's gut went cold. He shoved both hands into his pockets, Kaylee's leash slack around his wrist. She was sitting diagonally against his left leg, not at his side, not in front of him, as if unsure if she should block Josh or not. "What's that?"

"Tell me what to do if something happens." Josh shifted his weight closer to Michael without actually moving his feet. "If I should just . . . keep my distance and let you go, that's fine. But if there's something I can do . . ."

Michael's exhale was shaky with relief. "You can come with me. I'm not . . . I'm not *dangerous.*" A quiet laugh escaped him. "I was in supply, not Special Forces or something. And talking . . . talking *might* help, but if I don't make any sense . . ." He shook his head, resisting the urge to pull his hand out of his pocket so he could rub at the scar under his hairline.

Josh touched his arm gently, just like he had in the SUV. Michael glanced up, and when their eyes met, Josh smiled. "Follow you, talk to you. Easy enough."

To hell with discretion. Michael pulled his hand out of his pocket and touched Josh's fingers. Their hands turned naturally, fingers interlacing as if that was where they belonged. "How come you're so understanding?"

Josh gave a little shrug, fingers tightening. "I'm just willing to take a chance, that's all."

CHAPTER

FIFTEEN

The patio was lit with flickering torches and hurricane lamps, creating a comfortable balance between casual and intimate. Josh barely felt underdressed, though that could've also been because he and Michael were the only ones dining on the patio. *Tourists*, he thought, smiling to himself as he sat down at a small table next to the railing. The river was right there, thirty or forty feet down, and the breeze was cold and damp, though not too cold for a couple of New Englanders.

"Can I get you started with a drink?" the host asked, passing out menus. "Beer, margarita? We have an extensive wine list." He gestured to the drinks menu already on the table.

"Just water for me, thanks." Michael turned to Josh, saying, "But if you want something—"

"No, water's fine." Josh smiled briefly at the host. He wanted to stay focused tonight. Tempting as it was to have a drink or three to relax, he needed to pay attention. His father's "what if it's not casual" wisdom was too important to ignore, which meant Josh couldn't let tonight pass without what was sure to be an uncomfortable, frank discussion.

"And does your dog . . ." The host nodded at Kaylee, who had settled under the table, muzzle resting on the bottom railing as if she were looking out at the river. "A bowl of water or something?"

Michael shook his head. "She's okay, thanks."

The host nodded again. "Your server will be right back with those drinks," he said before leaving the table.

Michael took an eyeglass case out of his messenger bag. "I don't drink much. Almost not at all."

"Because of the"—Josh hesitated, wondering how to phrase it without offending—"health issues?" He imagined drinking would be a quick and dirty way to escape the trauma that had caused Michael's PTSD, but Michael seemed to be taking good care of himself, rather than going the self-destructive route.

Michael took a deep breath and gave a quick nod as he slipped the glasses on. The sight was distracting, flooding Josh's brain with inappropriate thoughts despite the seriousness of their conversation. He had to glance away, across the river, to gather his wits.

Hopefully unaware of where Josh's mind had gone for a moment, Michael answered, "Yeah. For a while I did—I have trouble sleeping—but alcohol interacts badly with almost everything."

Meaning meds, Josh guessed, looking at the menu without reading it. What was Michael on? Tranquilizers and sleeping pills as needed, or something taken more regularly, like antidepressants? Not that it was any of Josh's business, even if he was looking ahead toward a possible relationship.

"I usually don't drink either," he said, then winced. He'd been aiming for reassuring solidarity, not awkwardness. "I mean, there's nowhere really on the island, once you're out of college. I guess. Since I've never been to college."

He finally shut his mouth, but it was too late. *Brilliant, you idiot.* He'd cemented not just his awkwardness but his lack of higher education. It wasn't exactly a secret that he'd dropped out of high school, and he'd had a good reason for it—they would've lost the shop otherwise—but that didn't mean he wasn't self-conscious about it.

But instead of laughing, Michael just shrugged and said, "I dropped out after my first semester and enlisted."

Josh blinked at him. "Huh?"

Michael didn't quite sneer, but one corner of his lips twitched up. "I was supposed to graduate from Dartmouth. The day I turned eighteen, I quit and joined the Air Force instead."

"Dartmouth? But that's . . . one of the best colleges in the country, isn't it?" Josh asked, stunned. *Nobody* walked away from an Ivy League education to enlist in the military, right? Well, other than Michael.

Michael shrugged again and looked at him over the tops of their menus. "I wanted to see the world."

"Did you like it? I mean, until . . ." Josh trailed off, uncomfortable with the *idea* of Michael getting shot, much less saying the words.

"Yeah." Michael's smile was sad. Distant. "I would've stayed in forever, I think."

I'm glad you didn't, Josh thought, though there was no way he'd say that. Not now, when they were barely friends. Maybe not ever. Instead, he asked, "Is it a family thing? The military?"

Michael shook his head, wrinkling his nose, making his glasses twitch. "No. I'm the first. Maybe the only one, on either side."

Hoping to get that smile back, Josh said, "I have cooks on both sides. I suspect my family was making bagels ten generations ago, back in the Old Country."

Success! Michael laughed and asked, "Which old country is that?"

Josh shrugged. "Brooklyn. Even if you're an immigrant, once you get to Brooklyn, you're forever *from* Brooklyn."

"Does that count if you're adopted?"

"Damn right it does," Josh said proudly. "Otherwise I wouldn't have been entrusted with the recipe for Bubbe's matzo ball soup."

"Mmm. That sounds good," Michael said, looking down at the menu. "And I can't decide, crab legs or lobster."

A quick check of the menu showed that both were at the very top of the seafood section, with the ominous words *market price* instead of a number. The prices for everything else, though, were a whole lot higher than Josh was used to seeing, assuming he was reading them correctly and not getting his numbers mixed up. He started turning pages, looking for anything ten bucks or less, without success. The cheapest entrée—plain burgers—cost more than the most expensive sandwich combos he sold at Bagel End.

Would it be weird if he ordered a small plate of fries instead of an actual dinner? Maybe he could get a kids' meal, though even those started at twelve dollars.

This from a restaurant not twenty minutes away from the island? Was Bagel End undercharging?

Before Josh could figure out what to order, Michael set his menu aside and asked, "Want to get both and split them?"

"What?" Josh tried to estimate the price of fresh lobster and crab, but despite living on an island, he couldn't guess.

Michael gave him a wide-eyed stare. "Or not. I just—" He snapped his mouth closed and picked up his menu again, frowning down at it.

Also frowning, Josh quietly asked, "Just . . . what?"

"I haven't done a lot of dating," Michael said, eyes resolutely fixed on his menu. "Picking people up in clubs, yeah, but not . . ."

Caught up in the exhilaration of the word *dating*, Josh barely heard that second part. "Same here," he said. "Not clubs, but dating. Lizzie and I went out a few times, and there was an on-again, off-again thing with Freddy's nephew, Nate—Freddy, who owns the hardware store? It was"—he hesitated, catching the way Michael was watching him but clearly not following his rambling—"a summer thing . . . So yeah, not much dating."

After a moment, as though expecting Josh to keep babbling, Michael nodded. "I wanted this to be . . . nice."

Relief made Josh laugh quietly. "This *is* nice," he said, putting down his menu so he could lean on the table, getting closer to Michael. "This is a hell of a lot nicer than the diner or the pizza place or anywhere else, but they'd also be fine. I just want to be with you."

For only the second time that night, Michael's smile was bright and unburdened. God, he was gorgeous like that, confident and charming and captivating. "Then, can I . . ." He put down his menu and deliberately reached across the table, resting his hand palm-up before Josh, who slid his fingers over Michael's and took hold. Michael's grasp was strong and warm, and he didn't pull away when a server came out of the restaurant with their drinks and crossed the patio to their table.

"Evening," she said cheerfully. "Are you ready to order, or do you need a few minutes?"

Josh froze, glancing at the menu. Michael had made it clear he wasn't worried about the prices, but still . . .

"What do you say?" Michael asked while Josh was wavering. "Want to split the crab and lobster?"

There was no way Josh could resist Michael's hopeful expression. Smiling, he relented. "Sounds great."

"Crab legs and the lobster," Michael told the waitress, eyes bright.

The server nodded, grinning. "What sides did you want?"

After glancing at Josh, who shrugged, Michael said, "Surprise us. Everything's good here, right?"

"That it is . . . Are you a regular?" she asked, head tipped to one side as she studied Michael. "I don't recognize you—or your dog there." She ducked a bit to look at Kaylee.

Michael nodded. "I was, over ten years ago."

"Ah, got it." She picked up the menus. "I'll get your food right out to you. If you need anything, just give a yell," she said before bustling away.

Once they were alone again, Michael glanced down at their clasped hands and asked, "I guess you're out?"

"Yeah. Dad was disappointed for about thirty seconds. Not that I'm bi—just, he wants grandkids." He grinned. "It took him that long to remember I'm adopted. Now it's like he's got twice as many people to try and set me up with."

Michael laughed, fingers curling around Josh's. "At least he's okay with it."

Aha. Either Michael's family didn't know or they weren't okay with him being gay or bi or whatever. Poor guy. Trying to keep his voice casual, Josh asked, "How about your family? Do they know?"

Michael's fingers twitched. "No. Well, my sister does. And, uh . . . I guess there are people down in DC who know. While I was in therapy—before I could take Kaylee out—I, uh, went to a lot of nightclubs. Gay nightclubs."

There was an odd significance to how he said that, as if he felt guilty, but Josh couldn't imagine why. "Was it not . . . fun?" he finally asked.

Michael groaned quietly and leaned back in his chair without letting go of Josh's hand. Under the table, Kaylee's collar tags rattled. "It was . . . I went *a lot.* Three or four times a week for a few months."

Josh couldn't keep from raising his eyebrows. He wasn't exactly one to judge a person's social life, but that sounded excessive.

"It was a bad coping mechanism." Michael sighed. "A really bad coping mechanism. I mean, I was always *safe*, but . . . I couldn't tell you any of their names."

Oh. *Oh.* Josh glanced out at the river, hoping the firelight wouldn't show how his face had surely gone red. "That's—"

"It's not—" Michael said at the same time. When Josh nodded, he said, "It's not something I do anymore. I was . . . right out of the hospital, and Kaylee was still in training, too green to come out with me, so it was that or just . . . sit at home, all the time. But that's not what I want. Going to nightclubs and . . . you know. Not, um, anymore."

Maybe Josh hadn't had the most exciting sex life to date, but he understood. Michael must have been alone in DC, with all of his military friends back wherever he'd been deployed. Fresh out of the hospital, barely off death's doorstep, without even the dog who'd become what Josh suspected was his only friend . . . Josh couldn't blame him for looking for any distraction, any scrap of affection or connection, even from strangers.

Josh gave Michael's hand a reassuring squeeze and quietly asked, "So what *do* you want?"

"Someone who understands me. Someone who wants to be with me." It came out quickly enough that Josh knew Michael had thought about it. A lot, in fact, considering he didn't hesitate or stumble over his words.

"Then can I ask you something?"

Michael shot Josh a nervous glance. "Sure."

"What you said, about me not understanding what you might say, if something"—he couldn't remember the technical term— "upsets you . . ."

Michael's shoulders eased a bit, as if he'd expected a more difficult question. "It's called anomic aphasia. Sometimes I use the wrong word, but I don't know it. What comes out might be something similar in meaning or sound, or the complete opposite of what I meant to say."

It sounded like a rehearsed answer, but considering the potential for misunderstanding, Josh understood why he would've memorized it. And it explained some of the strange things Michael had said, especially when flustered.

So Josh smiled reassuringly and rubbed his thumb against Michael's hand. "I've done pretty well understanding you so far, right?"

Michael's lips parted, and he looked shyly down with a quick little nod. "Yeah. I guess you have."

Between Kaylee's leash, the keys to the SUV, and the to-go box of fries and steamed vegetables, Michael had his hands full, but Josh stuck close to his side anyway, close enough that their shoulders bumped with every step. He only moved away when they reached the door, so he could hold it open for Michael.

"Go through," Michael told Kaylee, smiling at Josh. "Thanks."

"No, thank *you*." Josh followed them out and took his place next to Michael again, as if he belonged there. "That was fantastic."

"Better than I remembered." Michael twitched the to-go box and offered, "You're sure you don't want this?"

Josh shook his head and patted his stomach. "I can't eat another bite. And Kaylee deserves a treat, doesn't she?"

Michael grinned, warmed by the affection Josh had for Kaylee. She'd been Michael's whole world for so long, he couldn't imagine being with someone who didn't like her. "Yeah. Here," he said, drawing Kaylee and Josh off to the side of the walkway so he could put down the box for Kaylee. She was too well-behaved to nose at it. "I don't like feeding her in the car. Sometimes food ends up under the seats. Take it," he told her, opening the lid.

As Kaylee dove into the food, Josh took hold of Michael's free hand. "I'm really amazed at how good she is. The way she didn't even flinch when I dropped my fork on her . . . Any other dog would've freaked."

Michael tried not to laugh, but it was a losing battle. "You stabbed a crab shell."

Josh snorted and looked away, failing to hide his smile. "I've never had crab in a restaurant before. Just the beachside shack. Place like this, I figured I'd need proper table manners."

Without looking away from Kaylee, Michael turned his hand so he could lace their fingers together. "She's a rock. Without her, I don't think I'd be here."

Josh's hand tightened. "Good girl," he said quietly.

Kaylee finished her treat, but Michael let her lick the Styrofoam container all the way to the edge of the walkway, where it got caught against a bush. He picked it up with his free hand, and when he stood up, he glanced at the night sky. The light pollution here was almost nonexistent compared to DC, which made for great stargazing but ominously dark roads.

He walked toward the trash can by the parking lot and threw away the to-go box, assessing his current state of mind. The date had gone better than he'd imagined, so far. He was relaxed and calm, completely in control of himself. *Safe.*

But as he headed for the car, unlocking it with a press of the key fob, he frowned up at the sky again. It was dark, and he hadn't driven these roads for a decade, and he wasn't alone in the SUV. He had Kaylee to worry about. He had *Josh* to worry about.

"So, uh . . . The ambush. The shooting, I mean. When I got shot." Usually, he didn't know when he was misusing his words, but he couldn't even put his thoughts together coherently. He took a deep breath and glanced at Josh, who was just watching him, patient, not trying to fill in the words. That helped Michael say, more steadily, "It happened in a heavy dust storm, in the desert. Sometimes, when it's dark . . . I don't like driving."

Josh nodded, still holding on to Michael's hand. "Want me to drive home, or are you okay?"

Relief stole Michael's breath. "You're—" He shook his head. "You don't . . . You don't think that's weird?"

"You were *shot,*" Josh said quietly. When had he stepped closer? Michael could almost feel the warmth of his body. "I'd think it was weird if you *weren't* . . ." He waved a hand.

"All fucked up?" Michael suggested wryly.

Josh laughed. "You said it, not me. But yeah. You were shot and in a coma and in the hospital for *ages,* but you're here now. You made it."

Michael's laugh was a bit hysterical. He hung his keys over one finger so he could run his hand up Josh's arm. And when Josh closed the distance between them, it was as natural as breathing for Michael to pull him into a hug.

"Do you want me to drive?" Josh asked, barely above a whisper, breath hot against Michael's shoulder.

"I'm okay." If Michael was reading the signs right, this would be the perfect time to kiss Josh, but . . . what if he was wrong? Josh wasn't one of Michael's one-night stands. And after *telling* Josh about that period of idiocy . . . No. He'd let Josh make the first move. Or, well, second move, if holding hands now counted as the first.

"Okay." Josh rubbed the small of Michael's back, then stepped away, putting an inch of space between their bodies. It was an inch too much. "If you change your mind, let me know. I drive the delivery truck for catering gigs, so I won't run over any trees or anything."

Michael laughed and pressed the keys into Josh's hand just for the excuse to touch him. "Then you drive."

Josh took the keys but also caught Michael's fingers, holding him in place. "You'll be okay if you're *not* driving?"

Michael let out a breath and looked down at Kaylee. "The thing is . . . if I see something—something innocent and normal, like tree branches in the wind or a piece of paper on the side of the road— sometimes it . . . it doesn't look so normal. During the day or when it's bright out, like in DC, it's fine. I just— That's why I didn't drive up here. I took the train."

He met Josh's eyes, expecting a look of calm understanding, but Josh was frowning in confusion. "Something Innsmouth?" Josh asked.

Shit. Michael fumbled for the right word. He'd thought he knew what he said, but now it wasn't coming to him at all. "Something . . . not harmful. Not guilty."

"Innocent?"

Michael nodded, jaw clenched, though he was angry at himself, not at the smooth way Josh had guessed such a common word. "Yeah. It's safer if you drive," he said in a rush, hoping Josh wouldn't say anything more about the momentary slip.

"Okay." Instead of pulling away, Josh laced their fingers together again. "But, uh, it might be a little weird if I brought you home with me. I don't know if I told you, but I still live with my dad."

Was that a hint for Michael to invite Josh back to the barn? It was damned tempting, but the thought blurred the boundary between his life in DC and his new life here. Josh wasn't a quick, easy fuck, and while Michael *wanted* him, the waiting—the anticipation—was a new pleasure he wanted to savor.

"That's all right," he said, rubbing his thumb against the back of Josh's hand. "I, uh . . ."

"It's not that I've *never* brought someone home," Josh said quickly. "It's just, Dad will want to talk. Ask questions about dinner and stuff. I haven't dated anyone for a while, and he's kind of a pain in the ass about it."

Michael laughed. "Keeping away from your dad. Got it." Conscious that they'd been standing in the parking lot for what felt like ages, he stepped back and went for the passenger side of the SUV.

Instead of circling around to the driver's side, Josh followed. "Hey, Michael?"

Michael opened the back door for Kaylee. "Yeah?"

"Can I just—" Josh reached out, sliding his hand around to the nape of Michael's neck. Shivers raced down Michael's spine, and he opened his mouth, only to have Josh press in close, stealing his breath and thoughts. Josh's lips were soft and hot, and though the kiss was brief, it left Michael dazed.

"Uh," he managed. And then, "Yeah."

That earned him another kiss, this one a quick brush of lips and a huff of laughter. "Sorry," Josh whispered, just an inch away. "The parking lot isn't exactly romantic, but if we did that at my house . . ."

Michael grinned. "Your dad?"

"Mm-hmm." Josh grinned back at him. "With my luck, he'd take pictures and send them to my aunt as proof I'm finally in a relationship."

Michael blinked. "You're not serious."

Josh's laugh was a little bit ominous. "If you stick around, you'll see. Never underestimate an aunt from Brooklyn when it comes to her unmarried nephew."

"Consider me warned," Michael said. Then he leaned in and gave Josh another kiss, reveling in the knowledge that he *could*.

The next day, Josh practically danced through the lunch rush at Bagel End, lips still warm from the memory of that last quick kiss, soft as a falling leaf. When he'd parked outside his house, and he and Michael got out of the SUV, he'd considered trying for another kiss, but no. He hadn't wanted to ruin the memory with a kiss that would've been full of self-consciousness and the awkward suspicion that his dad was probably watching through an upstairs window.

Not that he was exempt from all teasing. Dee's shift started at the same time as Josh's, and he endured all of ten minutes of "Well?" and "How'd it go?" and "When's the next date?" before he retreated to the kitchen to check on the soup for a catering order, only emerging when the front of the shop was packed and nobody had time for idle chatter.

He lost himself so completely in the chaos of greeting customers and taking orders that he didn't recognize Lizzie at first. "Welcome to Bagel End! Can I take your order?" he asked her.

She tipped her head and gave him a knowing smile. "Hey, Josh."

"Hey." He blinked, then sheepishly smiled back. Was he so caught up in last night's kiss that he'd forgotten about his ex-girlfriend-turned-accountant? Apparently. "Oh, hey. Is it one thirty already?"

"In about two minutes, yes. I'll just wait for you?" she offered, glancing around at the barely thinning crowd. "Want me to wait in back, or did you want to go somewhere else?"

"Uh . . ." Josh hadn't thought their meeting through. He was used to going over the shop's monthly accounts, which involved little more than plugging numbers into spreadsheets. That, he could tolerate while surrounded by the staff. This was the business plan meeting, though—as in, the business plan he *hadn't* begun to write.

Before he could think of an answer, Dee bumped into his side, grinning like a fiend, eyeing Lizzie. "Another hot date? You go, Josh! You're on a roll."

Anger flared, hot and sudden. Teasing was one thing, but this—as if he'd go out with someone *else* the night after his date with Michael, and Dee saying it in front of his ex-girlfriend from a million years ago . . . "Take over," he snapped at Dee, dropping the order pad and pencil on the counter for her. "Lizzie, let's . . . I'll meet you outside."

"Sure." Lizzie gave him a curious look, then headed for the door.

Josh wrestled out of his apron, ignoring Dee's concerned frown. He dropped the apron in the back, then rushed out front without looking at anyone behind the counter—not Dee and especially not his dad, who was too sharp-eared to have missed how Josh had snapped.

Outside, the air was thick with humidity and the threat of rain. Josh sighed and told Lizzie, "Sorry about that. Dee's a little . . ."

"Jealous?"

Josh blinked at Lizzie. Flaky, maybe, or overenthusiastic. But jealous? "What?"

Lizzie shrugged and gave Josh a nudge to start him walking toward the corner. "What, what? You're a great catch."

"I— We—" Josh stammered, face going hot. He glanced away under the pretext of checking traffic. There was no way in hell that Lizzie was hitting on him. Not two years ago, not six months ago, and certainly not now, the day after a fantastic date with Michael.

"No, not 'we.' *We* were awful together," she said, rolling her eyes. "But that doesn't mean that I can't see you *objectively* as someone who'd be a fantastic boyfriend-husband-whatever. I'm an accountant. I'm professionally objective. Diner?"

"Yeah." Josh snorted and nodded, turning to cross the street. "And thanks. I think."

Lizzie shrugged her laptop bag higher onto her shoulder and threw an arm around Josh's waist, giving him a quick hug. "So who is she? Or he? Anyone I know?"

"He, and no." Josh knew his smile was a bit goofy, but he couldn't hide it. "Former tourist turned townie, after being away for like ten years."

"Former tourist?" she asked, raising an eyebrow. "You sure he's good enough for you?"

Josh laughed, knots in his chest finally easing. "He's great. And Dee's a pain-in-the-ass gossip."

"She's a shift manager. Number three in command, after you and your dad."

"Yeah, that too," Josh admitted as they started across the green. "Still a pain in the ass."

"Are you just saying that because your dad—"

Josh smiled wryly at her. "Hasn't changed? Yeah. If Michael and I go out on two more dates, Dad will be picking china patterns and booking a hall."

"Michael, huh? Is he Jewish?"

"No, but Dad seems to like him anyway." Josh rubbed the back of his neck, trying to ease the tension building up again. "Not that they're ever going to talk to each other without me there to supervise."

Lizzie let go of his waist. "Be nice. Your dad's awesome."

"Yeah, uh . . . speaking of," Josh began, eyes fixed on the diner. He couldn't help but scan the parking lot for Michael's SUV, but there was no sign of it. "You've gone through a lot of our papers. Have you ever seen Dad's business plan from when Bagel End opened?"

"Mmm . . . no," Lizzie said, tipping her head to frown up at Josh. "But wasn't the money to open the store a wedding present?"

Damn. So much for plagiarism. "So I *don't* need a business plan if I don't want a loan or investors?"

"Josh . . ." Lizzie shook her head and sighed. "We've been through this before. A business plan will keep you on track. It'll—"

"Why can't I just write a list?" Josh interrupted with such force that he silenced her for a few steps.

Only when they reached the sidewalk on the other side of the green did she ask, "Did you do *any* work on the business plan?"

Josh let out a sharp breath and checked oncoming traffic. "I was busy."

"Busy? Josh, this is important."

"Why?" He forced himself to keep walking across the street instead of stopping in his tracks. As soon as he hit the diner parking lot, though, he turned to face her, demanding, "Why is it so important?

I don't have some teacher waiting for me to turn in an essay. I know what my customers want. I know what we have. I know how to get from here to there. Why does it have to be *written down*?"

Lizzie's eyes had gone wide, and she backed away a step. "Huh."

"'Huh'?" Josh quoted, trying not to scowl at her. Bad enough he'd already snapped at her for no good reason. "Look, I'm sorry—"

"You really are serious about this, aren't you?"

Josh sighed. "Yes, I'm serious. I've been serious since I first asked for your help."

She waved a hand dismissively. "Not the business thing. Your new guy."

It was Josh's turn to ask, "Huh?"

She smacked Josh's arm and got moving again. "Michael. Your new guy? You're really serious about him."

Josh shook his head—not in denial but to clear out whatever rust had gathered in his brain. "We've been on *one date*." Then he winced, glancing through the diner window at the corner booth. "One and a half. Maybe one and two halves, if you count breakfast."

Lizzie made an effort to hide her laugh, but it came out as a choked snort. "Oh my God. There. Proof. 'One and two halves'?"

Josh had to laugh at that. He pulled open the diner door, saying, "What does Michael have to do with my business plan?"

"Nothing, except maybe to distract you." She smirked at him. "But the way you snapped at Dee back there? You're the first guy to be playful and, you know, self-deprecating about your love interests when they're not serious. Back when it was you and me, you'd let your dad tease me about dating you for hours. You were the opposite of my knight in shining armor, buddy."

Josh gestured for her to lead the way to a table. "On what planet does that make sense?"

"I've known you since kindergarten." She dropped onto a bench and grinned. "You have no secrets from me."

"Because living with my father isn't bad enough?" Josh muttered as he sat.

"Small town, baby," she said triumphantly. "You snap at the first hint of someone teasing that your relationship with Michael isn't serious, and your 'jokes' are thinly disguised attempts at proving that it *is*. That, old pal, is proof."

"Oh my God. You're insane," he said with a groan. Somehow, he managed not to add *but you're also right.*

"Geniuses often are. Now," she said, unzipping her laptop bag, "do we talk about your business plan or Michael? Profit or gossip. Your choice."

Josh scrubbed a hand across his eyes. "Profit or gossip," he muttered. "Kill me now."

Politicians are never on vacation. The government doesn't take holidays. Michael had heard that mantra all his life, growing from a disappointed boy who wanted his parents to an uninterested teen grateful that they were too busy to keep watch over him every minute of the day. He was still grateful, because it meant their vacation home had a small but fully equipped office.

Now that he was out of the Air Force, he needed something to do *besides* training Kaylee. He could live on his trust fund, but that would end with him rotting in isolation or obsessively focusing on Josh to the point of driving him away.

He let himself into the office and logged on to the computer as Guest User . . . and then froze up. What *could* he do? ADA laws meant he could work in almost any job with a service dog, but he didn't relish the thought of being trapped in a cubicle all day. Kaylee would probably hate it too. His aphasia meant any customer-facing or telephone work was a disaster waiting to happen. Hell, any job that involved interacting with people was probably a bad idea.

What did that leave him? Forest fire lookout? He was good with dogs, so maybe he could be a dog walker or groomer. Not exactly the prestigious career his family had pictured for him, but fuck them. If he'd wanted prestige, he would've stayed at Dartmouth.

He leaned back in the fancy leather chair and looked over at Kaylee, sprawled on the carpet. "Think it's too early to call Josh?"

She looked up and thumped her tail in answer, which wasn't helpful.

"We had a good date," he told her, spinning the chair to better face her. "I should at least thank him for it, right? I mean, it might be too soon to ask him out again, but a friendly hello?"

Probably sensing no treats or commands were forthcoming, she laid her head back down. Even her tail-wagging had gone slow and half-assed. She wasn't wearing her vest, so she knew she didn't need to pay more than cursory attention to him.

"You're a lousy relationship counselor," he accused, turning back to the computer. Instead of reaching for the keyboard, though, he picked up his phone. He'd text Josh. It was more impersonal than a phone call, but there'd be no pressure—no expectation of an immediate response. Besides, Michael's aphasia didn't affect texting as much as speech, since he could read his words a few times before hitting Send.

Abruptly, Kaylee's head came up. A low growl rumbled through her chest, ending in a yip that jolted Michael's heart. He shoved the chair back into the bookcase and stood, hand clenching around the phone.

Since the house had been remodeled, he didn't know the sounds, but he thought that faint whisper was the front door opening. Kaylee rolled up to her feet and trotted to the door, silent now that she'd issued her warning to him.

Who had keys? His parents, but they were campaigning, weren't they? Amanda, but she'd made it pretty clear she wouldn't be visiting before taking off on her world tour. Best-case scenario would be the caretaker.

Whoever it was, they had him trapped. The office was down the hallway from the kitchen, nowhere near the back or side door. Short of diving out the window, there was no way to get out of the house unseen from the foyer.

Footsteps came down the front hallway, past the stairs. Michael moved to look down the side hall in time to see someone pass by—short, thin, carrying grocery bags. He took a deep breath and told his pounding heart to calm down. He was safe. More than safe. His mother was tall and wouldn't be caught dead carrying her own groceries.

"Heel," he told Kaylee as he headed out to investigate. "Hello?"

There was a quiet gasp from the kitchen, followed by a soft voice asking, "Mr. Baldwin?"

"Michael," he corrected, rounding the corner. The stranger unpacking groceries onto the counter looked barely out of high school. "Yeah. Hi?"

She beamed at him and said, "I'm Felice. I'm covering for my mom—her allergies are acting up. Did you need anything?"

"No." He scratched at Kaylee's head, wondering if he should mention that he was living in the barn, but he didn't want to make her pack everything back up. He'd just bring the groceries over there later. "Look, you don't— The house is fine."

"It's no trouble. Dad's mowing the lawn, so I've got time," she assured him. "He's trying to get it done before it starts to rain."

"Okay." He was still holding the phone, which gave him an excuse to escape. He held it up, muttering, "I've got to . . ."

"Oh. No problem." She lowered her voice. "I'll stay out of your way."

He retreated to the office and closed the door, trembling from the adrenaline lingering in his system. Kaylee followed him to the desk, but instead of sprawling on the rug, she leaned against his legs, muzzle resting on his knee.

Josh, he thought, looking down at the phone in his hand. A few quick taps had the phone unlocked, and he set it to his ear, only remembering he'd meant to text when Josh answered, "Hello?"

"Hi." Michael's mind went blank and light, full of simple contentment at hearing Josh's voice.

"Hey, you," Josh said warmly. "Good timing. I just finished lunch."

Michael glanced at the antique clock on the desk. Two fifteen. "I haven't had lunch yet," he admitted.

Josh made a displeased sound, almost like Kaylee's warning growl. "Have you had breakfast?"

Michael winced. How did Josh know him so well, so quickly? "Uh."

Josh huffed. "Come to the shop. I'll make you soup and a sandwich."

"You don't have to," Michael protested, though he was quietly thrilled at the idea. In DC, he'd been surrounded by doctors and therapists and caretakers, but that had been their job. The thought that Josh *wanted* to take care of him . . .

"The lunch rush is over by now. The place is probably empty. So get your butt in gear and get over here. And don't walk," Josh warned. "It's going to start raining in the next couple of hours."

"Okay, okay." Grinning, Michael logged off his dad's computer and stood up. "Give me about twenty minutes."

"Twenty minutes or else. And drive safe." Josh hung up.

Michael shoved the phone into his pocket and looked down at Kaylee, who was watching him curiously. "Want to go see Josh?" he asked her.

Naturally, she wagged her tail. A clear yes. She liked Josh just as much as he did.

"Good girl."

CHAPTER

SEVENTEEN

S eventeen minutes later—not that Josh was counting—Michael walked into Bagel End with Kaylee clomping along at his side, her steps made loud by bright-red doggie boots. Josh couldn't help but grin at them both.

He met them at the register, saying, "Okay, that's probably the cutest thing I've ever seen." He nodded down at the boots.

Michael smiled, glancing at Kaylee. "It's easier to dry her boots when it rains. You wouldn't believe how much water her feet sock up."

Sock? Probably soak, Josh guessed, though he didn't ask. Instead, he kept his grin focused on Kaylee and said, "Too cute." They both were, but *that* he didn't say outright. "Chicken and vegetable or broccoli cheddar?"

"Uh, chicken and vegetable? I'm guessing you based it on your bubbe's recipe?"

"Damn right." Josh went to fill a bowl, asking over his shoulder, "Kaylee can't have onions, right?"

"No. Onions, garlic, raisins, and chocolate, all bad for dogs. But I've got dinner for her at home. Ground beef, brown rice, mixed veggies."

"Hmm." Josh scooped the soup carefully, loading the bowl with diced chicken and carrots, leaving a thin layer of pure broth in the warming pot. Chicken and vegetable was the shop's most popular offering and rarely lasted past the lunch rush, so there was no point in saving the remnants for another customer. "What about roast beef for her? And does she want soup? The broccoli cheddar should be safe."

"You really don't have to go to all this trouble."

Josh moved the full bowl onto a tray, then brought the tray to the register. "No, but if we feed her here, then you don't have to rush home to feed her tonight. I can make you a couple of roast beef paninis with provolone and tomatoes."

"Isn't it sacrilege to *not* have a bagel sandwich here?" Michael teased, leaning forward to sniff the soup. His eyes closed briefly, and his lips twitched into a smile. "God, that smells good."

Josh pulled on a pair of plastic gloves and went for the bread basket. "You should've heard my aunt screaming when she found out we bought a panini press for the shop." He picked up the bread knife and put on his aunt's heavy Brooklyn accent, saying, "What're ya doin', catering to the hipsters, with their beards and music pods and fancy-shmancy mackey-etto coffee? Oy!"

Michael burst into laughter. "Can you call her right now? I want to hear her say that."

"Absolutely not." Josh sliced through two pieces of focaccia with practiced ease. "You're never meeting the Brooklyn branch of the Goldbergs."

Michael's voice went a little flat. "Because I'm not Jewish or because I'm a guy?"

"The word you're looking for is 'goy,' and neither. It's because you're from New Hampshire. Damn Northerner."

"You know, the rest of the country thinks New Yorkers are Northerners," Michael said, leaning comfortably against the counter. What a change it was from the first time he'd come in, barely able to meet Josh's eyes, much less give Josh his order.

"Yeah, but in Brooklyn, New Jersey practically counts as the Deep South—at least in my family." Josh took the roast beef out of the deli case and unwrapped it. "Last chance. Roast beef or something else?"

"Roast beef is fine for both of us. No soup for her—it'll be a mess. And thank you." Michael smiled sweetly.

"No problem." Josh said it casually, hiding how much he really did enjoy taking care of Michael. Kaylee too, in fact.

Michael ducked his head, glancing at Kaylee the way he usually did when he seemed to be feeling shy. "I'm surprised they let your dad leave Brooklyn."

"It was a close call, the way he tells it." Josh put the roast beef on the slicer and set the dial to medium thickness. Before he could start up the machine, the bell at the front door rang, and Michael jerked back from the counter, looking over his shoulder. Two retirees walked in, probably tourists, judging by the matching cardigans they wore. Josh's smile faltered—he'd wanted to have some time alone with Michael—but he called, "Hey, welcome to Bagel End. Be right with you."

"I'll just . . ." Michael looked to the tables at the front of the shop, by the window, but then pointed back to what Josh had begun thinking of as their table.

"Take the soup before it gets cold. I'll bring the sandwiches out," Josh told him, turning on the slicer.

Josh finished slicing the roast beef but set it aside to take care of the other customers first. There was no sense in heating up the sandwiches only to serve them cold. And it was a good thing he decided to wait.

The tourist couple, as part of their trip of a lifetime along the East Coast from Florida to Nova Scotia, would only eat locally sourced food. The beef and ham weren't problematic, since both were from New Hampshire farms, but the questionable origin of the ingredients in the bagels led to a five-minute discussion that Josh ended only by pointing out, "If it helps, we *make* the bagels right here. I can show you the dough that's proofing for our next batch, if you want."

It felt like hours before he escaped and could bring hot sandwiches over to Michael's table, along with two cups of water. Michael had finished the soup and was watching Josh with a grin. "Does that"—he gave a nod in the direction of the tourists, who were eating their authentic New Hampshire bagel sandwiches by the front window—"happen often?"

Josh lowered his voice to just above a whisper, saying, "It's like the bridge lures in all the crazies. The normal people keep going north to Maine or south to Boston. And it's only going to get worse here on the island. There's talk of building one of those Winnebago campsites on the northwest shore, out past the elementary school."

Michael snickered and picked up one of the sandwiches. "At least you'll get good business out of it."

"Right? I know," Josh answered a little too emphatically. "I can't wait."

"For it to get worse?" Michael pushed the plate with the other sandwich toward Josh, who shook his head.

"That's for Kaylee, when it cools, remember?" Josh pushed the plate back to Michael. "But the campsite? They'll probably have a café on-site, which means they'll need baked goods. Like bagels."

Frowning, Michael unwrapped his sandwich and asked, "Doesn't that mean competition?"

"Not if we supply the bagels," Josh said before he realized he'd never discussed his expansion plans with Michael. He was tempted to backpedal, but maybe an outside opinion would help bolster his own flagging confidence. Lizzie was more indulgent than encouraging, and Dad was against anything that involved a risk. As a neutral third party—or somewhat neutral, anyway—Michael could provide a welcome new perspective.

"With your catering business, you mean?" Michael took a bite, then closed his eyes with a soft groan that sent shivers down Josh's spine, momentarily scrambling his thoughts. Michael swallowed, mumbling, "Oh, that's good."

"Uh. Yeah. I mean, sort of." Josh shook his head. "I think we should go bigger than just catering one event at a time. B&Bs, the cafeterias at the elementary school and the college, even a couple of hotels right across the bridge—all potential customers."

Michael tipped his head, taking another quick bite, looking off into the distance. "You know," he said slowly, and Josh braced for criticism or condemnation, "you could probably also do one of those beach kiosks."

"They're all rented out this year," Josh said automatically. His brain was slower to catch up. "You think it's a good idea, though?"

"Hell, yes." Michael waved the sandwich. "This is fantastic. And the bagels are even better."

The unconditional support made Josh go warm and tingly all the way to his toes. "I, uh, don't suppose you've got any business experience, do you?"

Michael bit off a corner of the sandwich, chewed, and swallowed. "Sort of. Supply and logistics, remember? Figure out who needs what, project future mission requirements, work out how to get stuff from point A to point B, that sort of thing. Mostly it was a lot of paperwork, but yeah."

Josh took a deep breath, bracing himself. "Then . . . mind if I ask you a few questions?"

"Go for it." Michael smiled encouragingly.

Here goes nothing. "My accountant wants me to come up with a business plan . . ."

Evening darkened the sky by the time Josh walked into the pizza place. Michael beckoned him over to the table and tried to ignore the way his heart lurched. Just the sight of Josh filled him with warmth, melting the tension out of his shoulders and spine.

"Did you bring your laptop?" he asked, trying to remain businesslike despite the smile tugging at his lips.

"Got it." Instead of taking the seat across from Michael, Josh stopped next to him, first glancing at Kaylee under the table. He moved Michael's glass of water out of the way, then put his backpack down on the table, shoving everything else off to one side. When he let go of the straps, he braced a hand on the table and leaned toward Michael.

Yes! Michael indulged in his grin and stretched to accept Josh's offered kiss, right there in the pizza place. So much for being afraid the locals would all turn out to be homophobes. The kiss tasted sweet, like peppermint candy, and Michael couldn't resist a quick lick at Josh's lips despite the public setting.

When Josh sat down, his cheeks were flushed. "You, uh, don't have a laptop of your own?" he asked, unzipping the backpack.

Michael shook his head, a little surprised that he didn't feel a jolt of anxiety at the question. He really was getting comfortable with Josh. "No. I couldn't read for like a year and a half, so I didn't bother buying one."

Josh froze except for his startled blink. "You—" He bit his lip and slid the laptop out of the bag. "I understand. I, uh, sometimes have trouble reading."

"Do you need glasses?" Michael guessed, remembering to get his eyeglass case out of his bag. "I needed mine before I got shot. They're only for close up. I can't do laser surgery because of the"—he forgot the word, but rather than struggling to find or explain it, he waved a hand—"whatever. Starts with an *a*."

Josh shrugged as if he didn't know what Michael was talking about. "Maybe. I haven't had my eyes tested since elementary school, I think. I just . . ." He moved the backpack onto a spare chair so he could make room for the laptop. He slid it over to Michael. "Do you mind? If we're going to take notes, it'll probably be easier if you do it."

"Sure, no problem." Michael pushed open the lid and hit the power button, then got his glasses out of the case. "Is there wi-fi here, or do I need to use my phone as a hotspot?"

Josh winced. "Yeah, probably the phone. Otherwise, we'll have to give the library a try tomorrow. I think there's internet there. The town board was talking about open wi-fi in some public places—the town hall, the green and some parks, the beach—but I think it was too expensive. What do we need internet for?"

By the time the rush of words ended, the laptop had booted, not to a password screen but to the start menu. Years of Air Force training had Michael prepared to give a lecture, until he met Josh's eyes—and noticed the way he was staring. Self-consciously, Michael touched his glasses and asked, "What? What's wrong?"

"Nothing," Josh blurted, turning fully away toward the counter. "Your, uh . . . They look good. Really good. Did you want a refill? Or some pizza?"

He was adorably flustered, but why? Was it the glasses? Hiding his smirk at the thought, Michael touched the glasses again, settling them into place, and met Josh's eyes. "I ordered us a small pizza to split. Pepperoni okay?"

"Fine. Yeah." Josh gestured at the laptop. "So, the internet?"

"Right." Michael got out his phone and unlocked it, then started working out how to configure it as a hotspot. "We're going to work online, so everything we do is automatically backed up to the cloud. Less chance of losing anything. How was the rest of your day?"

"Good. Busy. We have a big catering order in a couple weeks."

Michael darted a look at Josh to confirm he was still staring. *Definitely* the glasses. "Anything interesting?"

"Library fund-raiser brunch. Tickets are around twenty-five bucks."

"Huh." Michael frowned, thinking about his trust fund. He'd set up automatic charitable donations when he turned twenty-five, but maybe it was time to take a more active hand in things. He'd have to find out how much support the local library got from the local government. "Want to go?"

Josh laughed. "I *am* going. Someone's got to serve up those bagels."

Michael grinned and nudged him under the table. The movement made Kaylee wag her tail, though she didn't stand up. "Okay, want to hang out with me after the bagels are all gone?"

"Well . . ." Josh drew out the word, leaning back in his chair. "I suppose. If I don't get a better offer, that is."

Laughing, Michael asked, "Better than me?"

"It *is* a library," Josh pointed out. "It could be full of hot librarians. And while you might look the part, you're—"

"Aha!" Michael interrupted. "You *do* like the glasses."

Josh's face flushed, but his grin didn't disappear. "Yeah, yeah, okay," he admitted. "I like the glasses."

Not a one-night stand, Michael reminded himself, though he was tempted. Damned tempted. Coax Josh back to the barn, show him a fantastic night . . . It wouldn't even have to be just one night. They'd gone on a couple of dates. Or one disaster, one date, and one working dinner. Sex didn't mean the end of the relationship. It could be the beginning.

"So, where do we start?" Josh asked, startling Michael out of his speculation.

"The—" he began before he went blank. The thing on the computer. The thing for Josh's bagel place. The thing he couldn't remember the word for, because he couldn't think over the sudden pounding of his heart.

But instead of stammering out all the words that did come to mind in hopes of luring out the *right* word, he pushed the computer an inch back, making room for him to brace his forearm against the edge of the table. With his other hand, he touched Josh's face, tracing over scattered stubble and soft skin, sliding back to bury his fingers in Josh's hair. Josh's eyes had gone wide, and when his lips parted, Michael leaned closer.

Josh had said he didn't care if they were in public, and Michael . . . Michael felt safe here, as safe as he'd been in the dark parking lot where they shared their first kiss. The heat of the pizza ovens was cut by the cold evening wind off the ocean blowing through the windows, bringing a salty tinge to air heavy with oregano and garlic. Kaylee was a warm weight across Michael's feet, tail swishing lazily over the floor.

Michael curled his fingers around Josh's nape, drawing him in, and silenced his exhale with a kiss. The world fell away under the soft press of Josh's lips, the hot brush of his tongue, the way his breath hitched. When the kiss ended, Josh blinked his eyes open, one corner of his mouth twitching up.

"What was that for?"

Instead of coming up with a coherent answer, Michael's brain stuttered and caught up to itself about a minute too late. "Business plan."

Josh gave a short little laugh. "Are you going for 'hot accountant' instead of 'hot librarian'?"

With anyone else, Michael would've stammered out an excuse and run off. With Josh, though, Michael just shook his head and said, "Business plan first. And pizza."

Josh's smile turned sly. Heated. "And then?" he asked, lowering his voice.

There it was, the invitation Michael had known he could coax out of Josh. Two hours to write up a business plan outline and finish dinner. Ten minutes to get Josh to the privacy of the barn behind the family vacation house. It would be nothing like DC—not a quick blowjob in the men's room or rutting together in an alley. Michael would take his time learning Josh's body, discovering what he liked, making him gasp and cry out. It would mean something.

"Tonight—"

"*Shit*," Josh interrupted, looking away before he rubbed at his eyes.

Michael's heart lodged in his throat. "What?" he asked, body going tense, braced against the rejection that had to be coming.

"I open tomorrow. It's my dad's day off," Josh said with a groan.

He's not done with me. Relief made Michael smile despite his disappointment. "We're calling it an early night, then?"

Shoulders slumped, Josh scooted his chair closer and put his hand on Michael's arm. "I'm sorry. It's just, if I don't get at least seven hours, I'm worthless. And you do *not* want me operating ovens if I'm half-asleep."

"Then I promise I'll get you home early." Michael covered Josh's hand with his own and smiled—genuinely, to his surprise. As much as he wanted Josh to himself, he had time. They both did.

CHAPTER

EIGHTEEN

"You sure you don't want a cup of coffee?"

Michael smiled faintly up at the waiter, Duke, and shook his head. "It's too late for caffeine."

"Milk shake?" Duke asked hopefully, refilling Michael's water glass for the third time.

"He'll be here any minute." Michael tried to sound certain, but it came out a little too hopeful. Pathetic. And for no good reason. Josh was coming here straight from work. There'd probably just been a problem. Paperwork or something. If the last couple of weeks had taught Michael anything, it was that Josh hated paperwork.

With an understanding smile, Duke said, "Take your time," before he walked away.

Michael drummed his fingers on his phone, then flicked the power on to check the time. Thirty-two minutes. He resisted the urge to bang his head on the table. Barely.

But then the door opened, and Michael straightened, looking over in time to see Josh walk in and glance around. When their eyes met, Josh smiled tiredly and headed right for the back of the diner, where Michael had taken what was fast becoming his usual table.

"Have I mentioned how much I hate opening?" Josh asked as he dropped next to Michael instead of sitting across the booth.

The diner was empty except for a family of early-season tourists, not that a crowd would've stopped Michael from wrapping an arm around Josh's shoulders to give him a comforting hug. "Want coffee?"

Josh groaned, dropping his head onto Michael's shoulder. "I have to sleep tonight because I have to open tomorrow. And the next day, and the next."

Michael kissed the top of Josh's head. "Switching up your schedule again? Don't tell me you have another special early-morning customer . . ."

"Dad ran off to Brooklyn." Josh sat back up, sighing at the effort, and leaned in close for a sweet kiss. "Hi."

"Hi," Michael whispered against Josh's lips, all the irritation and worry and self-doubt vanishing like smoke.

He had no idea how long they sat there, smiling across the bare inch of air that separated them, before a quiet cough sent a jolt of adrenaline right through Michael. He flinched back with a sharp inhale, eyes wide, and it took him a second to recognize Duke, who had a hand up in apology.

"Hey. Uh." Duke shot Josh a tight smile. "Did you . . ."

Kaylee sat up under the table a moment too late, but he'd never trained her to alert him to serving staff. Sensing how his nerves were jangling, she shoved her head between his thighs and the underside of the table and pushed against him, looking up with love in her deep-brown eyes. Distantly, he heard Josh and Duke talking—they seemed to know each other—but all Michael cared about was that he was safe. Josh was here, Kaylee was here, and Duke wasn't a threat. Michael focused on reminding himself of that, scratching behind Kaylee's ears until Duke left again.

Then Josh's hand slid over Michael's thigh, fingertips brushing Kaylee's muzzle. "You okay?"

There was no condemnation in his voice. No mocking. Just patient understanding. Michael nodded and let the touch ground him further. "Yeah." He summoned up a smile, adding, "It's your fault."

Josh blinked. "What?"

Michael kissed Josh's cheek and let his voice drop to barely above a whisper. "You're distracting."

Josh's fingers twitched hard against Michael's thigh. "Oh." He laughed nervously, then said, "Of course I am. I'm awesome."

That deserved another kiss, though Michael was too keyed up to lose himself in it, which meant that when Duke returned with a second glass of water, Michael didn't jump out of his skin. Duke was flushed and anxious looking, but there was no hostility in his expression. No sense of *Ew, guys kissing.*

"Do, uh," Duke stammered. "Do you guys know what you want?" As soon as the question was out, the blush went even darker, and he deliberately turned to Josh, not Michael, as if pleading for a rescue.

Michael bit back a laugh, but he let the innuendo pass without comment. "Burgers, right?" he asked Josh. "And steak fries?"

Josh's smile was full of gratitude. "Yes. Bacon double cheeseburger for me."

"Two," Michael said.

"Don't forget the steak fries. Lots of fries," Josh added. "Oh, and a chocolate chip milk shake."

Duke darted a quick glance Michael's way. "Regular or to, uh, share?"

"Share," Michael said, just as Josh said, "Regular."

Josh grinned and held up one hand; the other remained on Michael's thigh. "Share it is."

Smiling once again, Duke picked up the menus. "I'll have that right up for you."

As Duke walked away, Michael turned to face Josh a bit more, though he tried not to pull away from Josh's hand. "Speaking of having things, do you have the—"

Josh cut Michael off with a groan. "The numbers. Shit. I forgot to email Lizzie."

Michael's disappointed sigh wasn't entirely genuine. "We're almost done with the business plan," he reminded Josh. Of course, that also meant they were almost out of excuses for nightly working dates. "All we need are the numbers."

"Here, let me . . ." Josh made room on the table, then pulled his laptop out of his backpack. "I'll email her right now. I just . . . With Dad gone, it's like everything is ten times more complicated, and I was doing interviews through lunch to try and hire more summer help."

"You skipped lunch?" Michael forgot all about finishing the business plan. He was so used to Josh's instinctive need to feed and take care of him, it hadn't occurred to him to do the same for Josh.

"I had half a bagel between interviews." Josh shook his head, staring blankly at the laptop as it booted. "We need another shift manager or two. Dee and I are going to be *wrecked* by the time Dad gets home, what with the catering gig in three days."

Josh needed a break. Deliberately, Michael closed the laptop and pushed it away. When Josh turned curiously, Michael rubbed his hand up Josh's back, slow and firm, and dug his fingers into the tense muscles at Josh's nape. Over Josh's contented sigh, he said, "After the catering gig, it's just you, me, and a whole library full of excuses to wear my reading glasses."

Josh snorted, trying to choke back a laugh. "Oh my God. I'm never going to live that down, am I?"

Michael leaned against Josh's side and pressed a kiss to the curve of his ear, making him shudder. "I hope not. I was going to order a couple of extra pairs, just in case this one breaks."

Dad's vacation was going to be the death of Josh. Two days after the sleepy, business-plan-free date at the diner, Josh's to-do list had grown exponentially, and he'd ticked off exactly one item. This morning, in the lull between the Millers' morning coffee and the start of rush, he'd emailed Lizzie to get those numbers, and that was only because Michael had given him a disappointed-puppy look at the pizza place last night.

But that one accomplishment was enough—especially when he was consumed with prepping for tomorrow's catering order. The instant his afternoon crew came in, he retreated to the kitchen and lost himself in making batch after batch of bagels and flatbreads. In the intervals of rising and baking, he chopped herbs and vegetables, then whipped up tubs of flavored cream cheese.

He stopped only for the lunch rush, then went back to the kitchen as soon as things started to die down. But the next time the oven dinged, he checked the time, and . . . *Shit!* He should've been on his way out the door already, heading to wherever tonight's date was.

He almost burned his wrist on the edge of the oven door as he pulled out the baking tray. A quick flip sent the bagels onto a cooling rack, and Josh was free to bolt for the office. "I'm off! Shop's all yours, Dee!" he shouted, ducking his head to escape his apron.

"Got it, boss!" Dee yelled from up front, which she probably shouldn't have done in front of customers, but whatever. The customers probably wouldn't care. The shop was casual like that.

He hung his apron and shoved today's bright-blue polo shirt into his backpack, making a mental note to do laundry later tonight so he didn't end up catering for a bunch of stuffy librarians and stuffier donors in his underwear. Michael could pull it off, but not Josh. Not without losing a good thirty pounds and doing something horrible, like stomach crunches.

And that thought filled his stomach with a flock of all-too-familiar butterflies. Cuddling and holding hands and kissing were all well and good, but at some point in this relationship, the pants were going to come off. Would Michael still find Josh appealing without the support of a good waistband holding back a percentage of those extra pounds?

So much for getting up the courage to invite Michael over tonight. Maybe tomorrow—which was what Josh had been telling himself ever since Dad went to Brooklyn. But this time, tomorrow was a good idea. Michael would hopefully be in a cheerful mood after the event at the library, however stuffy the other attendants would surely be. And Josh had put extra effort into the everything bagels. The roast beef, lox, and smoked turkey would all be sliced fresh. The chili and chicken soup would be piping hot and spiced to perfection.

"Tomorrow night," Josh muttered as he smoothed down the T-shirt he'd brought to work for tonight's date. Tomorrow night, he'd invite Michael back home, and he'd put his queen-size bed to good use once more after the long, lonely three years since Nate left Hartsbridge Island.

For tonight, though . . . Josh picked up his phone and typed in his passcode, only to be met with nothing. No notifications. No emails, no texts, no voice mails, no missed calls.

Had Michael set up tonight's date last night? Josh had already been half-asleep when Michael drove him home. He had no memory of actually leaving Michael's SUV, unlocking the house, or anything else until his alarm had gone off at 3 a.m.

God, he was going to look like an idiot, but he had no choice. He quickly typed a text: *Sorry to flake on you. Where are we meeting?*

He had to deal with autocorrect three times, but he finally got rid of the squiggly red underlines and sent the text to Michael.

Too tired to stay upright anymore, he sat down and braced a foot against the desk drawer that was stuck open. When his phone went dim, he swiped at it, waking it up again. And again.

The third time the screen darkened with no response from Michael, he thought to check the timestamp on his own text. Almost fifteen minutes had passed.

He had the usual three bars of service, which meant the island's one cell tower hadn't gone on the fritz. The next nearest cell towers were on the mainland, too far north and south to properly overlap Hartsbridge Island.

Maybe the text hadn't gone through?

Suspicious, he copied the text, pasted it into a new one, and resent it. He immediately regretted it. Retexting was clingy. Demanding. Potentially dangerous if Michael was driving. Definitely inappropriate and pushy if Michael was having a bad PTSD moment. And just to keep himself from becoming a pest, Josh put his apron back on and went to see if the team up front needed any help.

"Thought you were outta here, boss," Dee told him as he went to check the soups.

Momentarily tongue-tied, he busied himself stirring what was left of the tomato basil. He was *not* going to admit to being stood up. "Just . . . trying to get a jump on tomorrow. See what we need done before I hit the library."

Dee sighed. "We're *fine*, Josh. Really." She stepped away from the deli counter and elbowed him. "Go on. Get out of here."

Go where? he wondered, hanging the ladle and putting the lid back on the pot.

Thankfully, he got a text as he headed into the kitchen. He nearly strangled himself with the apron in his rush to take it off, and he dropped his phone when he pulled it out of his pocket.

Swearing in whispers—there were a few customers out there, after all—he gave up on the apron and retrieved his phone. Buzzing with excitement at the thought of seeing Michael soon, he had to enter the unlock code twice.

Trapped at the VA in Manchester. See you tomorrow instead?

Josh read the text twice, and his heart sank. Michael hadn't mentioned going to the mainland, and that text was borderline rude, considering their standing date should've started a half hour ago. More.

Was Michael pissed at him?

No. No, it couldn't be. Last night's kiss had been sweet and hot and so damned tempting, making Josh want more. He'd just been on the verge of undead, so he hadn't—

He hadn't invited Michael in. He hadn't even *hinted* at moving their relationship beyond cuddling in restaurants and sharing sweet good-night kisses. *Shit.* And while Michael had made it clear he didn't want this to be anything like his old one-night stands, surely he hadn't been expecting things to move so glacially.

Michael was bored. He had to be. By now, he was helping Josh out of a sense of obligation. That was why he'd been so quick to ask about the bookkeeping figures for the last couple of days. Once they were done with the business plan, he'd be free to move on to better, sexier, smarter, thinner prospects.

Josh made it to the office before his legs gave out. He sat down hard, making the chair creak, and stared at the text through eyes that had gone blurry. *Trapped at the VA in Manchester.* That was practically code for *Anything is better than hanging out with you*, right? Otherwise, Michael would've said something about heading to Manchester last night. Or he would've at least texted *before* their expected date. Hell, he would've answered Josh's first text. Waiting until text number two was practically a warning for Josh to stop bugging him.

Message received, loud and clear.

Thanks to Josh's stupid business plan and his lack of experience and his even worse lack of sex appeal, the relationship was over before it had ever really started.

Fucking shit.

CHAPTER

NINETEEN

Opening the store was hard enough for Josh on a good day, without a sleepless night, packing up freshly sliced meat for the catering gig, and going through the usual morning routines. He was a zombie, one hundred percent certified undead and ready to star in a postapocalypse survival drama. Well, not star. He'd be an extra at most. Even as a zombie, he was more dumpy than terrifying.

When his phone alarm buzzed at 6 a.m., he turned off the meat slicer, stripped off his gloves, and went to unlock the front door. After propping it open to let in some fresh air, he made it halfway back to the counter, only to turn midstep, remembering the sandwich board.

God, he was going to be useless at the library today, but there was no one else he could send. This was a one-person event, and he and Dad were the only ones on the insurance for the delivery van. More paperwork Josh had neglected, come back to bite him in the ass.

And of course the sandwich board fought him this morning, when one of the hooks at the bottom finally worked free of the wood frame. "Fucking *fuck*," he muttered, shoving the screw-end of the hook back into the now-too-large hole, only for it to fall out again. Anger burned through his fatigue and despair, giving him the strength to screw the hook into the wood without predrilling a hole, but he knew that wouldn't work. The four hooks at the bottom of the sign needed to be even so the chains between them would be the same length. Otherwise, the sign would wobble. And that was assuming he didn't split the wood by shoving in the hook.

He propped the sign against the wall and sank down next to it, letting his head fall back with a thud that did nothing to help him focus. There was no point in trying to do anything else for the rest of the day. The librarians wouldn't starve; they could always call for an emergency pizza delivery.

Caught up in his self-loathing, he didn't notice the shadow that blocked the rising sun's warmth until a soft voice asked, "Josh?"

It took him a couple of blinks to clear his eyes. "Dr. Miller!" he yelped, feeling heat rise in his face at her smile.

"Are you all right?" Her British accent made the question sound perfectly normal, not like she was asking if he was having a breakdown. Which he was, of course. A life breakdown instead of a mental one. Not that he was going to go into details with her.

"Broke the sign." He held up the little brass hook, as if to explain further.

She gave him a curious look, head tipped to one side. Then she turned and walked away, heading for her car.

Wonderful. Now he'd alienated his not-really-a-boyfriend *and* his best customer. He closed his eyes for a few seconds, trying to will the ground to open up and swallow him, but he wasn't that lucky.

After a couple of beeps and the *thump* of a car trunk closing, Dr. Miller returned, holding up a roll of duct tape. "Will this help?"

Revitalized, he accepted the tape and twisted up onto his knees so he could get to work on the sign. "You're a saint." He could wrap a piece of tape through the last link in the chain, then tape the makeshift tab to the leg of the sign. It would hold for a few days, until he could arrange a more permanent solution.

"So I've been told," she answered wryly. "Be glad it's me and not my wife who found you in your moment of distress."

Over the sound of ripping duct tape, he asked, "Why's that?"

"She's not to be trusted with power tools. She's an emergency room visit waiting to happen."

Josh glanced over his shoulder at her. "Uh. She's a surgeon."

"Yes. Quite trustworthy with a scalpel. Never let her near electricity. Or plumbing. Or wood, for that matter." She wrinkled her nose.

The tension knotted up in Josh's chest broke apart. He laughed and continued taping the chain in place. "I'll keep that in mind." He scooted back and set up the sign, then grinned when it didn't immediately collapse. He got to his feet and turned, offering the duct tape to Dr. Miller. "Thanks. You're"—he blinked—"in jeans?"

"Not an office day," she said, taking the tape from him. She slid the roll over her hand, turning it into a hipster-chic chunky bracelet. She could make anything look good. "I'm going to the library fund-raiser. Have you heard about it?"

A little bit of that tension came back, but it was nothing Josh couldn't handle. "Yeah. I'm doing the catering."

Her smile turned pleased, almost smug. "Then it looks like a two-bagel day for me." She walked with Josh to the doorway, then nodded her thanks when he gestured her in first. "Are you certain you're all right? You seemed a bit distressed."

Josh glanced across the green at the view that was so familiar. The diner's neon sign flickered. The shadow of Hercules the stag spread in a long, dark patch over the grass. The air was full of salt and the promise of summer.

There wasn't a hint of Michael anywhere.

"Yeah," Josh said, only half lying. He'd been alone for most of his life. He could manage it again. "Yeah, I'll be fine."

Josh stayed fine all through the morning rush, wrangling regular customers, the first tourists of the official summer season, and the two new staffers he and his dad had hired before the Brooklyn trip. Work was a welcome distraction, even if his heart did give a lurch every time the bell rang. He had to tell himself not to look, that his staff could handle the crowd; he needed to focus on the tail end of breakfast and the catering order. He had only an hour of breathing room before he needed to pack the truck, so if there were any last-minute emergencies, he needed to be ready.

And shit, had he checked the gas in the truck? Dad had taken it out last time, and while he was usually good at topping off the tank, sometimes he got busy.

Josh would have to check. Ignoring the bell as it rang again, he stepped back from the slicer, saying, "Dee, take—"

"Oh crap," Dee interrupted, looking past Josh at the front door.

Any reprimand for unprofessional conduct died before Josh could figure out what to say. Michael slipped into the restaurant, wide-eyed and pale, gaze flicking between the knots of people at the tables, the register, the ordering counter. He looked about two seconds from bolting, as if only Kaylee straining at the leash kept him inside. She was heading for the ordering counter, or trying to; even when she stopped pulling, her tail was wagging, like she at least knew what she wanted and where to get it.

There was no way Josh would get through that crowd. Instead, he rushed into the kitchen and out the side door to the back hallway. Before he could open the swinging door to the front, it opened, nearly slamming into his face.

"Shit," Josh gasped as he jerked back, forgetting professionalism. He had time enough to blink once before Michael was right in front of him, pulling him into a hug so tight it crushed the air from his lungs.

Josh's abrupt exhale was halfway to a laugh of crazed relief. Apparently they *hadn't* broken up after all? He wrapped his arms around Michael's body, feeling the rock-hard tension in his back, the faint hitching of his breath. He was leaning to the right, thanks to Kaylee pressed hard against his right leg, which was something she did when Michael was on the verge of one of his . . . episodes. Whatever.

"Hey," Josh whispered into Michael's ear. He rubbed his hand up and down Michael's spine, wishing he knew what else to do. "It's okay."

"I'm— I feel—" Michael huffed in frustration and buried his face in Josh's hair, breath coming in hot, quick pants. "The thing. Feeling bad."

Josh had only the vaguest idea where Michael was headed. He shook his head, saying, "It's really okay."

Michael let out a broken laugh. "I'm sunny."

He had to mean *sorry*. Josh hid his smile at the choice of word replacement, wishing that *sunny* was the right word after all. He couldn't stand seeing Michael like this.

"For last night?" he asked, still rubbing Michael's back. It didn't seem to be helping, but it wasn't hurting either, as far as Josh could tell.

Michael nodded, stubble rasping over Josh's cheek. And that was weird. Since they'd started dating, Michael had taken to shaving, even though Josh liked his five-o'clock shadow almost as much as he liked those reading glasses. So why hadn't he shaved this morning? It wasn't even that early—not for a guy who'd previously shown up here at 6 a.m., cheerful and awake.

"Don't worry about it," Josh said. Four little words dismissing fifteen hours of anxiety and self-doubt, but it was worth it to feel the way the taut line of Michael's shoulders eased.

"It was—the, um, VA—the people—" Michael's fingers dug into Josh's back.

"Hey, it's the government, right?" Josh asked, trying for a light, casual tone. "I can imagine how much it must have sucked."

Michael sighed again and nodded. "So much."

Josh gave Michael a kiss on the cheek, way back by the hinge of his jaw. "Want to sit down?" When Michael tensed up, Josh quickly added, "In the office. It's quiet. Nobody will bug you. I can bring you breakfast."

"Um. Making food place. The *kitchen*," Michael said, the last word carried on a sharp exhale, as though relieved he'd remembered what to say. "Kaylee can't go there."

Josh lowered his voice to a whisper. "We'll sneak her through. Nobody will know."

"But all the people," Michael protested weakly. "They'll see."

"I'll go ahead of you and close the kitchen door. Everyone's out front, dealing with the rush. Nobody goes into the office except for me and Dad." Josh laughed softly. "It's cramped and kind of annoying, what with the fluorescent lights always flickering."

Michael huffed out a laugh of his own. "Sounds nice."

Josh gave him another kiss, throwing in a quick squeeze around the waist. "Is that a yes?" he asked, leaning back to look into Michael's bloodshot eyes.

With a faint smile, Michael nodded. "Yeah. And . . . thanks."

"He wasn't kidding," Michael muttered to Kaylee, though he was looking up at the ceiling. They both were. The long fluorescent bulb wasn't strobing on and off, but the flicker was definitely there, happening just frequently enough to keep him from really relaxing.

Another ten minutes, and it'd probably give him a migraine—not to mention what it was probably doing to Kaylee. He had a vague memory of reading something about dogs not responding well to fluorescent light.

"Back, Kaylee," he finally told her, and she backed away from the chair, giving him room to stand. He turned on the desk light, then reached across the tiny room and flipped the switch, killing the misbehaving fluorescent.

With a sigh of relief, he sank back into his chair. A twitch of his fingers got Kaylee to rest her muzzle against his thigh again. He closed his eyes, listening to the muffled sounds of the restaurant, the hum of conversation, the whir of the meat slicer, the scrape of metal pans from Josh cooking breakfast, despite Michael's protests that he didn't have to.

Really, Michael would be happy with a cup of strong coffee—just enough caffeine to get him safely home. He'd driven the last five miles in a daze. He had zero memory of leaving the mainland, except for the obnoxious white sign for the new gas station positioned right where the bridge met the island. He hoped he'd remembered to park in a nonhandicap spot. Or had he left the placard on from his stop at the motel where he'd tried—and failed—to sleep last night? Again, his mind was a blank.

He had no idea how long it was before the door cracked open and Josh peered in, bringing with him the sharp scent of onions and smoky bacon. "You awake?" he whispered.

Michael sat up with a smile. "Yeah. Sorry. The fluorescent light was . . ." He waved a hand toward the ceiling.

Josh grinned and stepped inside, careful to avoid Kaylee's slow-wagging tail. "Everything bagel with egg and cheese, double side of bacon, and coffee," he said, balancing the tray on top of a stack of paperwork. "Want some water for Kaylee?" He reached for her ear, right by his fingertips, but stopped himself before touching. It was polite—proper etiquette, in fact—but Michael's stomach gave a strange little twist at the sight. Josh wasn't a stranger. He was family, and not just to Michael.

"You can say hi," he told them both, giving Kaylee a nudge toward Josh. She was happy to take the hint and nosed at his hand, probably tracking the scent of the bacon. "And you don't mind her eating in here?"

"Of course not." Josh didn't just scratch at her ears. He crouched and made kissy noises as she sniffed his face. "Such a good girl," he cooed at her. "Yes, you are, aren't you? A hell of a lot nicer than the mainlanders. Right, baby?"

Michael knew his smile had gone lopsided and silly, but he didn't try to hide it, instead drinking in the sight of his boyfriend—boyfriend?—being sweetly affectionate with Kaylee. "Did you want to share?" he asked, taking his plate off the tray. Kaylee didn't turn away from Josh, but she gave a quick sniff that betrayed her interest in breakfast. No surprise there. Last night, they'd eaten fast food from the place across the street from the motel.

Josh planted a kiss on Kaylee's muzzle, then stood up. "I need to get ready for the library job. You take your time. I don't have to leave for another couple of hours."

"The library—" Michael's broken brain finally caught up with the date. "The fund-raiser? It's today?"

"Yeah." Josh tipped his head. "Didn't— No, you look exhausted. Did you even sleep last night?" he asked gently, brushing his fingers against Michael's jaw.

It took effort not to lean into Josh's touch. "Not really," Michael admitted, closing his eyes. "I stayed in Manchester. Driving was . . . um . . ."

"Yeah, I get it." Josh leaned over Kaylee, bracing a hand against the desk, and touched his forehead to Michael's. "You want me to take you home so you can sleep? I can get a cab back here or something."

"No." Michael almost shook his head, but he didn't want to push Josh away. "I want to go. I'll be fine."

He was ready for a protest—for Josh getting insistent that he knew what was best for Michael—but it never came. Instead, Josh ducked to give him a quick kiss and said, "Okay. I've got to wrap up the breakfast rush, then get started on packing everything. But first, I'll be right back with Kaylee's water." He was gone before Michael could come up with an answer.

Michael had left his bag in the car—hopefully with the doors locked—but Kaylee was pretty good at drinking from a cup without splashing too much. She scarfed down the bacon in about three seconds, and Michael didn't take much longer to finish his bagel sandwich. Josh had added chopped onions and sun-dried tomato to the scrambled egg and cheese, giving the sandwich an extra kick of flavor that made his stomach rumble after just one bite. Weeks of eating home cooking and surprisingly good restaurant meals had made Michael lose his immunity to the evils of fast food. Last night's burger hadn't sat well with him.

But despite the excellent coffee, the hot, fresh meal left him feeling drowsy and content. *Safe.* All he wanted was to close his eyes and relax, immersing himself in the feeling of being home again, but he couldn't. If nothing else, he'd wreck his back dozing off in the chair.

"Settle, Kaylee," he told her, even though she'd sprawled out with her muzzle tucked under the desk. She wagged her tail in acknowledgment but didn't lift her head as he stepped over her and opened the door as much as her outstretched legs would allow.

The kitchen was quiet, so Michael let himself out, trusting Kaylee to stay where she was. He couldn't remember the last time he'd been separated from her, but he felt no anxiety at all. Bagel End had become a haven for him. A welcome refuge.

So he was smiling when he walked over to the door that led behind the counter and looked through the window. Josh was way up front by the register with one of his employees, the two of them talking and laughing. The crowd seemed to have died down.

Michael backed off, wondering if he should sneak out with Kaylee—but to where? If he crossed the kitchen and went up front via the hallway, it'd look like he'd been hiding out in the bathroom or something. If he left through the emergency exit, he might set off an alarm, and he'd definitely look ridiculous. He'd gone *into* the hallway, after all. The staff would probably all be wondering why he hadn't come back out.

Or they might just think they'd missed him in the press of customers earlier. The emergency exit was his best bet, but only after saying good-bye to Josh. Walking out on Josh even once was one time too many.

But he wasn't about to go behind the counter. For all he knew, that was a violation of health code rules. Bad enough he had Kaylee in the office.

I'm thinking of heading home for an hour or so. Anything I can do to help with the catering? He typed out the text, checked and double-checked it, then sent it, watching Josh through the window.

A few seconds later, Josh pulled his phone out of his pocket. He swiped at it, then looked back at Michael with a grin. He left the register to his employee and headed to the kitchen as if Michael, not work, was his priority.

"Maybe make it a couple of hours? Think you can take a nap?" Josh asked as soon as the door swung shut behind him. He took Michael's free hand and laced their fingers together. "You look better, but still . . ."

"I don't want to be late." Michael glanced past Josh, and all three servers behind the counter quickly looked away from the window. Self-consciously, he stepped toward the office, pulling Josh along with him. "A shower should wake me up."

"How about," Josh said, crowding close and wrapping his arms around Michael, "you go home and go right to bed, and I'll text you maybe a half hour before things really get going? That'll give you enough time for a quick shower and the drive to the library."

Or you could come home with me, Michael thought, though he didn't say it. Today was a work day for Josh, even if it was also sort of a date. Instead, he countered, "Forty-five minutes, and it's a deal."

Josh gave Michael a kiss that was brief but in no way rushed, leaving Michael's lips warm and tingling. "Forty-five minutes," Josh promised. "Now go home. And don't worry about shaving. Hot, scruffy librarian is a good look on you."

CHAPTER

TWENTY

At a quarter past one, Josh sent his text: *The party starts at two. No need to rush. You need rest.* Then he started laying out a spread of deli trays, condiments, and cream cheese, leaving everything covered for now. He used a paper-lined basket to present the halved bagels, carefully stacked to keep the soft insides from going stale in the open air. When he bent down to plug in the slow cookers meant to keep the soup warm, he almost bashed heads with a woman he'd never seen before. "Oh, sorry," he said, just as she said, "Oops."

Only when he straightened up did he realize the table next to his was full of thick paper cups, hot drink sleeves, and two crimson-and-chrome machines with heavy levers, power cords trailing down from them both. "Need to share an outlet?" he asked, finally recognizing them as portable espresso makers. He'd looked into that sort of thing for Bagel End.

"Got it covered." She turned to root through a backpack under her table, and came up with a power strip. Flashing Josh a cocky grin, she plugged both of her espresso machines into the power strip, then plugged that into the wall. "Always come prepared." She offered him the power strip, adding, "I'm Sam, by the way. From Sam's Caf."

"Josh, Bagel End," he said, accepting the power strip in lieu of a handshake. He'd never heard of Sam's Caf—which he assumed was a trendy new way of saying "café." The thought wasn't entirely comforting. While he could abstractly agree that it was nice to have more businesses on the island, hopefully livening up the town and drawing more tourists, he had plenty of customers who came in for a caffeine fix and ended up leaving with a bagel too.

"The deli?" she asked with a smile, leaning a hip against the wall to watch him set up the slow cookers instead of getting back to her own table. "I've heard you've got the best bagels on the island."

"To be fair, I'd have to agree," he said with false modesty. Considering they were the island's only supplier of bagels, the shop qualified for the "best" and "worst" titles.

"I love bagels. Trade you for a cup, whatever you'd like," she offered, taking a step to Josh's table, putting herself right on the edge of his personal space as he bent to tuck the power cords out of the way.

She was close enough that his heart—or maybe stomach—gave a little flip of surprise. Was she flirting or just excessively friendly? Out of habit, he gave her a quick once-over. On the tall side, with dark curls cut shoulder length, more curves than were strictly fashionable, and a smile that was barely more welcoming than predatory.

A month ago, he would've tripped over his own feet at the very idea that she was flirting with him. Now, all he could think was that he needed to stir the soup. Especially the chicken noodle, which he knew Michael would love.

"I've had like five cups already today," he said, keeping his smile friendly and professional. He set both slow cookers to warm and snapped a piece of waxed paper out of the box. "But take your pick." He waved the paper at the basket of bagels.

Her eyebrows shot up, and she gave him a puzzled look and a shrug. "Chef's choice."

He handed over a cinnamon raisin bagel with sweet cream cheese, then got back to his soup. Stirring filled the air with the warm, homey scent of chicken and a hint of onions and garlic. It took only thirty seconds before the first of the library's staffers abandoned setting out chairs and drifted his way to sneak a taste.

By one thirty, he'd fed most of the staff, as he'd anticipated; he had quart-size to-go containers of warm soup in an insulated bag under his table. As patrons and potential donors began to trickle in, he refilled the slow cookers and restocked the bagels. A small display took work to keep stocked but was more visually appealing than a huge, half-empty spread—one of the little tricks he'd learned after a few disastrous early catering efforts.

From that point on, he, Sam, and Betty from the diner, who was providing slices of pie for dessert, were all kept busy, but not too busy to chat. Sam's Caf, as it turned out, wasn't a brick-and-mortar café but a beachside kiosk owned and operated by Sam herself, who was a junior at the local college. Josh's relief made him feel a touch guilty, but business was business.

Still, it was easier to be friendly, and he genuinely smiled at her explanation: "It's *caf* instead of *café* because I couldn't fit the *e* on the sign."

He laughed over the sound of rattling plastic as he refilled the tray of forks and knives. "I figured you were being all cool or something."

"I *am* cool," she declared smugly, pulling a shot of espresso for herself. It was her third so far, and Josh was wondering how long it would be before she glowed in the dark. "What's with Bagel End? I can't figure it out."

"You kind of have to *see* the shop to get the full impact," he admitted. "My parents—they opened it, and they had a thing for Tolkien. And they always figured if anyone in Middle Earth invented bagels, it'd be hobbits."

"Aww, that's adorable," she cooed. "And you've kind of got the right look, with the hair."

"Don't you start," he warned, brandishing a blunt plastic knife at her. "I'm a crack shot with bagels."

She snickered and turned away, only to let out another "Aww."

"Come on," he protested, scooping up some of the plain cream cheese. He'd entirely forgotten skipping his own lunch—a hazard of working in the food business. The whole Tolkien–Bagel End connection was subtle. It wasn't like their menu board was written in Sindarin Elvish. "It's not like—"

"Puppy!"

Kaylee! This time Josh's heart definitely gave a lurch. He dropped the everything bagel onto his plate, along with the cream-cheese-covered knife, and leaned against the table to grin at Michael and Kaylee. They were standing by the reference desk, where the children's librarian, who'd apparently drawn the short straw, was handing out donation forms instead of mingling. Michael took one of the forms, but instead of excusing himself, he set it on the reference desk and snapped a picture of it, then started typing on his phone.

"Who's the hottie with the cute puppy?" Sam asked.

"My boyfriend." Josh blurted it out without hesitation, wanting to stake his claim before her caffeine-fueled brain latched on to any ideas. Besides, he was ninety percent confident that he and Michael could use the b-word. Or seventy-five percent. Well, considering that he'd thought their relationship was over just a few hours earlier, maybe sixty, but that didn't mean there was room for anyone else to butt in. Besides, they'd settled things when Michael staggered in this morning. Now it was just a matter of confirming their status, assuming Michael was more awake after his nap.

Hopefully he *had* napped.

It took a few more minutes for Michael to finish chatting with the librarian and checking his phone before he finally came over to Josh. He didn't even look twice at Sam—just slipped between their tables so he could give Josh a quick kiss. "Hey. Thanks for waking me," he said, his smile warm and relaxed. "Go ahead, say hi, Kaylee."

Josh put out a hand to scratch Kaylee's head, but most of his attention was focused on Michael. There were still dark circles under his eyes, but the whites were no longer bloodshot. And while he'd showered and changed his clothes, he hadn't shaved. "Hot, scruffy librarian," he all but purred, reaching for Michael's hand.

Michael juggled his phone and the leash, freeing his hand to lace his fingers with Josh's. "More like exhausted, starving veteran, but I'll take what I can get."

"Chicken soup, everything bagel, roast beef, deli mustard? Not all in the same bowl," Josh teased.

"You're spoiling me."

Reluctantly, Josh let go so he could wash his hands and put together Michael's lunch. "If I didn't, Bubbe would crawl out of her grave to yell at me."

"Need some coffee?" Sam piped up over the jingling of Kaylee's collar tags. Josh glanced back and saw Kaylee standing behind Michael, blocking Sam from getting too close. Only then did he realize that at some point, Kaylee had stopped doing that to him.

"No, thanks," Michael said, stepping back and to the side, putting himself closer to Josh. He even switched the leash to his right hand, keeping Kaylee on Sam's side, not Josh's.

That was a clear hint that he wasn't ready to engage. PTSD, fatigue, or both? Whatever the case, Josh felt no guilt saying, "Why don't you go sit down? I'll bring this out to you."

Apparently Michael agreed, judging by his relieved smile and the way he leaned in for another quick kiss. "Thank you. And shit, I shouldn't be back here anyway."

"What? Why not?"

"Food service areas and dogs don't mix." Michael twitched the leash and told Kaylee, "Go through." She made her way between the tables, and he quickly followed.

Josh refrained from rolling his eyes at how diligent Michael was when it came to the rules, though he supposed it was better than Michael ignoring them altogether. Random health department inspections sucked enough as it was, without adding in dog fur. He put together Michael's lunch with a warm bagel he took out of the insulated bag, filled a soup bowl, then carried everything to the deserted corner table Michael had chosen. No surprise there. Josh was coming to learn that Michael wouldn't be comfortable unless he could keep an eye on the exits and anyone who might sneak up on him.

"Give me twenty minutes and I'll be done. A half hour, tops," Josh said as he put everything down on the table.

Michael caught his wrist and pulled him close. "You really don't have to keep feeding me."

Josh smiled and turned his hand to catch Michael's fingers. "I like taking care of you. I like *you*." He was proud that he used *like* there, despite what his heart was whispering. He didn't want to push for anything Michael wasn't ready to give.

Michael squeezed his hand. "I'm really sorry about yesterday. And this morning."

Josh's first instinct was to wave it off as no big deal, but then he thought about how hard it was for Michael to open up to him—and how *important* that sort of honesty was for their future. "Tell me about it later?"

Michael's inhale was a little shaky, but his nod was firm. "Okay." He gave another squeeze, then let go, a faint smile on his lips.

"Okay." Josh looked down at Kaylee, who was sitting under the table, ears perked as if she were eavesdropping. "You take care of him until I get back." She wagged her tail.

Josh took that as agreement and returned to his serving table, feeling better about the day. Between him and Kaylee and his new resolve for honesty, they'd get this relationship back on track.

If Michael were to be perfectly honest with himself, something his therapist would applaud but he himself tended to avoid, he'd admit to timing his email check for right around when Josh was finishing with packing up his catering table. *Hot, scruffy librarian.* The thought made Michael snicker, though he didn't look up from his phone. The email he'd sent to his accountant was full of typos, because he hadn't bothered with his glasses. Now, though, he figured he'd put those glasses to good use, for Josh's benefit.

The donation form was simple enough—one page, typed and photocopied and photocopied again, slightly off-center. Someone at his accountant's office had re-created it digitally, filling in all but the dollar figures, not that it was particularly easy to read on his phone. It was attached to an email with a brief review of Michael's financial state. He'd paid cash for his car in DC, he had a single credit card he'd used to establish his credit rating and then paid off, and he was currently living rent-free, but he couldn't stay here forever. His trust fund would let him live in comfort for the rest of his life, especially supplemented by his disability and medical retirement benefits from the Air Force.

If he had followed the path his father laid out for him, he'd be making six figures at a law firm by now, probably in Boston or DC. Or he'd be drawing a minimal salary working as a congressional aide for someone with the right connections, probably with generous financial help from his parents. Either way, he'd be on the road to wealth and power instead of drifting through a tiny town that could barely call itself a vacation destination, where his only meaningful connection was with the bagel guy.

He wouldn't trade this life, aimless as it was, for all the power and money in the world.

The thought made him smile, and he was still smiling when Josh came over, taking the seat next to him. "Feeling better?" Josh asked, laying his warm hand on Michael's arm.

"Yeah." Michael put down his phone but didn't take off the glasses. "Yeah, I am."

Josh nodded, fingers rubbing circles against Michael's skin. "So, what do you say we talk, get it out of the way, and then I can give you a tour of the library?"

Michael tried to hide a nervous shudder. "Is there more to see besides books, desks, and computers?"

Josh laughed. "Reference section, kids' section. There's one of those figureheads from an old sailing ship, but this one's supposed to be from a pirate ship."

"How can you stand the excitement?" Michael teased, scooting his chair closer. Kaylee was entirely under the table, so there was enough room for Michael to get right up next to Josh.

"Uh-huh. See if I take you on a date to the town museum." Josh rolled his eyes, nudging Michael's foot.

And that was a perfect opening for Michael to suggest going back to his place tonight. He'd spent last night a wreck, curled up with Kaylee, barely daring to sleep for fear of nightmares. Even if sex wasn't on the table—or in the bed, as it were—he wanted the intimacy of having Josh close, of falling asleep to the sound of Josh's breathing, of waking to his smile.

But before he could get up the courage, Josh spoke again, asking, "What happened yesterday?"

Michael sighed, looking down at their hands. Josh's presence had him so relaxed that Kaylee didn't respond to the faint spike of anxiety that shot through him. "Everything went wrong from the start," he said quietly. "They tried to say I couldn't bring in Kaylee. They said she wasn't a real service dog because she's not a golden retriever or Labrador, and wanted to see her certification. They didn't, um, believe me when"—he took a deep breath, trying to corral his racing thoughts, to find the right words—"when I said there's no such thing."

Josh hadn't stopped his soothing massage. "But you got in eventually?" he prompted.

Michael nodded. "A volunteer saw what was happening and got someone who was in charge. Someone who knew better." He shifted to the edge of the chair, focused on watching Josh's fingers move. "Then it was just paperwork. Trying to get a local doctor and dentist, updating my contact information, getting authorization for local specialists..."

"Specialists?" Josh asked worriedly.

Michael darted a quick look at Josh, who was frowning. "Someone for, you know, PTSD. A physical therapist. A—" He stopped as the word slipped right out of his grasp. It started with an *n*, but all that came to mind was *necromancer*, and he knew *that* wasn't right. "A brain doctor. Nerves. Nerve-ologist."

"Neurologist?"

Frustrated with himself, Michael nodded. "Yeah. That."

Josh's hand went still, and there was tension in his voice as he asked, "Is there something... *wrong*?"

Michael shook his head, then shrugged. "Maybe. I mean, probably not. I'm still getting migraines, and they want to make sure it's not from..." He gestured at the scar under his bangs.

Josh's eyes tracked up, and he touched Michael's face with his free hand. "I hate even thinking about it," he admitted quietly.

"If it hadn't happened, I wouldn't be here. I never would've left the Air Force."

"Yeah, but you wouldn't have been hurt," Josh protested.

Michael turned, pressing a kiss into Josh's palm. "I wouldn't have met you."

"I'm not worth getting"—Josh hesitated for a heartbeat—"shot."

"But you're here, and I'm here with you," Michael said, leaning closer. Even in this public setting, he felt safe with Josh, as if the world outside didn't matter. There were people chatting, laughing, eating dessert, and taking selfies, and not one of them mattered to Michael. Only Josh did. "This is exactly where I want to be. *With you.*"

It was Josh's turn to look down, color rising in his cheeks. "You know, yesterday, with your text . . . I thought that was you breaking it off. I mean, this. Between us."

"No. God, no," Michael insisted when he caught his breath. "Josh . . . All I wanted was to come home to you, but I couldn't drive. I couldn't talk to call you."

But he'd tried. He'd tried so hard, but he hadn't been able to make the words come, not even to talk to Kaylee. Hell, he'd had to use his phone to write out his order at the fast food place last night, which had confused the hell out of the drive-through clerks.

"Maybe next time," Josh said softly, "I can come with you to start?"

Yes, Michael thought, though he said, "No. Josh, you don't—"

"Don't say 'have to,'" Josh warned with a gentle smile. "I want to. I may not be good with paperwork, but I'm pretty damn stubborn, especially with anyone trying to give you shit."

Michael knew he should refuse. Stand his ground. He was a grown man, one who'd once navigated the convoluted, shadowy world of government paperwork and the subtle currency of debts and favors. Just because stress stole his ability to speak in coherent sentences didn't mean he needed a babysitter.

But that wasn't what Josh was offering.

Choosing his words with exquisite care, Michael asked, "Is it too soon to tell you how much you mean to me?"

Josh's eyes widened a touch, and his lips parted. Slowly, he smiled, and he freed his other hand to cup Michael's face in his palms, his touch light as a feather. "Only if it's too soon for me to say the same thing."

With a soft laugh, Michael leaned in, allowing Josh to guide him, to pull him forward, into a deep, heartfelt kiss that said everything they had left unspoken. For now.

TWENTY-ONE

The library hovered on the border between outdated and antiquated, which explained the air of desperation hanging over the fund-raiser. The multimedia lab had two blocky computers, old CRT monitors, and a notice hanging nearby warning patrons that wi-fi was down. One corner of the reference area had suspicious stains on the ceiling and wall. And Josh's brief tour ended near the restrooms, next to a water fountain with an Out of Order sign, well away from the gathering. Michael would've welcomed the private, quiet moment if not for the odd odor filling the hallway.

He pushed it out of his mind—and lungs—and pulled Josh into his arms. "So, do you have to open the store tomorrow?"

Josh gave a theatrical sigh. "Three more days, yeah. I swear, when Dad comes home, I'm going to sleep for twelve hours straight. I'm not getting out of bed until *noon*."

God, that was tempting. Michael slid his hands down Josh's back until he could hook his fingers into Josh's belt. "Want some help with that?"

The way Josh's eyebrows shot up would've had Michael backpedaling if not for Josh's encouraging blush. "I think . . ." He smiled, resting his hands on Michael's hips. "I think I'd like that. It'd have to be at your place, though. You know. Avoid the weirdness."

"Your dad's *got* to have figured out we're dating," Michael pointed out. "How many times have I driven you home at night?"

"Oh, not that weirdness." Josh dismissed it with a shrug. "The weirdness of him calling Dee to open the shop instead so he can make you breakfast and interrogate you about kids and converting to Judaism."

Michael choked back a laugh. "Yeah, let's build up to that," he said, pulling Josh closer for a kiss. "Maybe we could start tonight?"

Josh inhaled, eyes widening a bit. But then he shook his head, face falling, and insisted, "You need to sleep."

It was Michael's turn to shrug. "I don't have to sleep alone, though, do I?" he asked, just as Kaylee tugged on the leash wrapped around his wrist. He took a step back, glancing past Josh as a tall, familiar black woman entered the hallway. In her jeans and T-shirt, she looked like a model trying to go incognito. Her smile was so friendly that Michael gestured Kaylee back, stopping her move to intervene.

"Hello, Josh," she said, and her British accent triggered Michael's memory. This was Dr. Miller, wife of the other Dr. Miller.

"Hey, Doc." Josh turned but didn't let go, ending up with his arm around Michael's waist. Kaylee's head was trapped between them, but she didn't seem to mind.

Dr. Miller smiled, eyes sparkling as she darted a glance Michael's way.

Josh took the hint. "Oh. Uh, Dr. Miller, this is Michael Baldwin." He turned to Michael, adding, "She's on the town board."

Dr. Miller extended her hand to Michael, saying, "Please, call me Sharon."

He shook her hand with a genuine smile. "It's nice to meet you. Your wife recommended the town veterinarian for Kaylee here."

"She's lovely." Dr. Miller smiled down at Kaylee, but she didn't try to pet her. "Baldwin . . . Are you by chance related to Governor Baldwin?"

Michael felt Josh stiffen, and his own throat closed up. He had a horrible vision of Dr. Miller trying to pull him into local politics because of his connections. She was a politician. Just because she *seemed* nice didn't mean she was. Hell, in Michael's experience, the nicer the politician, the more dangerous they were.

But she was waiting for an answer, and Michael couldn't think of any way out, other than honesty. "He's—" It came out a raspy croak, and he paused to gather his wits, conscious of how Josh's expression had turned into a concerned frown. "Yes. He's my father."

Dr. Miller nodded, and Michael braced for the realization that she'd stumbled upon a political prize. But instead of seizing the moment, she looked back down at Kaylee and asked, "Have any of our businesses challenged your right to bring her in?"

Michael had been holding his breath; it came out in a rush of relief. "No." He gave Josh a squeeze and added, "Your wife said to let her know if I had problems with that."

"Once again, she's confused 'surgeon' with 'elected official.' But her heart's in the right place. Only a few years ago, the town wasn't in compliance with accessibility laws. We still have a ways to go." She looked back up at Michael. "If you do have any difficulty, stop by my office."

"I'm, uh . . ." Michael took his arm from around Josh's body and leaned down to unzip the center pouch on Kaylee's vest. Bending over made him dizzy, though, and he caught himself against the water fountain, which creaked and wobbled ominously. Was the entire library falling apart around him? He took out an ADA reference card and offered it to Dr. Miller. "This covers federal statutes in the Americans with Disabilities Act. We're supposed to call the police if we're challenged."

Dr. Miller flipped the card, skimming both sides, and nodded. "This is *very* useful. May I keep this? I'd like to show it to our police chief to ensure all of our officers are properly aware."

Oh. Michael smiled and nodded, wrapping his arm around Josh again, both for comfort and for balance. "Sure. The phone number at the bottom is my training school in DC. You can call them if you have questions or anything. I think they offer classes for businesses too."

"Thank you." She slid the business card into her back pocket and told Josh, "Lunch was delightful, as always."

Josh grinned proudly. "Two-bagel day," he said, which made her laugh.

"My wife will be jealous," she answered slyly. "A pleasure to meet you, Michael."

"You too." Michael shook her hand, then watched her walk off into the ladies' room without another word about his father. Not that he was out of the woods yet. He turned to Josh, braced for a confrontation all over again, but Josh was looking at the water fountain.

"Uh . . . We might want to move," Josh said, pulling Michael away from that side of the hall.

"What? Why?"

"There are mushrooms growing down there."

Michael ducked his head so he could see the water pipe under the fountain. Sure enough, tiny white mushrooms had sprouted right out of the wall. "Okay, that's it," he said, taking hold of Josh's hand.

"What's 'it'?"

Michael headed for the reference desk. "This library isn't just in need of donations. It's a health hazard."

"We had a really wet spring," Josh said, as if that were an excuse. "You're not going to volunteer, are you? Do you even know plumbing?"

"Not even close. But I *can* donate." Michael stopped on the far side of the reference desk from the librarian who was wrangling the forms and turned to Josh. "You didn't answer me about tonight," he said a little nervously. It was one thing to date a random tourist-turned-townie; it was something else entirely to date the governor's son.

Josh nodded thoughtfully, biting his bottom lip. "Okay. But I've got to clean up and drop the truck back at the shop. And I should make sure things are going okay there."

Relieved, Michael said, "I can follow you back there, then drive you to my place. Maybe we'll stop and pick up a pizza or something?"

With a sly smile, Josh asked, "This isn't your way of trying to get me to cook a private dinner for you?"

Michael laughed. "I was thinking breakfast."

"I'll grab some bagels, then. And oh! In the chaos this morning, I completely forgot." Josh's smile turned bright and hopeful. "I've got some prototype dog treats for Kaylee to try. You *did* say she'd help me perfect the recipe, right?"

"Absolutely." Michael squeezed Josh's hand, then got moving again, heading right for the librarian.

Tonight. Josh had no idea what would happen tonight—if Michael was awake enough for anything more than kissing and cuddling and an early bedtime—but they were going to spend tonight together. They'd wake up together tomorrow morning. And it had been *Michael's* idea.

Josh threw some assorted bagels into a bag and picked up the box of dog bagels he'd stashed under the register in the misguided hope he'd remember to give them to Michael.

"You're sure you're okay with closing tonight *and* opening tomorrow?" he asked Dee.

She looked past Josh to the front window, where Michael's SUV was visible. "When's the last time you went on a real, honest-to-God date?"

Josh groaned and checked the bag, wondering if he'd picked the right types of bagels. Eventually Michael would get sick of the two extremes—plain and everything—wouldn't he? "I've *been* dating, even if half those dates have been— Aha! Laptop." He dropped the bag on the counter pass-through and headed for the office.

She followed him into the kitchen, scolding, "I'm not talking about you two hunched over a laptop at the diner. I mean a *real* date." A wicked gleam came into her eyes as she added, "You know. A slumber-party date."

Josh couldn't outrun her. He went into the office and snatched up his backpack. "You did *not*—"

Dee laughed and leaned against the office door. "Your dad called to check on the catering order, make sure everything was okay. And he said that if you felt like taking advantage of having the house to yourself, you should." As soon as he had the backpack in hand, she took hold of his arm and tugged him out of the office.

Dad's just trying to help, Josh reminded himself. It could be worse. Dad had never been anything less than a hundred percent supportive of Josh's bisexuality. He'd never once hinted at "date guys, but marry a girl," despite how much he wanted grandchildren. But that didn't make it any easier for Josh to put up with Dad's incessant matchmaking—especially not if Dad was now dragging outsiders into it.

Caught up in his thoughts, he let Dee steer him through the kitchen to the counter pass-through, where he picked up the bagels. He slung the pack over his shoulder, feeling the weight of the laptop.

Should he leave it behind? Dee was right. After too many working dates, it was time for Michael and him to focus on each other, just like that night in Portsmouth. Their first real date. Their first kiss.

But Michael seemed genuinely interested in helping Josh with the business plan. There was a definite appeal to working on it at a cozy kitchen table over breakfast. And then going right back to bed for the rest of a warm, lazy morning.

Yes. Practically bouncing on his toes, he headed for the door, saying, "Call if you—"

"If I need anything. Yeah, yeah," Dee said, shepherding him out. "Don't forget condoms."

He almost tripped, he turned so quickly—just in time for her to shut the door in his face, which was becoming a habit. He was tempted to go back in and have a talk with her, but the greater temptation was just a few feet away, so he surrendered with grace. He didn't run around the front of the SUV, but he did jog, and seconds later, he was in the passenger seat, leaning over for a kiss from Michael and a friendly nudge from Kaylee.

As the kiss ended, Josh murmured, "So, uh . . . Tonight, are we . . .?"

Michael drew back enough to meet Josh's eyes. After a heartbeat, he asked, "Do you want to?"

Yes. Josh swallowed the word and tried to go for casual and cool instead. "If you want. I mean, you're probably still tired."

"Not *that* tired." Michael pressed his fingers against Josh's nape, pulling him into another kiss that sent tingles of anticipation through Josh's whole body.

By the time Josh pulled away, he was dizzy with desire. "We should—" He stole another kiss, this one fast and light. "Condoms. You know."

"I have, at home."

They were doing this. They were really doing this. Josh dropped the backpack between his feet and fumbled to put on his seat belt. As Michael pulled away from the curb into a U-turn, heading for the pizza place, Josh scrambled to come up with something to discuss other than sex. The backpack shifted, reminding him of the laptop. "Lizzie emailed me—" he said, just as Michael said, "About tonight—"

Josh's heart gave a lurch. Was Michael changing his mind already? Or was this where Michael confessed to something like an STI?

"Sorry, go ahead," Michael said, flashing Josh a quick, faint smile.

Josh shook his head and swallowed. "No, you go."

No longer smiling, Michael glanced over at Josh, then looked resolutely at the road ahead. "I, uh, have issues with my balance. Sometimes it's okay, but sometimes . . . there are things I can't do."

Josh hadn't anticipated *this* sort of health concern. He opened his mouth to ask if Michael was all right, but the answer was obvious. No. He wasn't. Instead, after a moment's consideration, Josh asked, "What kind of things?"

Michael shrugged, hands tight on the steering wheel. "I can't stand up if things are too"—he let go of the wheel and waved his hand— "intense. I can't be on top for more than a few minutes."

He fell silent. Josh waited for the other shoe to drop . . . but Michael remained silent. Finally, a little puzzled, Josh said, "Okay."

Michael shot him another look. "I don't want you to think . . . you know, that I'm lazy or that you have to do all the work."

Josh laughed, leaning further against the center console to get closer, running his hand up to Michael's shoulder and back down. "You call that work? Work is getting up at shit o'clock in the morning to deal with dough that rose too much and exploded all over the proofing cabinet."

Grinning, Michael asked, "Does that happen a lot?"

"Not for a few years, but bagel-making can be hazardous," Josh teased—and then realized how stupidly insensitive it was to joke about the dangers of making bagels to someone who'd been shot in combat.

He opened his mouth to apologize, but Michael laughed and let go of the steering wheel to catch Josh's hand. With his attention on the road, it took a couple of tries for him to lace their fingers together. "Do I have to worry about you sneaking into my kitchen in the middle of the night? The bedroom is a loft over the kitchen, and smoke rises."

"Hey," Josh protested. "I am a *god* of awesome breakfasts and brunches. Tomorrow morning, you and I are sleeping in, and then I'm going to make you the best brunch ever."

Michael's hand tightened around Josh's. "Sleeping in? I thought you were opening tomorrow."

Oops. Sheepishly, Josh said, "Uh, yeah. Dee agreed to close tonight and open tomorrow. That was supposed to be a surprise, so . . . surprise?"

"Excellent surprise," Michael approved. "And hey, what were you going to say before? Something about email?"

"Oh. Yeah," Josh said, regretting mentioning it earlier. If Michael wasn't hesitant about sex with Josh, there was no reason for Josh to be self-conscious and try to change the subject. Right?

Michael squeezed Josh's hand again. "Well?"

And now Josh was self-conscious about bringing up work at all. "It's nothing. It's just, Lizzie emailed me the numbers. For the business plan."

"Good!" Michael smiled at Josh. "We can finish that up tomorrow, over brunch."

"We don't have to," Josh insisted, no matter how relieved he was that the business plan part of the expansion nightmare was over. He wasn't exactly enthusiastic about the next step: getting his dad onboard. "This is practically a weekend vacation for us both."

Michael's smile turned indulgent. "Are you working tomorrow?"

Josh winced. "Yeah. Noon to closing, then prep for the next day. But it's just because Dad's still out of town."

"Still, like you said . . . practically a weekend vacation." Michael nodded. "I'll take it."

TWENTY-TWO

"This is great," Josh said, walking into the barn ahead of Michael. He looked to the kitchen in the back, the loft upstairs, then turned, swiping the pizza box temptingly close to Kaylee's muzzle. "This was really a barn?"

"Original to the property, yeah. Hell if I know how they got the permits to remodel." Michael closed the door and locked it for his own peace of mind, though he wasn't expecting anyone. The maintenance staff wouldn't be around for another four days. He and Josh were safe. Alone.

Josh made it as far as the coffee table in front of the couch, where he put down the pizza and his backpack. "So, uh . . . Do you want dinner now?" he asked quietly.

Something about Josh's tone made Michael glance up from taking off Kaylee's vest. Despite the hesitance in his question, there was no uncertainty in his eyes. He stared at Michael with such want . . . such desire. God, he was gorgeous. Michael knew that Josh thought himself unattractive, plain and overweight and boring, but Michael had never seen him that way.

"I wish I'd said something." The words came out soft, softer than Michael's footsteps as he dropped Kaylee's vest and walked right toward Josh, drawn to him.

Josh tipped his head questioningly, a tiny frown drawing his brows together. "What?"

"That first day, at your shop." Michael stopped inches away and brushed his fingertips up Josh's forearm, over blond hair so light, it was nearly impossible to see. "After I ate breakfast—after I settled down and could relax—I kept wishing I'd said something to you, more than just talking about food. Asked your name, asked you out . . ."

The corner of Josh's mouth quirked up. "No. You did not."

With a quiet laugh, Michael wrapped his fingers around Josh's arm and gave a tug, pulling him close. "You had the kitchen door propped open. From where I was sitting, I could see you at the table. I waited as long as I could for you to come back up front, but you were busy."

Josh narrowed his eyes, thinking, then sighed. "Right. I was meeting with Lizzie." He put his arms around Michael's shoulders, fingers teasing at his nape. "And then I switched to opening shift, in case you came in early."

Smiling, Michael rested his hands on Josh's hips, hooking his thumbs into Josh's waistband. "How about we promise to sleep in from now on?"

"Please, yes," Josh said, his voice heavy with exaggerated desperation. "I can't handle that much caffeine every single day."

"Yeah, it's not good for your blood pressure," Michael agreed. He looked down at the narrow vee of skin revealed by Josh's Bagel End polo shirt and thought about tonight. This was about more than just sex. They'd be spending the night together. Sleeping together. "I have enough trouble getting to sleep at night without adding caffeine to the mix."

Josh touched Michael's chin, lifting gently until their eyes met. "Do you have nightmares?"

Michael shrugged, ducking to kiss Josh's fingers. "Sometimes. I'm not . . . *dangerous* or anything when I do. And Kaylee's good about waking me up."

"Okay." Josh scratched blunt nails over Michael's neck, sending shivers down his spine, and his eyes closed. "You never answered me."

Michael had to force his eyes to open again. "What?"

With a quiet laugh, Josh asked, "Do you want dinner now, or can it wait?"

"Wait." Heart pounding, Michael took a deep breath and said, "It can wait."

Josh moved in for a kiss, needy and hot, fingers tight around the back of Michael's neck. Desire rushed through Michael's body, leaving him trembling, fingers clenched in Josh's waistband. His groan was lost under Josh demanding, "Upstairs. Now."

"Yes." Michael took a step back, pulling Josh with him so they didn't have to stop kissing. He needed more. Josh's mouth, his hands, his everything. "Josh."

"Hmm?" Josh scratched over Michael's scalp, then dipped his fingers into the neck of Michael's T-shirt.

Michael forgot whatever he was going to say. His skin was on fire with every new touch of Josh's fingers. They were both wearing too much clothing. He let go of Josh's waistband and tugged at his polo shirt, only to have Josh laugh and back away.

"Easy." Josh untangled Michael's fingers from the shirt and took his hands. "Upstairs first."

Michael nodded and let Josh lead the way to the stairs. Kaylee trotted along beside Michael, just as she'd been trained, but he waved her back. Even dizzy with need, Michael felt strong—stable—with Josh's fingers intertwined with his.

At the top of the stairs, he let go of Josh and flipped the switch to turn on the bedside lamps. "Kaylee, settle," he said, gesturing her to the dog bed she rarely used, rather than the big, cozy bed where she'd been sleeping since they came to New Hampshire. She had to think about it for a few seconds before she curled up out of the way.

"Don't tell me . . . she usually sleeps up here?" Josh asked as he sat down on the side of the bed, smoothing his fingers down the light quilt, still rumpled from Michael's nap.

"Usually," Michael confirmed, bending over to untie his shoelaces, one hand braced on the foot of the bed. "Not tonight."

Their shoes ended up kicked under the bed next to Michael's half-empty suitcase. Hoping Josh would take a hint, Michael pulled off his shirt and dropped it on the floor before crawling up the bed to where Josh sat, staring at him.

"You don't—" Josh began, then looked away with a long, slow exhale.

Michael swallowed and sat down a few inches away from Josh. "I don't . . .?" he prompted.

Josh smiled. "You don't have scars. I thought . . . After what you said happened, I figured . . ."

Relieved, Michael closed those few inches and rested his hand behind Josh. With every breath, his chest pressed against Josh's arm. "They're all under my hairline. It was pretty bad for the first year or so, but my hair's finally growing back."

Josh twisted sideways to face Michael, and looked down at his chest. "I wondered." He touched one finger to Michael's sternum. The touch was featherlight but pinned Michael in place, stealing his breath. "I was worried. What you went through . . ." Josh shook his head. "You're carrying enough scars."

"I'm here," Michael said simply, covering Josh's hand with his own. Josh splayed his fingers over Michael's chest. His palm was scorching hot, right over Michael's heart. "Exactly where I want to be."

Josh's eyes went wide and dark, and he surged forward, kissing Michael hard and deep, as if his life depended on it. He pushed, and Michael fell back, Josh following him down against the soft mattress. Their kiss turned messy and full of need until Josh ducked, pressing his lips against Michael's jaw, his chin, his throat. Michael got his hands under Josh's shirt and tugged, hinting again, and this time Josh went along with it, shifting and twisting and breaking the kiss for a heartbeat, just long enough for Michael to get the shirt over his head.

When Josh sank against him, he groaned and wrapped a leg around Josh's, pulling their bodies closer. They were still in their jeans, but Michael didn't want to let him go yet. He *couldn't*. He dragged his hands up Josh's back to his shoulder blades, then down again, along the soft curve of his spine.

"Josh," Michael said, his voice a rough growl. "You feel . . ."

"Mmm," Josh hummed into Michael's collarbone. He propped up on one elbow so he could run his other hand down Michael's ribs. Michael flinched, painfully aware that he'd lost weight in the hospital and never put it back on, no matter how much he worked out. Compared to Josh, he looked unhealthily thin.

Time for a distraction.

"Josh. Pants," he said, trying to stretch far enough to reach Josh's ass, but Josh was still inching down.

Josh lifted his head and met Michael's eyes, a wicked grin spreading on his face. "Good idea."

Then his hands were at Michael's waistband, and Michael gasped at the soft brush of fingers tickling against his abdomen. Josh took advantage of the moment's distraction to unbutton his waistband.

What about your pants? Michael wanted to ask, but he lost the ability to breathe as soon as Josh eased the zipper down. He'd been hard, but in a distant sort of way, too caught up in the feel of Josh's body to think about his own pleasure. Now he couldn't stop his hips from bucking up as Josh pushed his jeans out of the way.

Josh laughed, soft and smug and hot as hell, and teased his fingertips under the waistband of Michael's boxers. When Michael's breath hitched, Josh asked, "Too fast?"

This was the perfect moment for a witty response, something silver-tongued and seductive, meant to put control back in Michael's hands. Too bad Michael didn't have one. All he could manage was, "No. It's—it's fine."

"I hope it's better than *fine,*" Josh said—or Michael thought he did. His hearing went away, along with his speech, when Josh's fingers dipped low enough to brush over the head of Michael's cock.

Yes. More. Michael bit his lip and clenched his hands into soft curls. When had he grabbed Josh's hair? He kept it this side of polite as Josh tugged all the layers of clothes away from Michael's cock, over his hips.

"Up," Josh prompted, sliding a hand under Michael's ass. He let go of Josh's hair and braced his feet against the bed so he could lift his hips enough. The clothes hit the floor, and Josh sat back, tugging at Michael's socks, which was embarrassing but not nearly as awkward as leaving them on.

"Don't forget yours," Michael said, propping up on one elbow to look down the length of the bed at Josh. Somehow they'd ended up backward, with Michael's feet by the pillows, but he didn't care.

Josh's grin turned bright and mischievous. He tossed Michael's socks aside and followed them off the bed, standing so he could take off his own jeans. "We should probably talk about some things. Health. Preferences. All that."

Michael agreed. He really did. But not *now.* "Condoms and lube in the drawer," he said, pointing at the nightstand—and thank

God he hadn't left them in the bathroom downstairs, with the rest of his toiletries. His wishful thinking about his future with Josh had paid off. "I'd *really* like you inside me, but if you want to ride me instead . . ."

Josh licked his lips, staring into Michael's eyes. "Tomorrow."

"Or later tonight?" Michael suggested.

"That works," Josh said, going right for the drawer.

"God, look at you," Josh whispered, lifting his mouth from Michael's hip to stare up the length of his body. The bedside lamps gave Michael's winter-pale skin a soft golden glow, softening the stark lines of his hip bones and ribs. Josh pressed a slow, openmouthed kiss to the hollow of Michael's hip, and Michael's neck arched, drawing a heated groan.

All of Josh's self-consciousness about his weight melted away under his fascination with the strength of Michael's reaction. Josh was doing this to him. Plain, ordinary, townie Josh had broken through Michael's wariness and defensiveness to bring him such pleasure—and they'd barely begun.

Not that Josh was under any illusion that he was a great or expert lover. His past with Nate had been full of enthusiastic fumbling and attempts to emulate porn—never a good idea without a skilled chiropractor on speed dial. But what he lacked in experience, he made up for in his genuine desire to make Michael forget all about his DC one-night stands and anyone else he'd ever been with.

Josh nudged Michael's legs apart a bit more. He kissed his way down another couple of inches, until he felt coarse, springy hair under his lips. All he had to do was turn his head to nuzzle the base of Michael's cock. Michael gasped, rolling his hips up, and Josh slipped his fingers below Michael's balls. The lube was body-warm, slicking his way, and Michael's gasp turned into a groan.

"Can I . . . ?" Josh teased.

"Yeah." Michael bent his knees, feet flat against the soft mattress, giving Josh better access.

With a gentle push, Josh eased one finger inside. As he started to move, Michael lifted his hips even more and rubbed one foot against Josh's body. Encouraged, Josh slid a second finger inside him, eyes closed to better take in the heat and the tightness and the hitched, needy sounds Michael was making. With every gasp and twitch and moan, Josh moved faster, more confidently, until his world narrowed to his hand and Michael's body.

He didn't realize he was moving his own hips, rutting against the quilt, until Michael interrupted with a nudge of his foot. "Josh. Josh, it's enough," he said, reaching down to Josh's shoulder.

"You sure?" Josh asked, trying to be polite, though he wanted nothing more than to sink deep inside Michael.

"Yeah. Come on," Michael insisted, tugging on Josh's arm as soon as he was in reach.

Josh's laugh was breathy and strained. "Okay, okay." He crawled awkwardly up Michael's body for a kiss, then slid off him, bracing one foot on the floor. He used his shirt to clean his fingers, picked up a condom that had fallen off the bed, and got back on top of Michael as quickly as he could.

Michael pulled him down for a kiss before he could open the packet. Josh laughed and nipped Michael's lip, trying to tear only the packet and not the condom itself.

"Josh . . ." Michael's voice held more than a little complaint, and Josh kissed him into silence.

"Give me a minute." Josh sat back, grinning, and got the condom open. When he rolled it on, the touch of his own hands was enough to make him gasp. Thank God they hadn't drawn out the foreplay even more, or he wouldn't be able to last. His hands were shaky when he spilled more lube into his palm. Shivering at the chilly liquid, he slicked the condom and asked, "Do you want to turn over?"

"It's fine. Come here," Michael demanded, using one leg to tug Josh closer.

Josh huffed and settled between Michael's legs, reaching down between their bodies. "Demanding, aren't you?" he asked, wrapping his fingers around Michael's cock.

Michael's response was lost under his sudden moan. His head fell back, and Josh ducked to nip and kiss at his jaw. A couple of slow, slick strokes had Michael bucking his hips.

"*Josh.*"

Josh's laugh was sharp with the strain of holding back his own desire. "Okay, okay."

Michael's body was tight, almost too tight. Josh would've stopped, pulled back to try again with his fingers, but Michael locked one leg around his waist. "Don't stop. Come on, Josh."

"I don't"—Josh dragged in a breath—"don't want to hurt you."

"You won't." Michael met Josh's eyes and cupped his face in both hands. "Please."

They both wanted this. Both *needed* this. Josh nodded and leaned in for a kiss, pushing slowly, deliberately, without backing away, until the head of his cock slipped inside. "Oh God," he whispered, resting his forehead against Michael's.

They went still, breathing deeply, together, until Josh rallied enough to ask, "More?"

Michael nodded, hair rasping against the quilt. "More."

"Yeah. Okay," Josh whispered as he started to push again, then pulled back. With each thrust, he went a little deeper, and Michael rolled his hips up, raising his knees, until their bodies were pressed flush together.

"Josh. *Josh.*" Michael ran his hands down Josh's back, pushing insistently, as if trying to coax Josh even deeper. "It's okay. Move."

Toes curled, Josh did as Michael wanted. His efforts to keep it slow and gentle faltered under Michael's quiet demands, the way his fingers dug into Josh's shoulders, the press of his thighs against Josh's ribs. The sight of him beneath Josh, eyes closed, lips parted, was captivating.

Weeks of nothing more than sweet kisses left Josh defenseless against the thrill of being inside Michael's body. There was no way he was going to last, but he also wasn't going to be selfish about this. He shifted to brace himself on his left arm and reached between their bodies, but Michael caught his wrist.

"Later—after," Michael said between breaths. "Want to feel you first."

What? Didn't he want them to come together? Josh looked into his eyes, but he seemed sincere.

"Okay." Josh nodded, taking a hitched breath, and started moving again, this time chasing his own pleasure—not that it was an effort. Heat coiled low in his gut, driving him to move faster, harder, until he was gasping, eyes closed with the effort of drawing this out for a few more precious seconds.

"Come on, baby. Come on," Michael urged, lifting his head to press kisses against Josh's mouth and jaw. He stretched to reach Josh's neck and bit, and the sharp sting of his teeth and tight heat of his body were too much.

Between one breath and the next, the world fell away in a wash of blinding white, silent except for the thunder of Josh's own pulse. He soared, unable to remember ever feeling this good, this *right*. The aftershocks of pleasure left him gasping, trembling with the effort to keep from collapsing on Michael.

"God, you're gorgeous," Michael was saying, rubbing his hands up and down Josh's body in slow, sweeping strokes. "So perfect. You okay? Was it all right?"

Josh's first attempt at answering came out as a soft hum. He blinked a few times and tried to focus. Michael's eyes were dark, pupils consuming the rich brown, and Josh remembered that they weren't finished.

He pulled out without losing the condom and slid it off, sitting unsteadily back on his knees, scanning the loft for a trash can. Kaylee was watching them, and Josh quickly looked away from her. He didn't need a dog judging his performance.

"Under the nightstand," Michael said helpfully, pointing to where Josh had found the condoms and lube.

Josh threw out the condom and asked, "How do you want . . .?"

Michael shrugged. "Doesn't matter, as long as it's you." He ran a hand down his own body, taking hold of his cock, which was thick but only half-hard.

Right. Josh crawled up Michael's body, pausing long enough to swipe another condom off the floor. He was less distracted this time and ripped open the packet before getting caught up in Michael's kiss.

When Michael was good and hard, cock pressed against Josh's belly, leaving sticky drops between their bodies, Josh broke the kiss. "Then I can suck you off?" he asked, and Michael's eyes went wide.

"Yes. If you want . . . Yes."

Josh smiled at Michael's heartfelt response. He was so sincere, so concerned with what Josh wanted, even though Josh had already finished. "Yeah. I want."

Pleasantly sore and still buzzing, Michael staggered to the dresser he'd filled haphazardly when he moved his belongings from the main house to the barn. He'd never been much of a pack rat, but he'd squirreled away a few shirts that might fit Josh. Once upon a time, Michael had actually been in pretty good shape, with decently broad shoulders.

"Nice view," Josh said from where he was still sprawled on the bed, his voice a soft, sated purr.

Michael's answering smile was more than a little goofy, but Josh deserved it. Most of Michael's DC experiences had been blowjobs up against a wall or on a bathroom counter. He'd become something of an expert, and Josh had blown away all of Michael's hookups.

Blown away, Michael thought, snickering, as he started digging through a drawer full of soft, well-worn T-shirts.

"What's so funny?" Josh asked.

"Nothing. I'm—" Michael stopped, realizing at that moment what was missing. He dropped the shirts and turned back.

Josh's smile melted into a worried frown when he met Michael's eyes. He sat up so fast he kicked a pillow into the nightstand, almost toppling the lamp, sending shadows dancing across the wall. "What is it? What's wrong?"

"Nothing," Michael repeated. He abandoned the dresser and went back to the bed, staring at Josh in wonder. They'd known each other for only a few weeks. Before tonight, they'd never done anything more intimate than kissing.

And now, he couldn't imagine *not* having Josh at his side.

Josh moved closer, and they met in the middle of the bed, where Michael wrapped a hand around Josh's nape to pull him into a kiss. Josh sighed, shoulders relaxing, and returned the kiss enthusiastically.

When Michael backed off, Josh asked, "Does that mean everything's okay?"

"More than okay." Michael looked into Josh's eyes and cupped his cheek, and a twinge of nervousness silenced him. What if Josh was still treating this relationship as casual? What if this was just postsex euphoria and not real?

Bemused, Josh tipped his head and dropped a quick, playful kiss on the tip of Michael's nose. "Good. You, uh, forgot the shirt, though."

Michael nodded, thinking Josh was beautiful as he was, naked on the bed they'd be sharing tonight, but Michael had picked up on how self-conscious Josh was about his body. "Just for a minute. I, uh, have something important to tell you."

"Is this something important we should've discussed before, or—"

"No." Michael shook his head. "No, nothing like that. I'm healthy. I had about a million blood tests in DC, the last ones right before I left. Besides, we took precautions."

Josh gave a wry smile. "Sorry. I trust you," he said, staring down at himself. "Too many safe-sex lectures from my interfering relatives who want to see me safely monogamous and married. Oy." He rolled his eyes.

Michael couldn't help but laugh, despite how his heart skipped at Josh's words. *Someday, maybe?*

"Well, uh . . . would they settle for hearing that I think I love you?" he asked, taking Josh's hand.

"Probably, but not for very—" Josh stopped. Looked up at Michael. "You what?"

Shit! Michael tried for a casual smile and said, "I don't— You shouldn't—"

"Me?" Josh slowly smiled. "You do?"

Michael swallowed, trying not to read too much into Josh's expression. Trapped by his own admission, he could only nod. "Yeah."

"God . . ." Still smiling, Josh freed his hands to touch Michael's face. "Me too."

Yes!

Josh blinked, then shook his head. "I mean—you. When I said, 'me too,' I meant you, not me." He was blushing now, avoiding Michael's eyes until he looked up again and said, softly, "I love you."

They sat there, staring at each other with what Michael was sure were equally ridiculous smiles. Someone had to say something, but Michael was just too happy for words. He couldn't remember the last time he'd been this happy. Two years ago—six months ago—he would've bet his trust fund that he'd never be this happy. And he owed it all to Josh.

"Hey," Josh finally said, giving Michael a nudge.

Michael shook his head. "Yeah?"

"Get me a shirt, babe."

Michael laughed and kissed Josh's cheek, then got up. The loft rocked and swam around him, but his legs were braced against the mattress. He closed his eyes, riding out the momentary dizziness, until he felt Josh touch his arm. The touch was grounding, steadying, helping the world settle into place once more.

"You okay?" Josh asked.

"Yeah." Michael nodded, quietly amazed at how wonderful this man was. And how lucky he himself was to have found him. "I'm just fine."

The window was glowing with bright morning light when Michael woke to Kaylee's cold, wet nose prodding at his face—behavior he'd trained so she could prevent him from rotting away in bed during a bad bout of depression a few months back, unnecessary as it was now. He rolled over and changed that thought to *especially now*, because there was Josh, sprawled facedown beside him, softly snoring.

I love you, Michael thought, though he didn't say it. He wanted to give Josh a kiss, but he didn't want to wake him up. Instead, he kissed his own fingertip and touched it lightly to Josh's cheek, then turned the other way to deal with Kaylee.

Her good-morning lick was insistent, and Michael picked up his phone to check the time as he slid out from under the quilt.

Eight thirty? Wow. Then again, he probably shouldn't be surprised. He and Josh had done their best to exhaust each other last night.

He bent down to get the sweats he'd intended on wearing to sleep, until he got a better idea of Josh's stamina. Grinning at the memory, he stood, waiting for his balance to stabilize before he quietly dressed and headed downstairs to the bathroom.

The front door was new, so he didn't have to worry about squeaky hinges when he opened it to let Kaylee out. While she did her business, he left the door cracked and went to get the empty pizza box from the kitchen. The leftover two and a half slices were wrapped in the fridge. He was tempted to grab the half slice for breakfast, but that would ruin Josh's plans for brunch.

Instead, he gathered up the kitchen and bathroom trash and headed out, enjoying the feel of the grass under his bare feet. The sun was warm, the ocean breeze was cool, the water was a glorious steel blue, and everything about the world was perfect this morning.

When he tossed the trash into the garbage can in the garage, Kaylee bounded over to investigate. He ruffled her fur, asking, "What do you think? Want to keep Josh?"

Her tail wagged so hard, her whole body vibrated. She bounced, dropping her chest to the ground, butt in the air. Feeling better than he had in weeks, he leaned down to boop her nose with one finger, saying, "Tag!"

She took off running, and he gave chase, slipping and skidding on the dew that hadn't yet burned off. They ran back and forth across the yard, all the way to the rocky beach, stopping only at the sound of applause.

Michael turned and saw Josh standing in the doorway, wearing jeans and Michael's old service squadron T-shirt, and his heart leaped. "Come on, Kaylee!" he called, jogging back to the barn, where he pulled Josh into an exuberant embrace.

Laughing, Josh hugged him back and kissed him, tasting of toothpaste. "Morning, sunshine," he said dryly, though he was still grinning. "You have way too much energy without coffee."

Michael couldn't resist ruffling his hands through Josh's bedhead curls. "I blame waking up next to you."

"Oh my God. *Sentiment* before coffee?" Josh gave him a playful shove, then headed back inside.

Michael followed, beckoning for Kaylee. "Hint taken," he said, catching Josh's hand so they could walk to the kitchen together. "I'll make the coffee. Is it too early for brunch?"

"It's too early for anything, but . . ." Josh stopped abruptly and turned, wrapping his arms around Michael's waist. "I slept really, *really* well last night. So we'll overlook the not-sleeping-in part."

"Me too." Michael hugged Josh against his chest and closed his eyes. "No nightmares at all. I blame you."

Josh kissed Michael's cheek. "I'll take that blame."

"I really don't mind helping with dishes," Josh said, slouching comfortably back in his chair. He had a great view into the kitchen, where Michael was standing at the sink. His sweats were loose, hanging deliciously low on his hips, and his T-shirt was short enough to reveal a strip of skin every time he moved. *Damn*, Josh had gotten lucky.

"You're a guest," Michael said for the third or fourth time. "Besides, you cooked breakfast."

"Early brunch," Josh corrected, taking the phone out of his jeans pocket. He needed to do something with his hands, or he'd insist on drying the dishes and putting them away. "*Breakfast* is what you do when you have to be awake before noon. *Brunch* is what civilized people do on days off."

"Aren't I dropping you off at work later today?"

Josh snorted. "Half days off," he said, raising his eyebrows when he saw that he had social media notifications. Bagel End and Hartsbridge weren't exactly topics of interest to the public at large, but apparently the library had found someone who was media savvy to publicize the fund-raiser. Interesting.

"You do get *actual* days off, though. Right?" Michael asked hopefully.

"That's the problem with owning your own business," Josh admitted. There were a couple of requests for volunteers and links to donation pages, but someone had taken a surprising number of pictures. He started to scroll through them, absently saying, "Hell, we promoted Dee months before we were able to let her open and close without freaking out. It's like . . . your kid's first day of kindergarten or something."

"I understand. I'm not pushing or anything. Just, you know, planning." Michael turned to get the cooled pans off the stove and smiled. "Anything interesting going on in the world?"

"A recap of the fund-raiser yesterday." Josh laughed. "It's not like Hartsbridge Island is a big news capital. When the diner added their expansion, it was front-page news."

Michael's sigh sounded happy and content. "*That's* why I came back here. For exactly that reason. I got so sick of the bullshit in DC."

Josh nodded, trying to stay casual as he asked, "Because of your father?"

Michael glanced over at him, smile fading. "Yeah." He stacked the pans in the sink, frowning. "It's, uh . . . Both sides of the family have members in politics, and the ones who aren't politicians are lawyers."

Hoping to get that smile back, Josh asked, "Is that better or worse?"

"You know . . . that's a damned good question," Michael admitted, one corner of his mouth quirking up. Close enough.

"What about your sister?" Josh asked, scrolling back through the pictures. Had he spotted Kaylee? Yes! Someone had taken a zoomed close-up of her sitting next to Michael at the table. Cute dog plus Michael's cuter ass. Josh saved that one to his phone.

"Amanda? She's . . ." Michael shook his head as he started scrubbing the frying pan. "She's always had a plan. I mean, she was intimidating, even as a child. She had her whole life mapped out. What she'd study, what sports she'd play, where she'd go to college, all of it."

Josh glanced up in surprise. "That's kind of terrifying."

"You're telling me? I mean, I spent most of my time in boarding school trying to figure out if I was really gay and how not to get my ass kicked for it, and when she was sixteen—*sixteen*!—she sat down with our parents' financial advisor so she could be 'mentally prepared' for when she turned twenty-five and came into her trust fund."

"Okay, correction. Not *kind of* terrifying." Josh gave an exaggerated shudder and looked back down at the phone. "She's going to give me the 'hurt my brother and they'll never find your body' speech if I ever meet her, isn't she?"

"Oh, absolutely not." Michael's snicker sounded just a little bit evil, and Josh eyed him suspiciously. With an innocent smile, Michael said, "She'll pay someone with a bag of unmarked bills and have *them* do it instead."

"Right. Putting body armor on the shopping list." Josh snorted at Michael's laugh and kept swiping through pictures. Something caught his eye, and he swiped back one picture—and stared. Someone had caught a shot of him and Michael kissing by the water fountain. Josh's head was tilted away from the camera, but the shot had perfectly captured Michael's profile. There wasn't an inch of space between their bodies, and they looked . . . they looked *perfect* together, like they were meant to be in each other's arms.

Save. Josh had just gotten himself a new background.

"Josh?"

"Huh?" Josh glanced up from his phone. "Sorry, what?"

"I said, you don't have to worry, for now. She's going on some sort of world tour. It probably has something to do with her charity work."

Trust funds and world tours. Josh exhaled, trying to push away the inadequacy creeping through the back of his mind. Rich tourists and poor townies didn't mix, but Michael wasn't a rich tourist, and while Josh might be a townie, he wasn't *that* poor. He and his dad got by, the business was in the black, and . . . and Michael had said "I love you" first.

"Hey." He locked his phone, then smiled down at the lock screen. There they were, kissing. "Come here."

Michael turned off the water and ripped a paper towel off the roll. Drying his hands, he walked over to the table, asking, "What's up?"

Josh put the phone down, spun it around, and pushed it over to Michael. "Like my new background?"

Michael picked up the phone—and then smiled, his whole face lighting up. "Where— Josh, where did you get this?" he asked, delighted.

"A few people were taking pictures at the fund-raiser yesterday. Want me to send you a copy?"

"Yes." Michael's eyes lit up, and he sat down, handing the phone back to Josh. "Hey, send one to my sister too."

Josh held up a hand. "Only if you can guarantee my safety."

"I thought you're a crack shot with a bagel."

"For an amateur. If your sister's going to hire a hit man, I'm hiding behind Kaylee." He unlocked the phone and opened a new email, then attached the photo. "Here. Put in your email addresses," he said, sliding the phone back across the table.

Michael picked up the phone and started typing. "We've still got a couple of hours until I have to take you to work."

Josh grinned. "If you suggest anything that doesn't involve going back to bed with you, the answer's no."

Laughing, Michael said, "I was thinking bed first, then shower? It's big enough for both of us."

An invitation to play with Michael, with both of them naked except for soap bubbles and steam? *Oh my God, yes.* Josh had died and gone to heaven.

He had to catch his breath before he could nod and say, "I *guess* that's all right. This time. But next time, I expect more."

TWENTY-FOUR

B agel End had closed for the day, but the lights in the front of the store were still on, making the raindrops on the front window sparkle. Holding the umbrella angled against the wind, Michael gestured for Kaylee to sit as he tapped on the door, grinning when Josh came into view. Josh jogged across the store and unlocked the door, saying, "Sorry. I was just on the phone. Two minutes?"

"Take your time." Michael brought Kaylee in as far as the welcome mat, but the floor looked freshly mopped.

Josh made it halfway back to the counter pass-through before he glanced over his shoulder. "You can come in."

"I forgot Kaylee's boots," Michael admitted sheepishly. "Her paws are soaked. *Somebody's* getting a bath tonight, if you don't mind waiting."

Josh disappeared into the kitchen. "Actually, I have news," he shouted back.

"And bagels?" Michael called, because he knew Josh by now.

Josh's laugh rang through the shop. He returned a few seconds later, flipping off the kitchen light. He had his backpack over one shoulder and—as Michael expected—a bag of bagels in his hand. "And bagels, including a fresh batch of dog bagels I made after lunch today, so I hope your girl's hungry."

"I think she can manage some taste testing," Michael said, scratching at Kaylee's ears. "What's the news?"

"Let's get in the car," Josh said, using his keys to point to the SUV parked outside. "My feet are killing me." He activated the alarm system, then pushed open the door.

"Want a foot massage when we get home?" Michael offered, leading the way with the umbrella.

"Oh my God, yes. You're the most wonderful person ever." Josh locked up, then jogged around the SUV before Michael could offer to walk him there. A few seconds of rain wouldn't kill him, and Michael had left the SUV unlocked—something he could do here on Hartsbridge Island without worrying about theft.

Michael got Kaylee into the back, then climbed into the driver's seat and shook off the umbrella. Already, the interior of the SUV smelled like fresh bagels. "Are we stopping anywhere? We still have groceries from yesterday, but do you need to pick up anything for your dad?"

"That's the news," Josh said, slouching in his seat as much as the seat belt would allow. "Dad's staying in Brooklyn an extra week."

Michael started the engine, glancing over at Josh. The Goldberg family tree was more like a convoluted thicket, with too many repeated names and crosses with other families for Michael to follow, but he knew at least some of those relatives were getting on in years. "Is everything okay?"

"Great Uncle Hal isn't doing well. Dad wants to be close for Aunt Mitzi, just in case."

"Do you need to go down there?" Michael asked, thinking of last-minute train tickets and flights. He'd even drive down there with Josh, and to hell with New York traffic. He pulled out into the street and started driving, heading for the barn out of instinct.

"No, it's okay. The family knows I've got the shop to run."

The shop. Michael bit back a sigh, foreseeing a lot of early mornings and late nights and *not* a lot of Josh in his future. "If you change your mind, tell me, okay? I can even drive you down."

Josh glanced over as if surprised. "You'd—" He shook his head and smiled, reaching over to rub his hand up and down Michael's arm. His fingers were warm and gentle. "No, babe. You have doctors' appointments, remember?"

"I took care of my physical today, the support group meets every week, and the physical therapist has no openings until next month." The stoplight was red, so Michael took advantage of the moment to lean over and kiss Josh. "So I'm all yours."

"Mmm, I hope it didn't take a doctor for you to figure that out," Josh teased. "But really, it's okay. And there's some good news that's come out of this."

"What's that?" Michael sat back before he could get distracted. Josh's kisses were addictive.

"Dad and I gave Dee a raise, and she's officially on opening shift five days a week from now on," Josh declared as the light went green.

Michael grinned and risked pissing off any nearby cars by leaning over for another quick kiss. "Brunch, every day."

"Every day," Josh promised, nudging Michael back to his own side of the SUV. As Michael got it moving again, Josh said, "And when Dad gets back, we're going to look into hiring or promoting another assistant manager, so we can have *actual vacations*."

"Vacations . . ." Michael nodded, trying—and failing—to picture Josh in a swimsuit on a beach. He was more the hike-in-the-woods type. "Where do you want to go first? We could take a weekend, go up to the mountains . . ."

"I, uh, have to go to Florida. We have about ten Goldbergs down in the Fort Lauderdale area. Places like Margate and Coral Springs?"

Michael shook his head. "I've only ever been to Disney World and Eglin Air Force Base."

"Well, do you . . . want to go to Florida one day?" Josh asked nervously. "Meet a whole pack of random Goldbergs and in-laws?"

Family. Michael couldn't offer it to Josh, but that didn't stop Josh from wanting to share his own, without even a hint of hesitation. As if he had absolute faith they'd all accept his gay boyfriend—that they'd welcome Michael with open arms.

Growing up the way he had, he'd never wanted family, until now. He reached out for Josh's hand and gave it a squeeze. "Yeah. I'd love to."

Josh faked throwing the tennis ball, but Kaylee was too smart for that. He settled for arcing it high over her head to bounce against the front door at the far side of the barn, and she took after it like a shot. "Your dog's too smart," he complained to Michael.

"Yeah, she is," Michael said absently. "Uh, is stir fry supposed to look like this?"

That sounded ominous. Josh took the ball from Kaylee, who was panting and staring at it maniacally. Figuring she was more dangerous than Michael, Josh threw the ball for her, then climbed to his feet, rubbing at his ass. The floor was some sort of fancy, aged wood in desperate need of cushioning.

"Should I not have let you cook?" he asked, sniffing experimentally. Soy sauce, garlic, a hint of spice . . . At least nothing was on fire. Yet.

Michael beckoned Josh over without turning away from the frying pan. "Maybe the wok wasn't optional?"

"A pan's a pan, right?" Josh ducked under Michael's arm to cuddle close, only then looking down into the frying pan. The stir fry was a uniform brown and looked . . . soggy. "Okay, maybe not."

Sighing, Michael put down the spatula and turned off the burner. "Plan B?"

"Which is what?"

Michael's answer was interrupted by an unfamiliar ringtone. "Good question," he muttered, heading for the phone. "See what's in the fridge?"

Josh went to check, even though he knew exactly what was in there, since he'd gone through it just this morning: eggs, milk, cheese, bacon, a drawer of thawed meat, and the remainder of the vegetables that hadn't gone to their soggy demise in the stir fry. The bread box—an *actual* bread box, something Josh had never seen outside antique stores before—held half a loaf of challah bread Josh had made yesterday at the shop, perfect for French toast.

That meant they were having breakfast for dinner, bagels, or takeout. He had the diner's number in his phone. Burgers didn't sound like a bad idea. They could even eat there, so the fries would be fresh, though that would mean enduring Betty's teasing.

A *thump* made him turn, surprised. Michael was staring down at the table where he'd dropped his phone, dragging in deep breaths. Kaylee abandoned the tennis ball she was systematically shredding and rushed over to him.

"Michael?" Josh followed, heart lurching as Michael took a step back and slid down the wall to the floor, right next to the kitchen chairs.

Michael didn't respond. Kaylee dropped right on top of his lap, ears perked sharply up. Her tail wasn't wagging. Michael moved his hands to rest on her back, but he wasn't petting her. He closed his eyes, resting his head against the wall, and went perfectly still except for fast, deep breaths.

Shit. Josh's stomach turned, and he slowly lowered himself to a crouch, though he didn't dare get too close. What was he supposed to do? They'd discussed Michael's speech problems and his need to escape tense situations, but Josh couldn't remember *this*.

"Michael?" he asked quietly, clasping his hands together to keep from reaching out.

Did Michael shake his head, just a little bit, or was it Josh's imagination? He had no idea, but he took the silence as an answer. And he'd learned to trust Kaylee. She was smart and well trained to provide whatever support Michael needed. Josh shouldn't interfere.

So even though it broke his heart, he turned away to deal with the disaster congealing in the frying pan. He scraped everything into the garbage disposal but didn't run it just yet. The pan went into the other half of the sink.

He tried not to look at Michael and gauge what was going on inside him, focusing instead on what Michael would need after . . . after he came back to himself. He remembered Bubbe's answer to every problem was chicken soup and tea, but they were out of both. French toast was top-notch comfort food, but it didn't reheat well at all. Quietly, he went to the pantry and looked through the cans and boxes. Mac and cheese, baked beans, condensed soup—no.

Time to improvise.

He took out dried spices, cheese, a jar of spaghetti sauce, and the bagels he'd brought home out of habit. The bag of dog bagels went on the end of the counter, so he'd remember to lavishly reward Kaylee for being so good to Michael. The bagels themselves, he sliced and arranged on a baking tray. He topped each one with a generous spoonful of pasta sauce and some strategic shakes of garlic and oregano, then took out the cheese grater. He should've been lazy when they'd gone shopping and insisted on buying pregrated cheese, but live and learn.

Once the bagel pizzas were assembled, he covered them loosely with plastic. They'd cook quickly under the broiler, once Michael was ready to face the world again. After remembering to turn off the water in the sink, Josh crept past Michael and Kaylee, picked up his phone, and went to the couch. When he sat down, he couldn't see Michael, which meant he wouldn't be tempted to watch for any sign that the episode was coming to an end.

Shit.

Michael opened his eyes and stared down at Kaylee, focusing on her comforting weight instead of the phone call. Fucking Wilkins. He'd called from an unfamiliar number, so Michael had been entirely unprepared for his voice—and his news.

"I'm sure it's photoshopped or a case of mistaken identity, but the Hartsbridge Gazette*'s website has a picture of you supposedly kissing someone. A man. Can you believe the nerve?"*

Hearing Wilkins's derisive laugh was like biting on tinfoil. Michael could barely remember what came after that—something about confirming the picture was faked, a lawsuit that would shut down the local paper . . . He had no idea if he'd even answered or if he'd just hung up.

At least he *did* know that he'd hung up, because it was programmed into him. *Always* confirm that he hung up the phone, turned off the webcam, closed the blinds.

He let out a breath and swallowed, then licked dry lips. His feet were tingling, so he lifted a shaky hand and signaled Kaylee to move off him. She stood and backed away, and the first rush of blood *hurt*, all the way to his toes.

Only then did he look around, wondering what had happened to Josh. Had he left, thinking Michael needed to be alone, or was this too weird for him? Love only went so far, after all. Besides, Josh deserved someone who didn't black out because of a damned phone call.

"Josh?" It came out a weak, dry croak.

"Hey. Yeah," Josh said from the living room, followed by the scrape of furniture being shoved out of the way. He ran into sight, skidding to a halt in his socks, and crouched by Michael's feet. Kaylee, angel that she was, didn't try to block Josh. "Do you need anything?"

Michael wanted to answer, but he knew his words would come out all scrambled. Instead, he held out his hand.

When Josh took it and inched closer, he nearly broke down in tears. A gentle tug was all it took to get Josh on the floor right next to him, close enough that he could turn into Josh's arms and bury his face against Josh's shoulder.

And Josh was as much an angel as Kaylee was. He didn't say anything, didn't ask questions or demand an explanation. He sat there and rubbed Michael's back and held him, offering his silent support and demanding nothing in return.

That helped Michael find the courage to try to say, "I'm okay."

Josh kissed the top of his head. "I made pizza bagels. All I have to do is throw them under the broiler, anytime you're hungry. They'll be ready as soon as the cheese melts."

Michael nodded, checking in with his body. Pins and needles in his feet, aching butt and spine from sitting on the floor, headache that would become a migraine if he didn't do something to stop it.

Water. Food. Maybe a hot shower, then bed. He wanted to explain that to Josh, but all that came out was, "Yeah. I'm, um . . ." *Hungry*, he thought, feeling the empty ache in his gut. "Um. Stomach."

"Okay." Josh gave him a quick squeeze. "Can I get up to turn on the oven?"

Michael sighed, relieved. He could handle questions that only needed a yes or no. He nodded again, shivering when Josh let go of him to go deal with cooking. A twitch of fingers signaled Kaylee to Michael's side, so he could hug her close, but she was a poor substitute for Josh.

For a few seconds—maybe a few minutes—Michael listened to Josh moving around the kitchen. Then things got quiet, until Kaylee lifted her head at the hiss of fabric. Curious, Michael looked up and saw Josh coming back into the kitchen, holding the quilt that had been tossed onto one of the armchairs up front.

"Here. It's cold on the floor," Josh said, crouching to pile the quilt on Michael's legs. "You need more carpets around here."

It was such an innocuous thing to say—such a *Josh* thing— Michael let out a quick little laugh. "Thanks." Keeping Kaylee close, he tugged at the quilt with one hand, and Josh helped to spread it over Michael's feet.

"Think you can make it to a chair?" Josh asked. "You'll be more comfortable."

Michael shook his head. He wasn't ready to walk—not by a long shot—and he didn't want Josh struggling to help him to his feet.

"Okay. I'm going to get plates and stuff. Want a glass of water?"

"Yes." Better a verbal answer than a nod.

"Two minutes," Josh said, going back into the kitchen.

Michael closed his eyes and leaned against the wall again, concentrating on each part of his body, from his toes up to his head. It was a relaxation exercise that didn't actually relax him but helped him focus on the here and now.

Josh came back with two glasses of water, which he set on the floor. Then he went back for a plate with four pizza bagels precariously balanced on it, hanging off the edges. He sat down, setting the plate on the quilt, and said, "I was going to make Kaylee dinner, but I didn't know what she gets tonight."

Michael couldn't hide his groan. He had zero energy to put together Kaylee's meal, but she was his responsibility. His therapist had said caring for her would help to keep him focused, help him adjust to civilian life, but his therapist was a pain in the ass.

"Hey. I'll take care of it," Josh said, nudging Michael's legs. "Eat your bagel."

Michael huffed a laugh and picked up one of the bagels. "Bet you sound like Bubbe."

Either he said it right or he got close, because Josh laughed. "Yeah, but she would've said it half in Yiddish. And don't feel bad telling me if it tastes like shit. I can always make French toast or run to the diner to pick up burgers or something."

"It's fine, I'm sure." Michael had no idea how long he'd been out, but it had to have been at least an hour, judging by how loudly his stomach was growling. He took a bite, only then remembering how dry his mouth was, and he had to work to swallow. At least his hand wasn't shaking too badly to pick up the glass of water. He drank without ending up wearing it, and he was able to finish off the rest of the pizza bagel in a few quick bites.

"I made plenty, so eat all you want," Josh said, gesturing back to the kitchen. "I figured there was no need to save them, because tomorrow morning, we're having French toast."

Tomorrow morning. Josh still wanted to stay tonight, despite . . . *this*. Even without the aphasia, Michael didn't have the words to express everything he was feeling. But there was *something* he could say, so he caught Josh's hand before he could pick up another bagel and said, "Love you."

Josh smiled, squeezing Michael's hand. "I love you too, babe."

TWENTY-FIVE

What happened last night?

All through the night, Josh had hoped Michael would open up to him, but Michael had stayed silent, and Josh hadn't pushed. Last night wasn't like what had happened at the diner on their first date. Michael had stayed, even if he'd shut down for a while. He'd stayed, and they'd eaten dinner, and they'd showered and gone to bed together. And even if Josh hadn't understood more than half the words Michael had used, they'd been *together*. Not once had Josh felt abandoned or unwanted—if anything, it was the opposite.

So Josh kept his mouth shut, talking only about the most innocent, immediate concerns, and he fell asleep with Michael curled up at his side. And best of all, Michael was still there the following morning, when Josh rolled over and opened his eyes.

"Morning," Michael said with a faint, almost undetectable smile.

"Hey." Josh leaned over for a quick kiss, morning breath and all. "How'd you sleep?"

Michael sighed. "I crashed hard." The blanket rustled, and Michael's hand crept over Josh's hip. "Sorry about last night."

"Don't be." Josh shook his head, inching closer. The bed was warm and soft and cozy, and he didn't want things to get awkward and uncomfortable. "Kaylee knew what to do, and you came back to me. That's all that matters."

Michael's short laugh had an edge of desperation to it. "How are you so understanding?"

Josh shrugged, trying to ignore the butterflies in his stomach at the raw, unguarded love in Michael's voice. "You explained enough after that first time. I figured you'll tell me the rest whenever you're ready." He regretted the words as soon as they were out. He didn't want Michael thinking he was being pressured. "I don't mean—"

"Last night—" Michael raised his eyebrows, looking calmly at Josh, who nodded. Michael took a deep breath and said, "The call was from my father's chief of staff. The picture. The one on your phone."

"Oh shit," Josh said, putting two and two together. A family-values governor, a gay son who wasn't out, and the picture of that kiss on social media . . . Talk about a recipe for disaster.

Michael winced. "Yeah. He wanted, um . . . conversation that it was, um . . . computer-made. *Faked*."

Conversation? Josh shook his head, saying, "But since it wasn't, are you in trouble?"

Michael's eyes narrowed, and his hand tightened on Josh's hip. "I don't care," he said, the words loud and distinct and crystal clear. "I want *you*."

Josh's whole world lit up at that, and he squirmed to get an arm under Michael's pillow for a proper full-body hug. "God, I love you," he whispered.

Michael took a deep breath and said, slowly and carefully, "I won't let *anyone* come between us."

"Neither will I," Josh promised. "And I don't care who tries."

"Did I really let Kaylee eat pizza bagels for dinner last night?" Michael asked guiltily over the sizzle of bacon, noting the too-alert way that Kaylee was staring into the kitchen. She only did that when she felt she deserved a better meal—one that involved actual meat.

"Yeah. You said she'd be fine for one night." Josh started whisking a bowl of eggs, milk, and whatever else he put into the batter for French toast. "Should I have fed her something?"

"No, she's fine. Dogs ate people-food long before anyone ever invented kibble." Michael flipped the switch on the coffeepot and went to the fridge. "I'll take care of her breakfast. Raw ground beef won't bother you, will it?"

Josh smiled. "As long as it's for Kaylee, not me, we're all good."

Sharing the kitchen with Josh was cozy, but not because the kitchen was small. No, it felt pleasantly *domestic*—something Michael would never get sick of feeling. Despite the close confines, they got three breakfasts prepared by the time the pot of coffee was finished brewing.

"What do you say we go over the business plan today?" Michael asked once they were all sitting down—or lying down, in Kaylee's case—for breakfast.

Josh nodded, sipping at his coffee. "Okay. But you really should teach me what Kaylee eats, just in case. I mean, what if I want to surprise you both with breakfast in bed?"

Laughing, Michael nudged Josh's foot under the table. "Then I'll know the zombie apocalypse has started, because you'll be awake without having to open the shop."

Josh kicked playfully back. "Brunch, then. I can do brunch in bed."

That was damned tempting, but Michael wanted to get the business plan finalized and out into the world already. He could help Josh realize his dream. What better way was there for Michael to show how much he loved Josh?

"We'll go over it while we eat," Michael suggested, getting up from the table.

"No, you—"

Michael was already heading for where his messenger bag hung by the front door. "Two seconds," he called back as he took out his eyeglass case. Since that first night Michael brought Josh home, personal boundaries had blurred. Michael felt no guilt at going through Josh's backpack to get the laptop.

"It's done," Josh said when Michael came back to the table, laptop and glasses in hand. "Lizzie's already got it for a final check. I emailed it to her . . . yesterday? Two days ago?" He shrugged and shoved a forkful of French toast into his mouth.

"You should do a complete check, too. Weren't you going to show it to your dad?" Michael opened the laptop and hit the power button. While it booted, he used his fork to point at Josh, adding, "And remind me to talk to you about computer security."

Josh frowned. "Wha' abou' ih?" he mumbled, still chewing. It should've been offensive to someone who'd been raised with perfect table manners, but Michael found it endearing.

Hiding a grin, Michael asked, "You lock your phone, right?" Josh nodded, curls bouncing on his forehead. "So, you should lock your computer too."

Josh swallowed and shrugged. "Nobody ever gets near it, except in the office. Besides, it's . . . I don't know, ten years old or something. Nobody would *want* to steal it."

"Probably closer to four or five years, but still." Michael kicked at Josh's shin, socks skidding over sweats. "You have business data on it."

"Okay— *Ah*," Josh interrupted when Michael reached for the touchpad. "You eat. I'll open the file. You haven't touched your food. Do you want me to think you hate my cooking?"

Michael rolled his eyes and obediently poked at his food with his fork. "Like there's a chance in hell of that."

Over the click of keys, Josh said, "Jews don't believe in hell. Just unappreciated cooking."

When in Rome . . . Michael took a big bite of French toast and mumbled, "I luff youh 'ooging."

Josh beamed at him, apparently understanding. "The secret is the challah bread." He snorted and went back to tapping the touchpad. "Texas toast, my ass. Fresh challah. It's all in the egg you put in the dough." He spun the laptop to face Michael, then turned his attention back to his plate.

Michael could only push bad manners so far. He swallowed before asking, "Aren't you going to read it?"

Josh's answer—"We can skim it together."—sounded casual, but he'd gone tense, eyes a bit too wide.

What am I missing? Trying not to frown, Michael said, "I've read it already, about a hundred times. I won't catch nearly as many mistakes as you will. Fresh eyes and all."

Instead of answering, Josh lowered his fork and looked down. "Michael . . ."

"What is it?" Michael asked gently. Had he pushed the business plan too hard? Josh hadn't wanted to look it over. Maybe he'd changed his mind about expanding Bagel End at all.

Josh's inhale sounded hesitant. Hitched. He glanced up just long enough to meet Michael's eyes, then turned to stare in the direction of the laptop. "I, uh . . ." He shook his head. "I have . . . trouble reading."

"Huh?" Michael blurted before snapping his mouth shut. Josh wasn't illiterate. Michael had seen him scribble orders at Bagel End—and he'd read orders other employees had written. He'd chalked daily specials onto the sandwich board outside. He read menus—

No, he didn't. At the riverside grill in Portsmouth, Josh had let Michael order. Everywhere else they went, he knew what he wanted to order before they'd even walked in the doors. Michael had never seen him with a book, a magazine, a newspaper . . . Even his phone was used for games. And while he did text, he was slow. Hell, he probably depended heavily on autocorrect, just like Michael did.

Josh's face had gone red, and he looked like he was trying to master the secret of invisibility. Michael reached across the table to touch his hand. "And I can't write. Not really."

Josh looked up, startled. This time, he was the one who asked, "Huh? But you wrote . . ." He gestured at the laptop.

Michael shook his head. "I copied templates. Aphasia, remember? The words are up here"—he tapped the side of his head—"but they don't always get out the right way, in speaking *or* writing."

For a couple of precious seconds, Michael thought he'd eased Josh's fears. But then Josh slumped, face going pinched. "Yeah, but you made it into a great college. I didn't even graduate high school."

"And you have a thriving business that you're looking at expanding." Michael got his fingers around Josh's hand and squeezed. "I'm living in my parents' barn."

Josh coughed out a laugh and gave Michael a flat glare, though the curve of his lips hinted at a smile. "Your parents' remodeled luxury vacation loft that happens to be in a historical barn, you mean."

"Still." Michael wanted to see more of that smile, so he smiled encouragingly and said, "Moo."

It worked, thank God. Josh burst out laughing, mouth open wide. "You're crazy, you know that?" he gasped out, rubbing his free hand across his eyes.

"Well, yeah," Michael said smugly, basking in Josh's restored humor. "But I guess you're the same kind of crazy, since you spent, what, an hour with me while I had a brain-reboot on the floor last night."

Josh caught his breath slowly, and though his smile faded a couple of notches, it was still there for Michael to enjoy. "Because you explained it to me, sort of. Plus"—he leaned over to look at Kaylee, who'd cleaned her food dish to a shiny polish and was now sprawled out beside Michael's chair—"I figured I'd follow her lead. But reading . . . That's something *everyone* can do."

"Not everyone," Michael said, hoping to cut this off before Josh could get too upset about it. "I had a few guys in Basic who had to take reading classes just so they could pass the ASVAB."

"The what?"

"Sorry. It's the military entrance test. It tells you what your MO—" *Stop with the acronyms, Baldwin.* Sheepishly, Michael said, "What your occupational specialty should be."

Josh shook his head. "Classes won't help. I just . . . *can't* read. I was in remedial classes, I had tutors, all that. It just never . . . clicked."

Michael had heard the horror stories of illiterate students getting pushed through crowded inner-city schools, but he couldn't imagine that happening here, in Hartsbridge. "You can read texts, though, right? And—"

With a frustrated exhale, Josh pulled his hand free and grabbed his coffee cup. "Look, it's not—" He shoved his chair back and went for the coffeepot, saying nothing until he'd poured himself a refill. "I *can* read, sort of. It just . . . It takes forever. Texts are fine. I mean, they're usually short and easy to figure out, but a whole wall of text . . ."

Months in the hospital and outpatient treatment had taught Michael not to pry into someone else's disabilities. But this was a conversation, not an interrogation, and Josh hadn't shut it down. Not yet, anyway.

"Is it dyslexia?" Michael asked gently, careful to keep even a hint of judgment out of his tone.

To his surprise, Josh shrugged. "Don't know. A couple of teachers said something about testing, but . . . it wasn't a good time for it. I had enough fucking doctors in my life, with my mom. And then there just wasn't a point. I didn't need reading to show me how to make Goldberg-style bagels. I'd been doing that since I could stand on a step stool and reach the prep counter." He sat back down, then stood up again, saying, "Shit. Did you want a refill?"

"Boyfriend, not waiter, remember?" Michael waved Josh back into his seat. "Last week, when I went up to the VA in Manchester, half of why I was such a damn wreck was because of the paperwork. It got to a point where the words didn't make sense, only I couldn't even get my own words out to ask for help."

Josh pushed his mug out of the way so he could take Michael's hand in both of his own. "Is it dyslexia for you? I mean, along with the aphasia?"

Michael shrugged. "I don't think so, but I don't know a damn thing about dyslexia. At first, maybe? *Nothing* made sense for . . . for forever after I got out of the coma. I talked in nonsense, I couldn't read an eye-test chart, nothing. It came back, but slowly, and it might not ever come back all the way."

With a wry smile, Josh said, "Too bad there aren't . . . What would they be called? Reading-eye dogs?"

Michael laughed and nudged at Kaylee, who rolled onto her side, demanding belly rubs. He obliged with his toes, since he didn't want to let go of Josh's hands. "Yeah, but the library might be able to help."

Josh blinked. "The library?"

"Remember their—" Michael winced. "You probably didn't see their wish list, huh? They had a whole write-up of what they wanted to do if they reached each donation milestone. One of the things on the list was an adult literacy program."

"No." Josh shook his head and tried to pull free, but Michael held on more tightly. "I *know* these people—"

"Not like a class," Michael said reassuringly. "One-on-one lessons. Private and confidential."

"But . . . Michael, look," he said slowly. "I've never told anyone. I mean, my dad knows I had trouble in school, but not that it's still a problem."

"He doesn't have to know."

Josh huffed, looking down at his plate. "It's a small town, babe. Give it a week, and *everyone* will know we're sleeping together."

Quietly laughing, Michael said, "I'm pretty sure they've guessed that already. Two straight weeks of us going out to restaurants? The laptop didn't fool anyone."

Josh relaxed, slouching as much as he could without letting go. "Just be glad my dad's still in Brooklyn. He'd be throwing us a pre-engagement party. The whole 'Jews are pessimists' stereotype is a myth for him, at least outside the business. He's the king of wishful thinking when it comes to love."

Michael had to swallow to get rid of the sudden lump in his throat. "Is that something you want? Marriage, I mean?"

Josh's cheeks went red again, and his hands twitched. "Um. Yeah," he said, licking his lips. "I mean, I know there's this whole 'marriage is for breeders' thing—"

"Ugh. Don't," Michael interrupted more sharply than he'd intended. "My sister's het. At least, I think she is."

"No, no. It's not—" Josh blew out a frustrated breath. "*I* don't feel that way. But for years, I thought that being bi meant I only had a fifty-fifty shot at a wedding—a real wedding, with family and a chuppah and a cheesy band playing bad cover songs. And now . . ."

Michael grinned. "A cheesy band playing bad cover songs? Count me in."

Josh's mouth fell open, and he blinked a couple of times. "You . . . Huh?"

Heart pounding, Michael said, "We shouldn't take things *too* fast." But he'd gone the opposite route before, and it hadn't been good for him. Josh was different, about as far from a one-night stand as possible. Michael couldn't resist playfully adding, "Unless you want to be pre-engaged."

Josh pulled a hand free to muffle his laugh. "I dunno," he choked out, eyes sparkling. "Bubbe might come back from the dead if she finds out I'm pre-engaged to a goy."

"Especially a gay one?"

Josh waved his hand dismissively. "Nah, you're cute. She'd just pinch your cheeks and talk you into converting."

Michael had never given any thought to converting—in his family, religion was just another means to grab political power—but for Josh, he'd consider it. Assuming their relationship actually stayed strong, once Josh really got to know him. "How's this: if zombie-Bubbe shows up, I promise I'll be the first one calling an emergency rabbi."

Josh's smile turned sweet. "That's one-eight hundred-*oy vey ist mir.*" He slid his hands free and picked up his fork, using it to point at Michael. "Now eat. And maybe help me get through this business plan?"

"Anything you want, babe," Michael agreed.

CHAPTER

TWENTY-SIX

Pre-engaged. Josh couldn't stop laughing at that. Hell, he was on the verge of singing—a perfectly legitimate shower activity—but he didn't want to scare Michael off, even though Michael wasn't sharing the shower this morning. They'd learned the hard way that a shared shower meant a subsequent hour-long visit to the bed upstairs, followed by another shower and an embarrassed "Sorry I'm late" when Josh stumbled into Bagel End with wet hair and a dopey grin at the tail end of the lunch hour.

But that thought—*pre-engaged!*—was enough to keep Josh company while he rinsed off the soap without an extra pair of hands to help. Michael must have meant it as a joke. If not, then yes, things were moving a little fast, but Josh was absolutely certain that they were moving in the right direction. Michael had opened up about his PTSD, Josh had admitted to his reading problem, and Josh had stripped naked in front of Michael and *hadn't* been mocked for his belly. Even Michael's gentle suggestion about the adult literacy thing had been supportive, not like some exes' hints that Josh get himself a gym membership. In Josh's experience, nothing said "I don't love you as you are" like an unasked-for fitness center guest pass.

He did see exercise in his future, though, and not just the horizontal kind. Michael's suggestion of going up to the mountains sounded wonderful, if aerobically exhausting. The walking trails on the north side of the island were a perfect start and a great way to be alone in a small town. Just Josh, Michael, Kaylee, and Mother Nature.

He got out of the shower and wrapped up in a couple of ridiculously thick, fluffy towels. The vent had done its job, keeping the mirror clean, so he flicked it off—

And froze when, the instant the white noise cut off, he heard an unfamiliar voice shout, "— raise you to be a *faggot*!"

What the *hell*?

Josh hesitated long enough to pull on jeans, only because he was *not* going to get into a brawl in a towel. While he'd never taken a martial arts course in his life, discovering his bisexuality meant he'd gotten into his share of high school scuffles before dropping out. And for Michael, he *wouldn't* hold back.

Josh threw open the bathroom door and rushed out, shaking the wet hair out of his eyes so he could see into the living room, where Michael was in a stand-off with a tall, hard-faced man Josh immediately recognized from TV commercials.

Governor Baldwin.

Even across the barn, Josh could see that Michael was so tense he was practically shaking. And he *wasn't* answering, which was the worst possible sign. Josh's first instinct was to dive back into the bathroom and hide, but the governor's head snapped up, and he looked right at Josh. And the way his face screwed up into a look of utter disgust hit Josh like a truck.

"Oh *God*," the governor said, lip curled back. "You—you brought him *here*?"

He was partially hidden beyond Michael, but the way he went stiff screamed not just loathing but rage. There was no way in hell Josh was going to let this asshole lay a finger on his boyfriend.

"Hey, Michael," Josh drawled, leaving a trail of wet footprints past the table as he stalked forward. "Who's your guest?"

The offhand, almost dismissive question worked its magic. The governor's fury locked on Josh, freeing Michael to gather his wits and regroup—or, better yet, escape.

The governor's sneer almost turned into a growl. "What do *you* want?" he demanded, pointing at him with a rolled-up newspaper that Josh suspected was the *Hartsbridge Gazette*. "Money?"

Oh, fuck you and *your politics, you rich asshole*, Josh thought, taking deep breaths so he wouldn't say it out loud. He stopped right beside Michael and took hold of Michael's hand. His arm was limp, his skin clammy, but Kaylee was in front of him, keeping the governor at bay, and Josh would handle this for however long it took to get this asshole out of their lives.

Maybe the pre-engagement thing was a joke, but it was also a damned good weapon.

"Money's an awfully impersonal wedding gift, don't you think?" Josh asked, channeling Aunt Mitzi in all her witty, biting glory. Every Rosh Hashanah, when she called to wish him a happy new year, she'd regale him with talks of protests she led back in the sixties.

The governor's face went purple. His eyes bulged. "*Wedding!*"

There was nothing sweet at all about Josh's smile. "We haven't registered anywhere yet, so you've got time."

The governor sputtered, but it was Michael's choked cough—one that hopefully hinted at a laugh—that had Josh's attention. When Michael's fingers twitched, Josh could've cheered. *You're not alone, babe,* Josh silently told him with a squeeze of his hand.

Michael squeezed back and gave a jerky nod. He turned his face toward Josh, though he didn't take his eyes off his father. "You want to finish getting ready for work?" he asked in that too-slow way that meant he was checking and double-checking every word.

Everything in Josh screamed not to leave, but this was Michael's decision. Michael's fight.

"Yeah, I probably should." Josh desperately wanted to give Michael a kiss, but he didn't want to make this situation any worse. And—oh God—he'd *already* made it worse. Why the hell had he taken last night's playful pre-engagement and turned it into a *wedding*?

He drew his hand back, but before he could bolt, Michael caught him by the nape and tugged. Even with the governor right there, Josh didn't hesitate, leaning in for a quick kiss.

"*Michael!*" the governor roared, though the only thing it accomplished was Michael pulling Josh back in for another kiss. It was only a few seconds, but for the governor, it probably felt like a lifetime.

Good, Josh thought smugly. After that second kiss, he felt a hell of a lot more confident about leaving Michael alone with his father. But when he went into the bathroom, he left the door cracked open, just in case. If things got ugly again, he wanted to know about it.

It took every ounce of self-control Michael had to keep from calling Josh back, but this wasn't Josh's fight. He'd done enough. He'd done more than enough, snapping Michael out of his panic with a single touch. And the things Josh had said . . . Michael hadn't thought he could love Josh any more than he already did, but Josh kept proving him wrong.

"What the *hell* do you think you're doing? Is this a game?"

Michael blinked and looked at his father, reflexively flinching away from his fury. Twenty-plus years of training had taught him to avoid that anger at all costs—that compliance was better than disobedience, that provoking his father never paid off.

But Michael had never really had something to fight for. Not until these past few weeks, when he'd been living *his* life—the life he wanted as a gay man with a wonderful boyfriend and absolutely no political obligations.

"It's—" He scratched hard at Kaylee's head, concentrating on the fur under his fingertips. He couldn't afford to lose his words. This was too important. "It's not a game. He's my boyfriend."

"And *this*?" His father gave the newspaper a sharp wave that made Michael flinch again and back up a step before he could stop himself. Kaylee—thank God for her training. She turned, keeping her head close to Michael, giving him a good three feet of space.

"Newspaper," Michael said, trying to channel even a tenth of the confidence Josh had shown. "So?"

With a brusque fury that nearly ripped the paper into shreds, his father opened it to the second or third page, then shoved it at Michael—or tried to. *He* flinched when Kaylee's tail, raised in a sharp curve, brushed against his arm, and Michael gave in to the urge to smirk. By law service dogs couldn't be trained as attack dogs, but he'd bet his father didn't know that.

The smirk almost vanished, though, when he saw a grid of black-and-white photos under the headline *Library Fundraiser a Smashing Success!* One of the photos was circled in blood-red ink—a picture of him and Josh sitting at one of the tables, kissing like the rest of the world didn't exist.

So there were *two* pictures of them kissing. Michael had the crazy idea of showing his father the other picture—the one that Josh had emailed to him and Amanda. She'd thought it was sweet and adorable.

"Do you have any *idea* what this is going to do to me?" his father demanded, rattling the paper. "Bad enough you dropped out of college to join the damned Air Force."

Oh, no. His father did *not* get to use that as a weapon. Michael was *proud* of his service. "I was serving my country," he snapped, positive that he got the words out flawlessly. "The first Baldwin to serve, probably since the damn Revolutionary War!"

His father sneered and flung the newspaper aside, sending pages flying into the armchair. "Don't give me that! You threw away your life! And now you're throwing it away again with some . . . money-hungry lowlife—"

"*Don't!*" Michael hissed in a breath through clenched teeth. Kaylee nosed at his thigh, and he gestured for her to stay still. He didn't need grounding from this.

"He's a *nobody*! A damned high school dropout who makes bagels for a living!"

After getting shot, Michael had spent months angry at everything. It had been a searing anger, a low-grade fire in his belly that would flare up like a volcano at the least provocation. Now that anger went cold, sharpening everything into absolute clarity.

"You researched him?" he asked, barely above a whisper.

"I have an election to win," his father answered flatly.

"This has *nothing* to do with you," Michael insisted, even though he knew that wasn't true. Politics meant it was open season on everything the Baldwin family did or said. That was how it had always been—until now.

His father took a breath, ready to launch into a tirade, but Michael shot back first. "It's always been about you, hasn't it? Everything's about you and your damned campaign and your fucking politics!"

"My *fucking politics* have led this state to its strongest economic growth—"

"This is my life! This isn't your campaign!" Michael interrupted, fists clenching.

"Your life? You call this a *life*?" his father scorned. "You threw away everything! You walked out of college and threw away your future, and for what? To play soldier?"

Damn right! Michael thought, agreeing with his father for the only time he could remember. "Yeah. To be a soldier! For the first damn time in my life, I did what *I* wanted with my life."

Lips curled in a sneer, his father said, "Don't give me that. You were barely eighteen! What the hell does a teenager know about life? Hell, what do you think you know about life now?" He made a quick, sharp gesture toward the back of the barn, where Josh had gone. "Eight years of being a soldier, and what's it taught you? The first thing you do is create a gay scandal to wreck my campaign."

His father didn't understand—his father would never understand—but knowing that didn't stop Michael from shouting, "*This isn't about you!*"

"It damn well is!" his father shouted back, stepping forward, right into Kaylee. She braced and stood her ground, ears flicking. "I'm not going to let some money-grubbing Jew fag sabotage—"

"*Josh!*" Michael turned his back on his father, even though the thought of being so defenseless and vulnerable made his skin crawl.

"Don't you—" He heard movement—his father's footsteps, the click of Kaylee's claws—and he knew she was twisting around to keep his father at bay, no matter how he moved.

Josh came out of the bathroom, dressed and ready to go. He hadn't shaved, but Michael guessed he hadn't wanted the hum of the electric razor to interfere with his eavesdropping. "All done?" he asked in a calm, steady tone.

Michael nodded, saying, "Grab the laptop," over his father's shouted demands that Kaylee get the hell out of his way.

Josh stopped at the breakfast table and picked up the laptop. He even remembered Michael's glasses.

Michael turned back to the delightful sight of his father standing there, defeated by a dog that wasn't even fully grown. Keeping Kaylee between them, Michael picked up Josh's backpack, surreptitiously bracing himself against the armchair when the floor tilted and wobbled under his feet. His heart was racing wildly, and his vision was going black around the edges, but he'd walk out of this barn under his own power if it killed him. He was *not* going to let his father win.

"Where do you think you're going?" his father asked in a dangerously low growl, one that would've had Michael shivering in fear just ten years ago.

He couldn't risk answering—not verbally. Instead, he pulled Kaylee's leash and vest off the hooks by the front door, then glanced back at Josh and gestured at the messenger bag. Either Josh caught the hint or he knew that Michael never left the house without it. Josh slung it over his shoulder, tucked the laptop under his arm, and said, "Ready when you are."

Like all politicians, Michael's father had to get the last word: "Don't you dare walk out of here," he said, his tone going sharp and threatening. "If you walk out, you're through with this family!"

After beckoning for Kaylee to follow, Michael pulled open the door and smiled over at Josh. "I have a *real* family now," he said, walking out into the sunlight.

J osh stopped the SUV in the loading zone next to the marina's little dry dock, where a dumpster would hide the huge vehicle from the road. His hands were unsteady and his mouth still tasted sour, but at least he could drive. It had taken Michael too many tries to press the unlock button on the keychain, and after the beep he'd shoved the keys into Josh's hands in a silent request for Josh to drive.

Not that Josh would've let Michael drive in his state. Even now, five minutes after Josh had raced out of the driveway, past the governor's black luxury sedan with its waiting driver, Michael was still a wreck. He'd climbed into the car and called Kaylee onto his lap instead of the backseat. He was holding her to his chest, face buried in her fur, muscles so taut they were trembling.

The sight made Josh want to go back to the house and ram the giant SUV into that asshole's car a few times. A few dozen times. The thought that Michael was *still* miserable because of his asshole father . . .

"Hey." Josh brushed his fingertips over Michael's forearm. "We're safe, Michael. We're alone here."

Michael started to take a deep breath, then coughed and lifted his head, wiping fur off his lips. The cough turned into a faint laugh tinged with desperation. "Thanks," he croaked, looking over at Josh with glassy eyes.

"Want me to go to the store for you?" Josh offered.

Michael frowned. "Huh?"

"We've always got some stale bagels. I can probably get back to your place before that asshole's gone. Bet I can give him a black eye from twenty feet if I use an everything bagel."

Michael snorted and choked instead of laughing at the stupid joke, but it worked anyway. He let go of Kaylee and caught Josh's hand. "My knight in a green apron?"

Relieved that Michael wasn't falling into one of those awful episodes, Josh shrugged and said, "You don't need me to fight your battles. I just distracted him for a couple of minutes. The rest was all you."

"I don't . . ." He shook his head and shifted under Kaylee, or tried to. "Kaylee, get in back. Go on," he told her, reaching between the front seats with his left hand, snapping his fingers. She crawled awkwardly over the center console, tail smacking Josh in the face a couple of times before she made it onto the backseat. Michael wiped at his face, then looked down at the fur on his shirt and jeans. "I don't remember most of whatever happened. Just bits and pieces."

"Good," Josh said honestly, taking hold of Michael's hand again. "You've gone through enough shit already in your life."

Michael nodded, giving Josh's hand a squeeze, and glanced around. Frowning, he asked, "Where are we?"

"The marina just down the road. I kind of figured your father's the type to send his flunky after you to drag you back for another 'talk.'" Josh shrugged. "Nobody will find us here."

"Thanks." Michael gestured at the door, asking, "Can we . . .?"

"Sure. I know the owners. They won't care if we hide out here for a few," Josh said confidently. He turned off the engine and got out in a rush, jogging around to help Michael out. The leash and vest were tangled around his feet, and Michael stared at them in confusion. Josh picked them up, saying, "We left in a hurry. Do you remember that part?"

Michael leaned against the side of the SUV and glanced at Josh's backpack in the footwell. "My messenger bag? Your laptop?"

"I got them. They're in the back," Josh assured him.

"Okay." Sighing, Michael turned to face the water. "I, uh . . . I think I need a hotel."

"You could do that," Josh said slowly, "or you could just stay with me."

Michael glanced at him, wary and defensive. "Josh, you saw what he's like. He won't stop. He'll come after me."

"You mean after *us*," Josh corrected. He shrugged, putting all the confidence he could muster into his voice, and added, "Besides, who cares? The police chief's an old friend. He's been coming to Bagel End for years. He'd get a kick out of arresting the governor for harassment."

Michael's laugh was short and a little mad, but it made Josh smile. "Would he? Really?"

"Hell, yeah." Josh stepped in front of Michael so he could take both of his hands. "He's a townie. We protect our own."

Michael squeezed his hands. "What about your dad?"

Damn. Maybe Michael would've been willing to move in with his boyfriend, but not his boyfriend's dad. Still, Josh had to try. "He knows about you. What he knows, he likes. And there's plenty of room."

"Yeah, but . . ." Michael glanced away. "It's *his* house."

"Just for now," Josh tried, heartbroken at the thought of Michael lying awake in some distant hotel room on the mainland. "You said yourself that you have trouble sleeping even somewhere that's familiar. You didn't sleep at all in that motel a while back, right?"

Michael met his eyes, a faint smile on his lips. "Is this your way of saying I should shut up and let you talk me into it?"

Josh smiled encouragingly. "All the brunch you can eat."

That got a laugh and another shrug. "Okay. But I'm going to be apartment hunting."

"Oh God, no." Josh shuddered exaggeratedly. "Most of the apartments around here are for college kids or they're over the shops downtown. I'm serious about the house. We have plenty of space."

Michael tipped his head back toward the window where Kaylee was panting into the glass, watching them. "What about Kaylee? Your dad—"

"Loves dogs," Josh interrupted. "Please, trust me on this?"

"I *do* trust you, but this is more than just us."

Josh gave in to the impulse to roll his eyes. He let go of Michael's hand so he could take out his phone. The picture of them kissing made him smile in grim triumph. *Eat that, Governor Shithead*, he thought before hitting speed dial one.

"Who—" Michael began, though he went silent when Josh held up a finger.

Dad answered after two rings, saying, "You're early. What's wrong?"

"Relax. Everything's fine," Josh assured him, even though everything *wasn't* fine. His dad was asking about the shop, though, so it wasn't entirely a lie. "Do you mind if Michael and his service dog move in with us for a while?"

"*Josh!*" Michael said in a choked whisper. Josh shushed him.

"Uh, no?" Dad said uncertainly. "This is . . . sudden, isn't it?"

"Yeah, but there were some problems with the whole gay thing and the whole Jewish thing," Josh explained in a deliberately casual tone.

He could hear Dad's sharp inhale, like a snorting bull getting ready to charge. "Oh, *were* there?" he asked ominously. "You want to clear out the guest room or is he sharing with you?"

Josh looked right into Michael's eyes. "He'll stay in my room. We're, uh, pretty serious about things."

"Good! Serious enough that I can tell the relatives?" Dad asked hopefully.

"Let me ask." Josh tipped the phone away from his face and asked Michael, "Can Dad tell the family about us?"

Poor Michael gave a deer-in-the-headlights blink. "Your family?"

Josh nodded. "They'll be thrilled to hear I'm finally settling down after my years-long wild dating spree."

Michael laughed and hooked his fingers in Josh's belt loops to tug him close. "Yeah. He can tell."

"Hear that, Dad?" Josh asked into the phone.

"I heard," Dad said, voice full of happiness. "And, uh, it wouldn't hurt if you brought him to talk to the rabbi."

"Dad . . ." Josh warned, even though he was grinning.

"All right, all right. But don't blame me when everyone starts texting you to ask if you're having a Jewish wedding."

"If Aunt Mitzi learns to text, I'll eat my phone."

"Then use plenty of mustard. Your cousin Rebecca showed her."

"We're all doomed. And I have to go, Dad. I need to get Michael settled, then get myself to work."

"Go. And mazel tov, both of you. Tell him I said so, all right?"

"Yes, Dad. Love you," Josh said, hanging up before the call could devolve into five minutes of "one more thing" and repeated good-byes.

Michael was staring at him, bemused. "I, uh, heard about three-quarters of that," he admitted.

"Dad gets loud every time he goes to Brooklyn. It's the only way to be heard over the chaos," Josh explained, pocketing his phone. He put his arms around Michael's shoulders and said, "I told you he wouldn't mind."

"We'll see how it goes," Michael insisted. "There's a big difference between liking your son's boyfriend and wanting him living with you. And Kaylee sheds, even if I bathe her every week."

"Oh my God, you sound like my grandmother," Josh said, rolling his eyes again. "Will you stop looking for trouble? We'll work something out. And worst case, it's temporary until *we* can find somewhere together—assuming you'd be interested."

Michael blinked, lips parting in surprise. "You'd want to? I mean, this whole thing wasn't planned. We haven't even really talked about it."

Josh sighed, wondering if Michael would ever realize just how great he was. "Yes. I want you to move in with me or for us to live somewhere else or whatever it takes for us to be together."

Instead of protesting or arguing or coming up with even more reasons it wouldn't work, Michael surrendered. Josh saw it in his smile and felt it in his sweet, soft kiss.

Time to move forward. When the kiss ended, Josh said, "Okay. First things first. Is he going to change the locks, or can I sneak in later tonight and pick up your stuff for you?"

"I'll do it," Michael said.

Josh hesitated. "Is that a good idea?"

Michael winced. "Honestly, he's probably too impractical to think of changing the locks, but he *would* have you arrested for trespassing. I can get my stuff. Or I can hire movers and just go supervise."

"That." Josh nodded. "Do that. At least you won't be there alone. He won't start anything in front of strangers, right?"

Michael's smile was thin. "No. And if he tries, I'll make damn sure to record every word he says, and send the file to every newspaper in the Northeast."

Josh probably should've said something about reconciliation or let bygones be bygones, but he was still seeing red. Instead, he leaned in and gave Michael a kiss full of love and approval. "Good. So what next?"

Michael took a deep breath and looked out at the water for a few seconds. "We get you to Bagel End in time for your shift. I'll call my sister and let her know what happened. If you don't mind me using your laptop to start scouting real estate, I'll hang out there until you close. Then you can show me where I'm going to be living."

"Sounds perfect." Josh took the SUV keys out of his pocket. "We just have to stop at the grocery store on the way home."

"No food at your place?"

"Mostly cans and frozen stuff, and tomorrow morning, I plan on making you brunch. Let's call it our first tradition," he said, turning to walk back around to the driver's side.

Michael caught him by the arm and tugged him close for a kiss that was hot and slow and full of the promise of many more to come, leaving Josh's heart pounding.

"I love you," Michael whispered, lips moving against Josh's.

Josh smiled into the kiss. "Love you too, babe."

EPILOGUE

The night was crisp and cold, with just enough wind to stir the tree branches and not a cloud in sight. If it hadn't been below thirty degrees outside, Josh might've suggested going to the north end of the island for some stargazing, but why leave the house to find romantic ambience when they had a perfectly good fireplace right here? Besides, they had plans for a night of TV until Dad went to bed, followed by a few hours of Josh and Michael in front of the fireplace, ignoring the TV.

After more than six months with Michael, Josh had yet to get sick of appreciating all sorts of romantic ambience.

"You know, these aren't bad," Josh's dad called from the living room, followed by a suspiciously loud crunching sound. Had they started in on the tortilla chips already?

Frowning, Josh leaned away from the fridge, but he couldn't see through the doorway to his dad's armchair. "What are you eating?"

"Nufin'!" Michael answered.

As if Josh was supposed to believe that? He finally found the jar of salsa behind the ketchup, which somebody had put back empty. "Okay, look. I know you both love ketchup—" He stopped in his tracks when he spotted a brightly colored box on the coffee table, in reach of both his father and his pre-fiancé. The box was printed with frolicking cartoon dogs and bagels raining down from the sky. The bag of tortilla chips lay untouched on the other side of the table.

Dad smiled sheepishly at Josh. "We were, uh . . ."

"Eating dog treats?" Josh finished, bringing the salsa to the table. The TV was tuned to the Portsmouth news station. Michael's laptop was pushed out of the way to make room for the dog bagels, even though he couldn't have finished his homework yet, which was no surprise. He'd been complaining about having to do homework ever since he enrolled in a couple of online courses last September.

Michael swallowed and shrugged. "They're better than I expected."

"Uh-huh." Josh sat down on the couch next to Michael, letting the worn-out springs tilt their bodies close. "You were supposed to be doing homework. And you." He pointed past Michael at Dad. "You were supposed to be *filling* the boxes. The New Year's sale starts tomorrow."

"I have two days to turn in this essay. And I'm helping make sure this new batch came out right. It's quality testing," Michael said, utterly sincere despite the absurdity of what he was saying.

He leaned forward for a kiss, but Josh put up a finger, blocking his lips. "Dog cookie breath."

Michael laughed and nipped Josh's fingertip. "Dog *bagel* breath. And we have more than enough to stock the shelves. You outdid yourself with the baking."

"Actually," Dad interrupted, surreptitiously brushing bagel crumbs off his fingers before he picked up the TV remote, "I think the sale might be delayed." He turned up the volume.

"—upgraded to a winter storm warning for most of New England," the meteorologist was saying, pointing back over her left shoulder. "We're looking at twenty-four to thirty-six inches of snow for the southeast part of the state as far west as Nashua, with wind gusts of fifty miles per hour."

"Wonderful," Josh said flatly. At his tone, Kaylee stood up and rested her chin on his knee. Michael was still her first priority, but she'd taken it upon herself to check in with the rest of her new family as needed. He ruffled her ears and explained to her, "I'm already sick of shoveling."

"Two to three *feet* of snow?" Michael asked, frowning at the TV. "That's not normal, is it?"

"I thought you grew up here," Dad said.

Josh snickered. "Give him a break, Dad. He's been away from snow for ten years. His blood's thinned."

"Hey," Michael protested. "It snowed like crazy where I was stationed in Japan."

"Uh-huh. And two inches of snow shuts down Southern cities like DC," Josh countered.

Michael shook his head. "Still, two to three *feet*."

Trying to find a hint of optimism, Josh scratched behind Kaylee's ears and said, "That's if it doesn't move out to sea instead."

The weather map on TV shifted to show all of New England. The meteorologist said, "Governor Baldwin has joined with the governors of nearby states in declaring a state of emergency. Residents are requested to stay home and stay off the roads, where blowing snow and heavy winds are expected to reduce visibility. Widespread power outages may affect the region, and residents in the affected zone, especially along the coast, are advised to take emergency measures, including evacuation for people with special medical needs."

The TV cut to the anchor desk, where two reporters began to discuss those emergency measures, and Dad muted the broadcast. For a few seconds, the only sound was the crackle of logs in the fireplace. Josh did a mental tally of how much wood was in the pile out back. Between that and their last delivery of heating oil, they'd be warm no matter what.

"Do we also want to evacuate?" Michael finally asked, looking from Josh to Dad and back.

"That's just the news being paranoid," Dad said with a dismissive wave.

Josh nodded. "I think they have to say that for legal reasons. We'll be fine."

"Still, it's not yet eight," Dad said thoughtfully, glancing at the clock on the fireplace mantel. "The grocery store's still open. One of us should pick up supplies."

"We're going to have to open the shop tomorrow," Josh said, getting to his feet. He was the one who did the nighttime driving in the household. "We have too much dough proofing to let it go to waste. And people might come in, looking to stock up."

Michael followed Josh over to the coatrack by the door to the garage. "Kaylee and I will come with you. We can get the shopping done twice as fast."

"Thanks." Josh gave him a quick smile and started to put together a mental shopping list.

"Should we get some plywood, board up the shop window?" Michael asked.

Dad frowned at the TV, where a list of emergency phone numbers was scrolling down the screen. "I think we'll be fine." He turned to Michael and asked, "Are you going out anywhere this week?"

Michael tipped his head, frowning. "Physical therapy at ten tomorrow, but I think that's it." He crouched to put on Kaylee's vest.

"You might want to pick up some tire chains, just in case." When Dad looked at Josh, it was with a sly grin, eyebrows raised. "I suggest you put up a sign to let customers know we might be closed once the storm hits, if the roads get bad, but that's up to you. Feel like opening tomorrow morning, boss?"

Josh snorted. "I think you gave me half your share of the business so you could sit on your ass and make me do all the work."

"If you two can be pre-engaged, I can be pre-retired," Dad said smugly, deliberately pulling the lever on the side of his recliner to put his feet up. "Best Hanukkah gift I ever gave you."

Ignoring Michael's snickers, Josh said, "Fine, I'll put up a notice. But we're still going to the supermarket now, before there's a run on bottled water and Oreos."

"And ketchup," Dad reminded him. "Oh, and pick up some eggs."

"Oreos, eggs, and ketchup," Michael said, getting back to his feet. "Are you two *sure* we don't need to evacuate?"

"We'll be fine. It's just snow," Dad said reassuringly. "We have a hospital down the road and plenty of firewood. Absolute worst case, the elementary school is an evacuation center, and it's not too far away, and we've got insurance on everything."

"Yeah," Josh said, trying not to let Michael's worry get to him. "Okay."

Michael nodded, relaxing. "If you think of anything else we need, text us."

Dad leaned forward and picked up his phone from the coffee table. "I will. Drive safe."

Once Josh had his coat zipped up, he led the way into the garage. Michael tossed him the car keys and went around to the passenger side. Josh had to suck in his gut to squeeze into the driver's seat, but keeping both vehicles inside was worth the hassle. None of them wanted to scrape ice off the windshield every morning.

Josh got the engine started, then turned to watch Michael get into the passenger side. Kaylee was already in the back, muzzle resting on the center console. "She doesn't need her boots?" Josh asked, reaching up to hit the garage door opener.

"She's fine." Michael touched Josh's arm, stopping him from putting the SUV into reverse. "Whatever happens, we'll be okay. Right?"

"Yeah." Josh looked into Michael's eyes, seeing the love and confidence that had grown over the last seven months. Seven months of dating and learning each other, of Michael adjusting to life on Hartsbridge Island, of tourists and college students, and both of them ignoring the reporters who occasionally came nosing around, looking for a scandal. "As long as we're together, everything will be fine."

Michael leaned in close so he could cup Josh's face in his hands, holding him still for a kiss. "Then everything will be fine."

Dear Reader,

Thank you for reading Jordan S. Brock's *Change of Address*!

We know your time is precious and you have many, many entertainment options, so it means a lot that you've chosen to spend your time reading. We really hope you enjoyed it.

We'd be honored if you'd consider posting a review—good or bad—on sites like **Amazon, Barnes & Noble, Kobo, Goodreads, Twitter, Facebook, Tumblr,** and your blog or website. We'd also be honored if you told your friends and family about this book. Word of mouth is a book's lifeblood!

For more information on upcoming releases, author interviews, blog tours, contests, giveaways, and more, please sign up for our weekly, spam-free newsletter and visit us around the web:

Newsletter: tinyurl.com/RiptideSignup
Twitter: twitter.com/RiptideBooks
Facebook: facebook.com/RiptidePublishing
Goodreads: tinyurl.com/RiptideOnGoodreads
Tumblr: riptidepublishing.tumblr.com

Thank you so much for Reading the Rainbow!

RiptidePublishing.com

ACKNOWLEDGMENTS

This book wouldn't exist without Katie and Michele, the greatest beta readers and cheerleaders to ever lurk in Google Docs with me; my husband, who gave me the time, space, and freedom to write; my service dog, Darian, who helped me reclaim my place in the world; and everyone at Riptide Publishing, who welcomed me with open arms and gave my creative side a way to shine. There isn't enough coffee in the world to thank you all!

ALSO BY

JORDAN S. BROCK

Harstbridge Island
Building Bridges (coming soon)

ABOUT
THE AUTHOR

Coffee-fueled author Jordan Brock writes engaging contemporary romance with a deliciously pan-romantic sensibility and an emphasis on consent, respect, and, of course, love. Her characters are constantly surprised by the way love's slow burn sneaks up on them.

Jordan's children are all four-legged and furry. They love to be oh-so-helpful with her writing. She can usually be found hiding from the sun with her service dog and her puppy-in-training. (She tried the training thing with cats first, since cats are so much smarter, but it was a no-go.)

Before she was published, Jordan worked as a tech writer in the semiconductor industry. She's also created labs and learning materials for auto, diesel, and motorcycle mechanics. The technology was the easy part; the hard part was trying not to slip in pop-culture snark.

Jordan lives in the desert outside Phoenix, Arizona, despite the fact she turns into gray goo and blue hair dye when exposed to heat. For fun, she hunts scorpions in the backyard, with a blowtorch, and a crowbar. She's chronically unavailable for at least a month after new game releases from Blizzard. She's an unapologetic fangirl and has been known to write an occasional fanfic to prove Bucky Barnes is not a villain. Oh, and she crochets the cutest amigurumi ever.

If you'd like to learn more about Jordan, check out her blog and website at jordansbrock.com.

Enjoy more stories like
Change of Address
at RiptidePublishing.com!

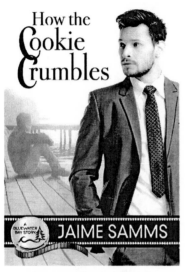

How the Cookie Crumbles
ISBN: 978-1-62649-389-6

Blueberry Boys
ISBN: 978-1-62649-342-1

Earn Bonus Bucks!

Earn 1 Bonus Buck for each dollar you spend. Find out how at
RiptidePublishing.com/news/bonus-bucks.

Win Free Ebooks for a Year!

Pre-order coming soon titles directly through our site and you'll
receive one entry into a drawing for a chance to win free books for
a year! Get the details at RiptidePublishing.com/contests.

CPSIA information can be obtained at www.ICGtesting.com
Printed in the USA
LVOW08s1636111016

508320LV00002B/518/P